One
Step
Beyond

Mum

You're not supposed to write
in books!

Cheryl

The King is Dead.
Long live the King!

WHEN THE SUBATOMIC CREW GOT TOGETHER to discuss themes for our anthology, we debated the theme. What pairing of subjects would get people interested? "Unicorns and the New Economy"? (Way too much fantasy for 300 pages.) "Existentialism and Donuts"? (Too indulgent, though we do love donuts.) What cool, rockin' niche is under-served by the publishing community?

And so "One Step Beyond: Tales of the Fantastical"—rock 'n' roll and speculative fiction—was born!

But not genre fantasy or science fiction. Nope, no unicorns or space operas in these pages. We looked for speculative fiction without the usual trappings of the genres it encompasses. No elves, no UFOs, no musclebound adventurers. We were looking for speculations that began with the most magical supposition of all time: What if…?

What if human sacrifice is the price of rock-star fame? What if your Camero crashes, and you're ushered into the underworld by Lynyrd Skynyrd's Ronnie Van Zant? What if society bans music, and musicians become outlaws? What if bio-engineered dinosaurs sing karaoke only to Elvis tracks… and they run out of material?

In our search for stories, several things quickly became clear to me:

1. Elvis will always, always be the King.

2. Hippies are still controversial, almost 40 years post-Woodstock.

SHARE AND SHARE ALIKE!

You can download free digital versions of Subatomic Books at our website, **WWW.SUBATOMICBOOKS.COM.** Our luxurious home on the web offers eBooks, audiobooks and podcast audio.

We believe literature should be shared amongst friends. If you enjoyed reading or listening to one of our publications, please buy a copy or persuade your friends to do so.

While this copy of *One Step Beyond* would feel right at home on your bookshelf, it also likes to travel. Should you decide not to keep it, pass it on to a friend or a stranger; leave it in a coffeehouse, at a party, or at a bus stop.

One Step Beyond

SUBATOMIC ANTHOLOGY 01

EDITED BY CHARITY HELLER HOGGE
WITH
VALERIE ENRIQUEZ
CHARLES BLANK
KEVIN WILSON

SUBATOMIC BOOKS
little is big

This is a work of fiction. All the characters and events portrayed in this novel are either fictitious or are used fictitiously.

SUBATOMIC ANTHOLOGY 01: ONE STEP BEYOND

Published by Subatomic Books.
616 SE 36th Ave.
Portland, OR 97214

www.subatomicbooks.com

ISBN 978-0-9793915-1-4

First Trade Paperback Edition: October 2008

Printed in the United States of America.

0 9 8 7 6 5 4 3 2 1

Table of Contents

3. Rock 'n' roll is to spec fic what a funky bass line is to an editor in rush hour traffic: It gets our groove-thang on.

Special thanks belongs to our contributors, who—in addition to being fantastic handlers of the grand What if—are a very patient, accommodating group. Thanks to Steve Libbey for his contribution of the cover design, and thanks to Kevin Wilson, William Thoma, and our intern, Valerie Enriquez, for their editing help.

CHARITY HELLER HOGGE
Portland Ore., April, 2008

Mr. Bad Man

C. L. HOLLAND

C. L. Hllld

"DEBS, WHERE'D YOU GET THIS?" Steve Summers, rock legend and coolest step-dad ever, is looking at me like he's seen a ghost. Not the reaction I'm expecting.

"The internet," I tell him. "It's on all the download sites."

"And it's listed under our stuff?"

I nod. "Isn't it you, then?"

Steve doesn't answer, just reaches out and hits play again. He frowns as he hears the muffled voices and I know he's trying to work out what they're saying. Someone growls out bitter-sounding words; out of the pause that follows comes a long slow sound. It sends a shiver down my spine, just like it did the first time I heard it. It sounds like someone died. Steve jabs a finger at the speaker as the cello works its way through a sequence of notes.

"That's Jonathan, I'd put money on it. And that," he gestures as a soft voice joins in, "is Adam."

I nod again. The voice that whispers silkily over the cello is definitely Adam Wynne. That or an imitator so good it's scary.

"That'll be Nick on cymbals. With one of those brush things," Steve explains for my benefit as a hissing sound comes in, and then the bass erupts into the song like a gatecrasher. "Sounds like me on bass, too," he remarks thoughtfully.

"So it is Mr. Bad Man, then?"

It's a moment before he replies. "It's definitely us," he confirms. "Trouble is, we never recorded it."

"Oh, come on, Steve," I protest. "You just said it was the band!"

"It is," he tells me soberly. "But like I said, we never made it."

"Then who did? You mean it's a tribute band?"

"No." Steve is dismissive. "I've heard a lot of tributes. The one thing they never get right is Adam."

I know what he means. There's something special about Adam's voice, like he's singing just to you. When he sings about love, you find yourself falling in love, and when he sings about breaking up, you feel like your heart is breaking, too. With that and his looks, it's no wonder half the girls in the world fell in love with him. I would have, too, except I was too young to understand what all the fuss was about. I only got into them later, when Steve married my mum.

"Maybe it's just Adam, recording with someone else?" I suggest tentatively. The look Steve gives me says it's not quite the stupidest thing I've ever said.

"It's us. It's the band," he insists. "When you've been in a band, you just know." He shrugs. "Adam wouldn't have sat on something like this. It's good. Besides, he hasn't been anywhere near a studio since our last album."

The song builds to a climax and Steve stops rather than talk over it. Adam's voice is raw, like he's shouted himself hoarse, or he's crying or something. Even the instruments sound strained. Steve looks uncomfortable as the bass and drums drop out until it's just Adam and the cello. I feel the same. It's too personal, like reading someone's diary or walking in on your parents having sex. It makes me wonder if they know it's one of Mr. Bad Man's most popular downloads.

Finally the cello fades out, its last note dying away in time to hear Adam's harsh whisper as he goes over the chorus in a rush of breath.

"If I could forget your face/Deny the love that left a stain/

Lose the warmth of your embrace/Lose the love to lose the
pain,/I wouldn't mind/I wouldn't mind/To lose the love to lose
the pain."

The CD player whirs as the laser goes back to the beginning.
In the silence I realize I have goose bumps on my arms. Steve sits
quietly for a long time.

"Mind if I keep this?" he asks finally.

"Sure. It's on my iPod, anyway."

"Thanks." There's a frown on his face that means he's trying
to puzzle something out, like when him and Mum are doing the
crossword. He's as hooked as I am, and I hope it means what I
think it means.

A fortnight later and it's obvious Steve's forgotten all about it.
The CD sits on his desk gathering dust and he doesn't mention
it again. I take matters into my own hands, switching it for the
one he's got in the stereo because he never checks. Sure enough,
when he gets home, instead of the Rolling Stones he gets an
earful of Adam angsting at him. He gives me a look, because
I'm not supposed to mess with things in the study, what with
it being full of guitars and awards and stuff, but he doesn't say
anything and he doesn't turn it off.

I start playing it in my room after that, loud enough that he
can hear. So long as he doesn't forget about it, the mystery will
bug him; he's like that. Normally I play Mr. Bad Man stuff while
he's out, because it embarrasses him to hear it on the radio, but
now I start being a pain on purpose. Maybe if he remembers
how cool it was to be in the band, he'll call up one of the others
and they'll figure out what's going on.

"Come on then, Debs, get your shoes on." It only takes
another two weeks of playing the song at top volume for Steve's
curiosity to get the better of him. He's off to see Jonathan, and
he's taking me along. Mum doesn't mind for once. She doesn't
normally like me meeting Steve's rock 'n' roll friends in case
they're a bad influence. But she met Jonathan at the wedding
and liked him, and anyway, he's a teacher, so you can't get much
more respectable than that, right?

"Are you sure Jonathan won't mind me coming? He's around kids all week, he probably wants the weekend off."

"Better not ask him to teach you anything, then," Steve replies. "He probably had enough of teaching kids to play the spoons at the wedding reception." I blush and he grins. "Don't worry, kid, I checked with him and it's fine."

We get in the car. When Mum introduced me to Steve, I was expecting him to drive something classy and expensive, or one of those camper vans. Something quirky. Not a regular road car like thousands of other people drive, a few years old and never quite clean. I put the radio on, not the CD, because the one place Steve can't stand to hear his songs played is in the car—that goes for all the stuff he's been a session musician in, too.

He can't escape the good old days, though. Less than ten minutes later a familiar, urgent-sounding bass line comes on, matched note for note by the guitar.

"Ch-ching," he mutters, like he always does whenever something's on that will get him royalties. I've always wondered how much he gets, because it can't be much with it being split four ways and all, but Mum says it's rude to ask.

"'Let me out, or I'll scream!'" I sing along. "'Let me out, or I'll scream blue murder!'" "Scream Blue Murder" is one of their earlier songs, back when Jonathan mostly just played guitar. You can always pick the early tracks because they didn't start using the cello and piano and things until later.

We drive for most of the morning. We're meeting Jonathan at his school, some rich boys' school in the middle of the countryside. It's so posh they've even got their own mini recording studio. When we get there, I gawp like I did when I met Jonathan and Nick at Mum's wedding. The school's huge, all grey stone like a castle, and it's got its own chapel that's bigger than the church in our town. Steve's been here before, so he goes straight in like he owns the place. We don't go to the studio though, but to the canteen where Jonathan said he'd meet us. I nearly laugh when we get there, because even though they're rich, they've got those crap plastic chairs like everyone else, all bright orange and clashing with the décor.

Jonathan's sitting at one of the tables, looking all teacher-y with his cup of coffee and pile of marking. He looks up as he hears us coming and smiles. He's got glasses now, which he never did in any of the band photos, and he looks a lot nicer with them. I blush as I realize I'm staring but it doesn't look like he's noticed. Maybe he's just used to it, because I bet even rich kids listen to Mr. Bad Man.

"Steve, Debbie, hi." He gets up and shakes hands with us and it's a bit like being at school, but then Steve pulls him into a hug and there's a lot of grinning and back-slapping. Nick comes in, then, and there's more of the same. He gives me a kiss on the cheek and looks around.

"No Adam?" he asks.

"Not yet," Jonathan replies mildly. "Give him time."

Steve snorts but doesn't say anything. Jonathan said the same thing at the wedding, and Adam didn't turn up. I was gutted, but at least I got to meet the rest of the band. Steve was really upset, even though Jonathan said it was probably because of the press. Photographers came to the reception and hung around outside and I got my picture in a few magazines, which shut up the people at school who didn't believe the legendary Steve Summers is really my step-dad. Adam's avoided the media like the plague since Mr. Bad Man split; he's even been in court for punching a photographer a couple of times. Steve always says the last album took it out of him, but I think it was the car accident while they were recording. Some girl died in it, and none of the songs on that album sound like his heart was really in it. Steve won't talk about that, though.

We get some drinks, then wait in the canteen for a bit. Steve, Jonathan, and Nick talk about when they were in the band and all the things they got up to. Mum doesn't let Steve tell those stories at home so I'm listening really hard, and then all of a sudden this voice says, "Steve, I swear your groupies are getting younger every year."

Everyone goes quiet. Adam's in the doorway, looking so different from the album covers that for a moment I'm not sure it's really him. His hair's longer, kind of hanging in his eyes like he hasn't bothered to cut it, and he hasn't shaved in several days. Steve's looking towards the door with a strange expression on his face, and I'm staring and just know I'm bright red, and then Jonathan gets up and extends his hand.

"Adam. Late as usual," he teases and they shake hands. There's no hugging and it looks like they prefer it that way. Nick gets up and shakes Adam's hand as he steps into the room. Steve goes over and there's this moment like when cats meet for the first time and aren't sure if they like each other, but then they shake hands as well.

I'm still trying not to stare when Adam glances over Steve shoulder and spots me. My stomach does this quivery thing like butterflies then, because Adam's still quite good-looking even though he's old enough to be my dad. Not that old, though, it's not like he's wrinkly or anything.

"This is my kid, Debbie," Steve introduces me. "Debs, this is the elusive Adam Wynne."

Adam comes over to me and shakes my hand. "Hello, Debbie."

I've got all this stuff I want to say, that I've spent ages practicing so it sounds cool and mature. But the instant Adam's hand touches mine I become an idiot fan-girl. All that comes out is a squeaky little "Hi!" and I blush so hard my ears go hot.

Jonathan gets some more coffee and leads us out of the canteen. I wander along with Steve while Nick makes small talk with Adam at the back. The rest of the school is as posh as the outside, with shiny floors and loads of trophies in cabinets. We end up in the music department, in this classroom that's at least twice the size of the ones at my school. There's a piano in the corner, all glossy and black. At the other end of the room there's a drum kit set up, and a guitar and bass on stands next to amplifiers.

"What's going on?" Adam's hanging back in the doorway looking wary like he expects someone to jump out at him.

"Sorry. Some of the boys had practice this morning."

Jonathan's casual about it but Adam doesn't look convinced, especially when Steve wanders over and starts checking out the instruments.

"Nice," he says. "I wish we'd had some of this at my school."

"And miss out on the working class rock musician scene?" Nick jokes.

"Yeah, 'cause the cello got that across so well," Steve replies ironically. He picks up the bass, glancing across at Jonathan to check it's okay. He shrugs the guitar strap over his shoulder then checks the strings are tuned and picks out a few notes. Nick's already set himself up at the drums when Steve picks out the bass line to my favorite song, "Dark Circles." Jonathan picks up the guitar and before I know, it they're all playing. Adam's still hanging back, looking nervous like he's the new kid in class. There's no way he's going to sing, so before things get awkward I head over to the mike.

My voice is a bit croaky at first, but it's mostly nerves—I'm actually performing with Mr. Bad Man! Well, most of them, anyway. The sound is raw because they've not played together in a long time, plus I'm no diva, but it washes over me and I get a buzz that feels like I'm floating. I glance over my shoulder and Steve gives me a wink.

Then I see Adam and nearly choke. He hasn't moved and he's watching us with an expression that's caught somewhere between hunger and loathing. It hits me clear as day that he hates the whole thing, being in a band and all. It makes me wonder why he came.

If the others notice it doesn't show in their playing. Maybe they're just used to him being weird. I close my eyes and get into it again, and when we reach the end of the song his expression is closed up and unreadable like it was when he arrived. He waits until the others have put down their instruments before he speaks.

"What's this about, Jonathan? You didn't drag me all the way out here for a jamming session."

"No, I didn't." Jonathan's as unruffled as usual. I guess he'd have to be, being a teacher. "There's something I wanted to show you." He goes over to the CD player. "The voices are barely audible, but I managed to find a cleaner version." He presses play and everyone goes quiet.

The first voices are still too muffled to make out, but then Steve's voice comes out clear enough to hear the words even though he sounds like he's underwater.

"Ad, you sure about this?"

"Let's get it over with," Adam says bitterly and then the song starts.

Adam and Nick look shocked, like Steve did the first time he heard it. Jonathan sits down and watches, while Steve's looking everywhere but at the rest of the band. The sound of the cello freezes them and Nick shoots Adam a startled look as the singer's voice whispers and then soars.

Halfway through, Adam sits down. He sounds like he's tearing himself apart with heartache; in real life he's gone pale. No one makes a sound, or even moves, and Steve exchanges a glance with me as the instruments fade out and the harsh whisper croaks out of the speakers.

Adam's gone very still, looking at the floor. Someone says, "Ad?" very softly and he looks up.

"What the fuck was that?" he growls, but he doesn't look angry.

"Debs found it on the internet," Steve tells him. "She wondered why we never released it."

"We never recorded that."

"But it's us!" Nick interrupts. "I can hear it even if you can't. And on the beginning, that's you and Steve. How can we not remember a song like that?"

"It's a hoax." Adam's voice is flat and angry. He turns away and starts towards the door.

"How?" Steve asks. "The instruments, yeah, that's possible, but the voices? Did you record it with someone else and not tell us?"

Adam turns back, looking trapped. "You know damn well I

haven't recorded a thing since the band broke up."

"No, I don't. We've hardly heard a word from you. How are we supposed to know anything?"

"Is it you?" Jonathan's voice, calm and reasonable, breaks in. Adam stares at him. "It's a fair question. If you recorded it, just tell us so we can all go home with the mystery solved."

"It isn't me. It can't be anyone else, but it isn't me." Adam sounds frustrated, and maybe a bit scared.

Steve sighs and rubs his eyes. "I don't suppose anyone fancies playing it, see if it jogs a memory?"

They all go quiet at that. Adam breaks first.

"I can't."

"Don't give me that," Jonathan chides gently. "You could sing it note for note right now."

"I don't know the words."

Jonathan hands Adam what can only be a lyrics sheet, crushing his argument. I can see a little-boy look on his face, and just know he's about to say he doesn't want to, but Nick's already nodding.

"I'm in. It'll be interesting."

Adam glances over at the instruments and the fight goes out of him as he realizes how neatly Jonathan set him up. He slouches over to the mike and waits for the others to get ready, which takes a few minutes as Jonathan has to get a cello out from a store cupboard. I creep over to a chair in the corner, trying not to draw attention to myself and break the soap-bubble moment. It's like a dream. I'm so busy watching Adam I don't notice when Jonathan's ready. The first note of the cello makes me jump. I've never heard one played up close before and it's louder than I was expecting. For a moment it doesn't look like Adam's going to sing, but Jonathan begins the sequence again and this time the singer joins him.

The music drifts through the room like smoke. It sends shivers over my skin, better live than it ever was on CD. Something's missing, though. Adam's singing the words but not the meaning. His deadpan delivery makes it sound seriously creepy. Nick and Steve start playing and I don't think they've noticed. The smell of rain comes in the open window. The downpour overlays the song, sounding like it's a part of it. There's the sound of a car going fast on a wet road although I can't see one. A note of desperation creeps into his voice just like on the recording.

Tires screech, people scream.

There's the twisting and crunching of metal and the sudden stink of petrol. Adam's staring out the window like he's seen a ghost. I follow his gaze and go cold. All I can see is the lush green grass right outside and a blue, cloudless sky. The band is still playing. Steve looks like he wants to throw the guitar down, and the cello sounds ragged. Adam's voice is almost lost beneath the instruments. His eyes are closed, tears tracking down his cheeks.

Someone's still screaming. It sounds like they're right in the room with us.

"Kate! Kate, no!" It's Adam's voice but when I look at him he's still singing, sort of. His lips are barely moving and his eyes are wide and staring at nothing, like he's stoned. Steve looks the same, his fingers moving automatically on the strings even though he looks like he's gone somewhere else. They all do.

"God, Kate, no," the other Adam says. He goes quiet and there's nothing but the music and the rain, and underneath them a quiet sobbing. The rain washes the smell of petrol away and I feel a sudden stab of relief as I hear sirens in the distance.

I'm the only one who feels it. Steve's crying, something I've never seen before, and Jonathan's face is twisted with grief. Nick gives a sob and throws his drumsticks. They clatter against the wall like old bones. Steve stops playing a moment later, turning away and tearing the guitar strap from his shoulder as if it's burning him.

It's just Adam and the cello. His voice rises to meet it, cutting it off in a scream of rage and grief as he sinks to his knees. He's rocking back and forth singing the chorus one last time, and I realize through his sobbing that he's singing different words.

"I wouldn't mind," he whispers, "I wouldn't mind, to keep the love and keep the pain."

Steve's the first one to him, dropping to his knees and holding him tight. A moment later, they're all there and it's like I'm invisible. I'm about to creep out and give them some privacy, but then Adam speaks.

"I lied about the accident. About what happened." His voice wavers as he chokes out more words. "We'd got engaged. Kate had just told me she was pregnant. We were going away, to celebrate. I was going too fast. I lost control."

"God, Adam. Why didn't you ever tell us?"

"I couldn't. I… I lied—about afterwards. I lied when I said I was unconscious. We knew what was coming. We talked about it. She was badly hurt, bleeding. We couldn't get out. I sat there and watched her die—her and our child. And then I waited until the sun came up and someone found us."

He's crying again. Before I know it I've put my arms around him.

"I'm sorry. I'm so sorry I made you remember."

"I wanted to forget so badly. I wanted it and I made it happen."

"We all forgot," Steve says softly. "I don't know how you did it, but that song…" He shudders. "I didn't even remember her name until today."

"I wanted it," Adam repeats. He clings to me like a child and we stay like that until he's cried himself out.

After a while Steve sends me outside. They've got a lot to talk about, the four of them, and I'm glad for the excuse to get away. It's a long time before they leave.

Steve comes out to the car looking drained. He turns off the radio and for once I don't complain.

"Will he be alright?" I say into the silence.

Steve nods then thinks better of it and shrugs. "I guess. As well as he can be. Jonathan's going to make sure he gets home."

"Do you remember it properly now, what happened?"

Steve negotiates his way out of the school grounds before he replies. The sun's going down already.

"After the crash, we wanted to take a break from recording, but we were bound by contract to deliver another album. The record company started putting pressure on us. Adam went on a four-day bender and when he came back he wasn't the same. He was so angry. That song was the first one we did, the first and only time we ever played it together. It was never meant to be recorded."

I don't say anything. I wonder what would have happened if they'd never written it, and what would happen now. After a while Steve turns the radio on quietly, and we don't hear another Mr. Bad Man track all the way home. ✳

That Smell

HORACE JAMES

SQUINTING THROUGH A MASSIVE BRAINFUCK of a head-ache, Dale Barrett stared down at the remains of his car. Despite drinking a fifth of Jack Daniels and eating a couple of the little tablets his buddy Dean called "pink fuckers," Dale was no longer buzzed in the least.

The back of his throat twitched at the acrid smell of automotive death: fumes of gasoline, antifreeze, and hot lubricants oozing out onto the asphalt. His pride and joy—his 1974 Camaro SS—was wedged like a doorstop under the back-end of an old tanker truck, which was now raised off its dual tandem wheels. The truck was otherwise undamaged. Even the chrome-plated girls on the truck's mudflaps were unscathed and maintained their bare-breasted windswept poise.

Rising up from the twisted corpse of the Camaro like demented birdsong were the frenzied guitar solos of "Free Bird," screechy and distorted.

How could a CD player live through that? Dale wondered. Shit. How did I live through that? I must have been thrown free, banged my head, and blacked out.

It was proof of his belief that seatbelts were a government plot.

The memory reloaded hard and fast. A ratty-looking Mustang.

A little backwoods highway NASCAR action. Dale had backed
off and waited for the dude to try and pass so he could fake him
out with a little swerve into his lane and then put the spurs on
the Camaro's horses and blow his ugly fucking doors off, but as
they came over a rise, Dale's eyes were on the rearview and—

"Hey, slick. Drive much?"

Dale never saw the man walk up. Didn't hear footsteps, no
crunch of gravel. He was just there. The driver's door of the
truck hung open.

"My Camaro, man… look at my fucking Camaro!"

"I seen worse."

"What the hell is this damn truck doin' parked in the middle
of the road? Are you fuckin' crazy?"

No response.

Dale strained to see his face, but it was eclipsed by the shadow
of a wide-brimmed leather hat. Long dirty blond hair, Neil
Young T-shirt, jeans, and a pair of boots—the standard redneck
hippie trucker uniform.

"Am I crazy? A fair question, friend, but it occurs to me that
trying to fuck an eighteen-wheeler in the ass with a Camaro is
what's crazy."

Dale started to say something, something his teachers would
have called "provocative," but he sensed a different kind of vibe
from this dude. He couldn't get a read on him, no signals from
the way he talked or the way he stood. Stone still. He could be a
snake on a rock.

"You must have been running that Chevy hard to make a
mess like that. Looks like a… a goddamn plane crash." The
driver laughed.

"What the hell's so goddamned funny? Shit, I must've sunk
ten grand in that car, easy."

"Too bad."

"Damn right it's too bad! And how come there's none a' them
orange triangle reflector things? I'll sue your ass for negligence."

"Do what you gotta do, kid. Maybe you better call the highway patrol. Then again, they'll probably make you blow in that

tube thing… what's it called?"

"A breathalyzer."

"Yeah, that's it. Maybe you might hold off on that call. Hell, I'm in no rush, I've done missed my deadline. Ten thousand gallons of gas but can't burn a drop of it in that diesel."

"You ran out of gas? That's fucking lame."

"You got that right. Running out of gas sucks left hind tit." The driver put his hand to his ear. "Ahh! You were listening to 'Free Bird'! The music of angels."

"My old man's disk. It's alright, if you're into old stuff."

"I don't mean that it sounds like angels. I mean that most of the people on that record are dead."

"Lynyrd Skynyrd? They're still around. I know for a fact they played Jamapalooza last year."

"How old are you, kid?"

"Nineteen. And a half."

"Your daddy never told you the story? Of the original band?"

"Who the fuck cares? Look, man, shouldn't we be exchanging license plate numbers or something?"

"Fuck that. You need to hear this."

Dale shut up. Something in the driver's voice… it seemed to fill Dale's head up so that there wasn't much room left for thinking on his own.

"October '77. The band finished a gig in Greenville, South Carolina and got on their piece a' shit chartered Convair to fly to a gig at LSU in Baton Rouge. The right engine was fucked up, shooting out flames on their last flight, and sucking up all kinds of fuel. Everybody was scared shitless of that plane, but there was a schedule and contracts and a shitload of money involved. Rockstar paranoia don't mean shit against that.

"Ten minutes out from Baton Rouge, the pilot figures out he's not going to make it. Probably the fact that the propellers weren't turning gave it away.

"They headed for McComb. The plane went down slow, but it went down. Hard. Into the trees, into a swamp. Not too far down that dirt road over yonder."

Dale looked over his shoulder. Across the highway, a black hole in the kudzu gaped like a cave. "No shit?"

"No shit. Whatsoever. The pilot, copilot, the road manager, and three band members died, and the rest got tore up real bad. Just 'cause the pilot didn't fill the goddamned tank."

"Man. What're the odds? Of you being right at this spot, out of gas, hauling a load of airplane fuel?"

"Odds? Odds don't mean jack shit, son. Luck, fate, and bad decisions. That's all that counts 'round here. C'mon, slick, what say let's go check it out."

"I don't think so. What if the cops show up?"

"Are you kidding? Cops? At this hour? This is the road to No-wheresville, slick. The Mississippi Twilight Zone. You look like you could use a hike in this good country air, it'll clear ol' Jack Daniels out of your pipes."

"You think?" It was hard for Dale not to like the idea. An adventure.

"Absolutely. Let's do it."

Dale took a last look at his Camaro. The music died. "You got a flashlight?"

"Don't need no flashlight; we got us a full moon."

They set out across the road and after a few steps, Dale's lungs were full of the scent of ancient decay unique to the southern swamp. The damp air was cooler, but the dense atmosphere and lack of a breeze more than made up for it.

The moon cast its cold gray light onto the path where it wasn't shaded by the tupelo and sweet gum trees. The nighttime chorus of whippoorwills and frogs and locusts paid no attention to the footsteps of the pair.

"This swamp's an old, old place," said the driver. "Back before settlers, even before Indian times, there were ancient people that lived around here. They died out, nobody knows why. There's an old burial mound right up past that ridge. The Choctaw and others that come later wouldn't go nowhere near it. Claimed it was full of lost souls condemned to wander until they could find a way out."

"Sounds like a story for a camp out."

"You wouldn't want to camp in here. During the war, a company of Union soldiers cut across here hoping to find a shortcut to Natchez. Thirty-two men went in, and one come out; but they couldn't make no sense of what he was saying."

Dale looked out into the moonshady woods. Shadows faded in and out of view quicker than they should, out of sync with his passage along the path. Some seemed to be moving along with them, like the shadows of clouds on a sunny day. "Dude? If you're trying to freak me out, you're doing a good job, man. Let's talk 'bout something else."

"Yeah. I can't say I wasn't scared first time I came here. Choctaw name for it is *chikamauga*—'captives of trees,' or something like it."

"How much farther? 'Cause I haven't felt drunk since before the crash and this place is seriously creepin' me out." And, Dale thought, when did I tell the dude I'd been drinking Jack?

"This is it, slick, just past those pines. See how it's still a little more open up through there? Not so much after thirty years, though. The swamp heals itself. Too bad it don't work on people. You know, you might want to get that looked at."

"What?"

The man in the hat pointed at Dale's head. "That."

Dale put his hand to the top of his head and felt wetness and the edge of something hard. The unique terror of unexpected indentation seized Dale's heart. It was hard and broken and jagged and filled with slimy softness. The hard and rectangular object jutting out from the mess, his fingers recognized as the rearview mirror from a 1974 Camaro.

He opened his mouth to scream, but nothing… The bugs and critters were dead quiet, too, as was the driver, who had taken his hat off and was gazing up into the sick moonlight. Maybe it was the eerie light and shadows, but Dale could have sworn that the man's head and face weren't made of flesh at all but was just a crude assembly of dry skin and bone and pieces of wood and dirt and leaves.

"Here she comes, right on schedule," the driver said in a hoarse whisper. "Best on-time performance in commercial aviation."

Dale looked up and around and saw nothing. Then he heard it: sharp whacks and thuds as something hard and heavy and fast came on him from high in the trees, louder, louder, the crack of big timber joined by the tortured howl of ripping metal. Then he saw it—a big old plane, wings shorn off. Dale caught the glint of moonlight off the cockpit window and in a second it was on him. He thought he could hear the screaming of the passengers. Or had his voice come back to him?

"Gillsburg, MS—A high speed collision with a tree just off Route 568 in rural Amite county claimed the life of a McComb man.

"It is believed that Dale Barrett, 19, fell asleep at the wheel as the car left the roadway 100 yards before the place of impact. The car was completely destroyed, and it was not until hours later that police discovered that Barrett managed to cross the highway and walk over a mile into the wooded area before collapsing and dying from massive head and other injuries.

"'Mr. Barrett was somehow able to extricate himself from the wreckage despite a massive brain injury,' said Sgt. Brad Garvis, the Amite County Sheriff's Department accident reconstructionist who testified at the inquest. 'I've been in this job for 20 years and have never seen anything like this.'"

"An autopsy is being performed to determine if alcohol or drugs were a factor in the accident."

"Coincidentally, the location where Mr. Barrett's body was found is the site of the 1977 plane crash involving the rock band Lynyrd Skynyrd. Six died in the crash, including front man Ronnie Van Zant." ✳

All the Young Dudes
(and one Hippie Princess)

J. Michael Shell

I couldn't stop thinking about Sarah. Why Sarah? I'd known her for two weeks back during the bicentennial. Curiously, she is the only person I've ever met, before or since, named Sarah.

Why would she suddenly saunter into my thoughts now, after all this time? It had been more than twenty-five years since I'd left her sitting there, amazed that I could walk away from her; all she wanted was to share a summer with me, a bed with me. Sarah was also, truly, the most gorgeous girl I'd ever seen. To this day I'd have to insist that's still true.

I met her in one of the most beautiful places I've ever been, too: Bar Harbor, Maine. Back during those summers of love, Bar Harbor was a gathering spot for many members of the brightly attired, beaded and feathered, Northeastern contingent of the hippie population.

For me it was a staging area. I had decided to take my hippie land-yacht—a '63 Chevy long-bed van—up into the Maine wilderness to ignore that bicentennial Fourth of July. I'd arrived in Bar Harbor the second week in June and was working as a dishwasher, sleeping in the van and stashing money away for my trip to the wilderness.

I can't remember where I met Sarah. I think it was at a party some freaks were throwing in a house they'd rented on Mount Desert Isle. It really doesn't matter—wherever it was, Sarah was all I saw that night. No description could do justice to the vision she was. Her shoulder-length blond hair always seemed lit in soft-focus, and her eyes were ice-blue and meltingly wet. When she'd had enough wine, they would cross ever so slightly and sparkle wildly.

I was in my element, back then—I was born to be a hippie. Sarah was a Hippie Princess. That first night, we talked; sitting under a tree that seemed to have stars twinkling in its branches. I'm certain that if it hadn't been for the wine, we'd have made love right there, but she'd had too much. I ended up carrying her inside and leaving her on a couch. I slept in the van, parked in the lot at the Blue Nose Ferry.

I only saw Sarah twice after that; once in a bar where she worked, and the last time in a house she and several other kids had just rented. It was July third. She took my hand, wove her delicate fingers into mine, then walked me up a flight of stairs. Her room was up there and she wanted to show it to me.

They were splitting the rent five ways, she told me. It was a big house. "We can make it six if you want to stay here," she said, sitting on the bed, "with me."

I could have said yes and spent that summer with Sarah. I could have lied, made love to her then and there, and left anyway.

"I've got to go," I said. I turned and didn't look back.

I remember feeling incredibly holy at that moment. I'd come to Maine on my hippie-quest and was going off into the wilderness… alone. Sarah and I could have been the Hippie Prince and Princess of Bar Harbor that summer. Walking her down those crowded sidewalks at night, my arm around her waist, all heads would have turned. But I left and never regretted it, until now. What, after twenty-five years, would make me think of those sparkling eyes, and want, so badly, to see them again?

"Old hippie" is a hard thing to be. The two words are anachronistic. But here I am, almost three decades later, my hair thinning above my ponytail, crow's feet etched like peace signs around my eyes.

If there can be such a thing as an old hippie, I'm it. I own nothing but this '69 Chevy van and the few things inside it, mostly clothes and my tools. I managed to become a carpenter after I left school. I was one credit shy of my BA in English when I quit, and I felt very holy about that, too. I had my education—that piece of paper just didn't impress me.

Carpenter seemed like an honorable way to make the Evil Necessity. Turns out I have an aptitude for it. So that's what I did and still do, here and there, up and down the east coast. Lately I've been following storm paths into the damage, where the money is good and the help comes and goes. Soon, I know, my body won't be able to take anymore. I work very hard, when I do, and my knees complain. What can I do? I know what Jerry Garcia did, and I wonder if he's grateful. After old hippie comes dead hippie. I don't think we get any "declining years." I think we've already lived them.

So there I was, hunched over the steering wheel, headed for the Florida Keys where Hurricane George had just left me plenty of work. They shouldn't name hurricanes after men—it just pisses them off. They are female and don't like having men's names hung on them. Look at a satellite view sometime of a full-blown hurricane. Only something female could be so beautiful and dangerous at once.

I'd been to the Keys many times, still have friends down there. I was looking forward to seeing them, but my knees were bitching. Every time I clutched the Chevy, my left knee would pop, painfully, twice. Once in, once out. *Don't go,* it was saying.

I was going. I hadn't worked in months, and that poor old Chevy liked lots of gas and oil. Besides, it was October and getting cold. Once on the interstate—95—I wouldn't have to clutch and my knee would shut up. I was almost to it, on 178 in South Carolina, when I saw a hitch-hiker. I don't always pick them up anymore. The world's gotten awful damn crazy, but I do feel guilty when I don't. It was beginning to cloud up and my knees were swearing it was going to rain.

My decision was made even before I saw her. For just a moment, I thought my van was brand new, that it was 1969. There, standing in that late-afternoon, cloud-shaded light, was an honest-to-god Hippie Princess. It almost scared me, after thinking about Sarah, 'til she hopped in and threw her back pack behind the seat. Her hair was nearly black and her eyes so dark they seemed to be dilated. She wore a buckskin jacket a size too large, the fringe of which dangled down her hip-hugging jeans. A red bandanna was tied around her right thigh.

"Where ya headed, gorgeous?" she asked.

"I think I'm supposed to ask you that," I replied.

"You think I'm gorgeous?" she asked. She had a slight Southern accent that fit her better than the jacket.

"Second most beautiful girl I've ever seen."

"Who's the first, your wife?" She smiled. There was a glint in her eye when she asked me that.

"I never married," I said, pushing in that painful clutch and getting the van into gear.

"Me either," she said. "Big waste of time."

"You can't be more than twenty," I laughed.

"I'm a lot older than I look," she said seriously, and her voice sounded old. Then she laughed and said, her voice young again. "About twenty-one."

I laughed, too, but I'm not so sure I thought it was funny. There was something about her, something strange that I couldn't put my finger on. "I'm Mitch," I told her. "I'm headed for Cayo Oeso, the Island of Bones."

"Key West!" she said, surprising me that she knew the old Spanish name. "If you can stand the company I'll go with you."

"That where you were heading?" I asked.

"I was heading south," she answered. "That's as south as yer gonna get in this Chevy. Gotta cigarette?" I reached down under my seat and tossed her my can of Bugler. "Ah," she said, again very seriously. "A real cigarette."

In less than a minute she'd rolled two perfect ones and pinched the excess tobacco off the ends.

"Here," she said, sticking one into my mouth. "On the house."

"My tobacco," I mumbled, the cigarette dangling from my lip.

"Roll yer own next time, you ungrateful shit." She scowled at me. "And I was just considering fucking you, too."

"You're awful damn foxy to be fucking old men," I said as she lit my smoke. "And thanks for the cigarette."

"You're welcome, and I never fuck old men. So if you're old and you want to get laid, you better not tell me. You're a Hippie Prince, aren't you? And you've lost your Hippie Princess? Let her get away? Well, you were lucky, trust me. She'd have fucked your lights out, but you'd never have escaped. Then you would be old and so would she. Instead you're still a prince and now you've got me for a little while. I'll roll your cigarettes and sing to you while you drive."

"What's your name?" I asked. I wanted to change the subject. The synchronicity of things was disorienting me. I felt strange, maybe even scared, by the things she'd said.

"What would you like it to be?" she asked.

I almost said Sarah but didn't. As pretty as she was, this girl was not Sarah. "How 'bout 'Pearl,' after the immortal Janis?" I asked.

"Naw, I'm way too tall to be Janis. I know what you were going to say—I'm psychic, you know. But you'd better not call me that. Call me Cricket, for now. That's what my friends call me."

"Okay, Cricket, but if you're really psychic, what was I going to say?"

"She's gone now, Mitch, a long time gone. And if you say her name while I'm balling you tonight, I'll cut you off, *coitus interruptus*, I swear."

"How do you know that's what I want? For all you know, I could be gay."

"I told you, I'm psychic. Besides, you're a prince and I'm a princess. We may be the last two. If we didn't make love it would be a sin against fate. You want that haunting your soul?"

"I don't want anything haunting my soul," I answered.

At the entrance to I-95 I stopped for gas. When I came out from paying for it, Cricket was sitting behind the wheel.

"I'll drive for a while, give your knees a rest."

"How did you know... oh, yeah, you're psychic. Right. Have you got a license?"

"You wanna see it, Mitch?" she asked, sarcastically.

"No. No, just drive, Princess. My knees are killing me. I'll roll us some smokes."

"Here," she said, tossing a baggie onto my lap, "roll some of this."

I actually didn't smoke much pot anymore. Thirty years of toking and it just got old. But I rolled a fat stogie out of Cricket's stash and fired it up, passed it to her.

"I grew this myself," she squeaked, holding the smoke deep in her lungs. "It's kick-ass. If you're a real good lover I might turn you on to some acid."

"Damn, Darlin'," I said, taking back the joint. "If we're a rolling pharmacy now, how 'bout not going so fast. The speed limit in Carolina's sixty-five!"

"Sorry," she said, backing it down to seventy. "Case you didn't notice, I'm a pretty fast chick."

"Fast is good to a point," I laughed. "I haven't done acid in a decade. I'm not sure there's another trip in me."

"Oh, you've got a trip in you, alright. You a hippie or what?" she said, producing that scowl again.

"Whatever you say, Darlin'." The pot was making me sleepy. "If I cat-nap a little you gonna keep it under a hundred? I've been driving since dawn."

"Sleep, gentle prince," she said. "When you wake up we'll be in Georgia at a Holiday Inn. I'm gonna want you to wash my back."

Somehow I managed to sleep with that thought on my mind.

When I woke up we were parked.

Cricket was gone and my view consisted of a Holiday Inn sign. Then I saw that oversized buckskin full of pretty-baby coming out of the office. She hopped in the van and tossed me a key. "Room 169," she said, "a fortuitous number."

I was going to ask her about money when she said, "Tonight's on me. I sold a pound of that grass I grew before I hit the road. I don't want you paying for anything the first night I fuck you. Do you understand?"

I did. I understood her perfectly. She wanted that feeling of "holy."

Cricket drove and parked us in front of room 169. I grabbed the door handle, but she stopped me. "Don't get out, just look at it. That's where it's going to happen. That's where the last two will mate, and love will be jealous that it hasn't been so in so long." She looked at me then said, "It's the wedding chamber of what once was. Do you like poetry, Mitch?"

"Yes, I do," I said, much impressed by her recitation.

"But we're gonna eat, first, and that's on me too," she said as she started the van.

We ended up at a place called "Steamers."

"I'm ordering for you, of course," she said. "Remember, I'm psychic. Besides, there's only one possible thing we could eat before what's going to happen tonight. Bring us two big pots of oysters," she told the waitress. "A draft for me and club soda for my prince." I had quit drinking years ago. She smiled wickedly at me and I no longer doubted her claim to clairvoyance.

As the waitress left, I leaned across the table and asked, "You didn't know I like lemon with my club soda?"

"They're gonna bring a whole plate of lemons with the oysters."

They did.

Cricket was skilled with an oyster knife, and shucked and ate her pot-full in no time. Then she started on mine. "I've got the feeling I'm going to need these more than you," she said.

"That's awful flattering, Cricket, but…"

"Call me Annie," she interrupted. "My *friends* call me Cricket." Then she looked into my eyes and I swear I felt something inside of me melt. "We're beyond friends, you and I," she said, and I suddenly felt that I loved her. That feeling never left.

We finished eating in silence. The rest of the diners disappeared in a haze. All I could see was Annie. We drifted out of Steamers and, again, Annie drove.

As soon as the door clicked shut to room 169, Annie was in my arms. I slid my hands under the shoulders of her jacket and dropped it to the floor. Our lips never parted as we deftly undressed one another. I held her naked body against mine as tightly as I dared. It had been too long. So long that it almost hurt to have soft young flesh pressed against mine again. Then she lightly pushed me back and took my hands. "You are truly magnificent, Mitchell," she said looking me over. I started to reply, but she put a finger to my lips. "It's time to wash my back."

You can't run a Holiday Inn out of hot water, but we did our best. Annie faced into the shower's spray and I ran my soapy hands down her back, around her thin waist and onto her smooth, flat belly. I rested my chin on her shoulder and slid my finger between her legs. "Be good and come for me," I said, gently massaging that most famous spot on a woman's anatomy.

She leaned her dark head back and moaned, "I'm a good girl, Mitch. Oh, God, I'm so goooood!"

I was about to get onto my knees and kiss her there, but she stopped me. "Don't hurt your legs, lover, stop. You can do that later. Now you be good for me."

Annie knelt in that spray and steam and took me into her mouth. It didn't take long for that to work. I was about to warn her when she said, "I know, I want it."

It seemed like I'd never stop coming and she swallowed and swallowed and swallowed, moaning as if she could feel the orgasm shaking me. Then she stood up, threw her arms around my neck, and kissed me so hard I thought my lips would bleed.

"Take me to bed wet," she said. "Take me there, now!"

There were two beds in that room. Annie threw the covers off of one and pulled me down into it, on top of her. "Now you can put your tongue on me. Now, please, now!"

I slid down her slick, wet body. When I gently began that delicate kiss she wrapped her legs around me and writhed. I've known girls to fake orgasms, but Annie was no faker. It seemed like hers would never stop. When, finally, I did, she was weeping. I climbed back up her and stroked her hair, looked into her eyes. "What's wrong?" I asked.

"Wrong?" she smiled through her tears. "I am a princess being loved by a prince. I'm so full of joy it's spilling from my eyes. Make love to me, Mitch. Come deep inside me and stay there till dawn. I'm empty without you."

Oysters or no, my stamina amazed me. I loved her in every position. We remained as wet as we'd been in the shower. Finally we left that soaked bed for the dry one and curled up together like spoons. I entered her again from behind and we stayed that way all night, joined. I'm not sure if I slept.

Annie was asleep when I saw dawn sneaking around those thick motel curtains. I was still inside her. Slowly I withdrew without waking her. She groaned lightly and rolled onto her stomach.

Quietly, gingerly, I got out of that bed onto knees that felt like new. When you pal around with pain long enough, its absence is very noticeable. On a whim I went down into a knee bend, something I hadn't been able to do for years. I did another and another. I wanted to laugh out loud but knew I'd wake Annie. Gently I pulled the covers up around her and headed for the shower. If she wanted to play with me in there later, I'd take another one.

I looked at my face in the mirror and silently complemented the Holiday Inn designers on the bathroom lighting. It made me look ten years younger. I could barely find the ghost of a crow's foot. Those lights even made my thinning hair seem full. In the shower I couldn't help singing. For some reason, Mott The Hoople invaded my mind and I yowled out "All The Young Dudes."

Then the bathroom door opened and I heard the toilet seat drop. "You sing like a frog, my prince," she said.

"I woke you, didn't I?"

"No. No, you didn't. Sing to me more. I am sorely worn out this morning. Sing 'Stairway to Heaven,' I think you'll do that well."

Much to my surprise, I remembered all the words and sang it in key. Annie got into the shower with me, and curled into my arms. We stood like that for some time, but that was all. She seemed truly exhausted. As I stroked her pretty, wet head, I thought I saw a gray hair. Those lights that had flattered me were playing bad tricks on poor Annie.

When we left room 169, I drove. As we crossed the Florida state line Annie seemed to come back to life. "When we get to Pompano, get off," she said. "That's where we're staying tonight."

"Any place in particular?" I asked.

"It doesn't matter, as long as it's on the water. We're going to make love in the surf, and then in the shower, and then in bed. But I think you'd better feed me oysters again. I'm not getting any younger, you know."

I laughed, but Annie only smiled. It seemed like a sad smile, too, as if she was going to miss me. I felt no such misgivings. I was in love with her and would tell her soon—in the surf or the shower or in bed.

Annie made me get off at the Deerfield Beach exit, just north of Pompano. Apparently she knew the area. "It's the quickest way to the beach," she said.

She had me stop at four motels, each time coming out of the office shaking her head. At the fifth one she came out smiling. "They had a room 69. Tonight's on me, too."

I started to protest, but she waved it off, told me I was buying her dinner. "And I'm going to need a damn lot of oysters, at least a dozen of them raw." Again, she insisted I drive around to the room and sit while she looked at the door.

"When I'm full of semen and sea-water, we'll come back here and hold each other all night," she said dreamily. "And we'll flow like the tide into one another's veins. Your lips will be wet on my neck and I'll hold you inside. Our bed will be the timeless ocean floor, and we'll float above it, sink down into it. We will be one love in solution, forever calling each other's name."

I don't think I breathed as she spoke. She turned to me and said, "Take me someplace nice to eat, Mitch. I'm very hungry tonight. Joe's is good, and it's just down the road. Let's go."

Joe's restaurant was very like Steamers: a serious sea-food joint. Annie ate her dozen raw oysters, then a full pot steamed. She insisted that I eat oysters too, so I did. I have to admit they were good.

After dinner we drove back to the motel but didn't go into the room. Annie was insistent that we go right to the beach. She seemed almost desperate and tugged at me until we were out of the lights, down at the water's edge. Then I felt it, too. We were practically tearing each other's clothes off when Annie stopped me, put a hand on my chest, and said, "Wait... be still." Then she opened her other hand. I could barely see the two tiny squares of paper she was holding. She licked her finger and touched it to one of them, then placed it onto my tongue. The other she licked off her palm. We finished undressing each other then waded into the gentle surf.

A slight luminescence dotted the water here and there as we stood chest deep in that still tepid ocean. Annie floated her legs through my arms and eased down onto me. She was holding me tight as that wee small surf raised and lowered us, made our love for us as we kissed like the depths of that sea. The moon was a sliver and the stars were bright. All of that heavenly light was shining only for us, for that moment that lasted wave after wave after wave. I'd forgotten about the drug, but if it had anything to do with that ecstasy, I sing its praise.

We never made it to the shower that night, but lay salty in bed as we had the night before. It seems I tasted the sea on her nipples, on her neck, behind her ears, for hours. I know I slept this time because a knock on the door woke me. It was the maid asking if she could clean the room. It was almost check out time. "C'mon, Annie," I said, gently shaking her. "Let's get a quick shower, we've got to go." She barely moved, just rolled on her tummy and groaned. "Do you want to stay another night? I'll go take care of it if you do."

"No," she moaned, trying to move. "Get the shower going, not too hot. I'm coming, I'm coming, I'm coming."

I did as she asked and shortly thereafter she literally dragged herself in there. She stepped right into the shower and my arms, barely able to stand. I turned her around, facing the spray, when I noticed she was peeing. I don't think she knew she was doing it.

I dressed myself and then dressed Annie. It was like dressing a living doll. She just couldn't move. I got her into the van and buckled the seat belt around her waist. She immediately fell back to sleep. I thought it must be the drug, but I swear she looked older. There was definitely gray in her hair. I was in such a hurry in the room that I hadn't even combed my own. I looked at myself in the rear-view mirror and was shocked by what I saw. My eyes were clear and white, my hairline, full and restored. It was a college kid looking back from that mirror, and it scared the bejesus out of me. I drove down the beach to a 7-Eleven and bought a quart of orange juice. Then I tried to wake Annie.

"Please, Annie, drink some of this. You've got to talk to me. What's going on?"

Finally, she sipped the juice, looked at me as if unsure of who I was. Then recognition entered her eyes. The wrinkles around them were unmistakable now. Still, she was beautiful, and I loved her. "Mitchell," she smiled. "No one has ever loved me like that. Drive south, now. I must go to Key West. Please, will you take me there?"

"Of course I will, but what's happening, Annie?"

"I'll tell you in Key West, on the Isle of Bones. Now you must let me sleep. You've worn me out, sweet boy," she said touching my cheek. Then she slipped once more into slumber.

From Pompano it was all of five hours to Key West. Somewhere near Sugarloaf Key, Annie slowly started to rouse. We were less than an hour away. She managed to roll two cigarettes. Her once nimble fingers seemed to fight all her efforts. Finally, she stuck one into my mouth, said, "Say thank you." I did.

We crossed Stock Island and entered Key West. "Do you know the "La Concha?" she asked me.

"Yes, I do. Pretty uptown."

"Get us a room there, Mitch. I want to shower and change."

In the parking lot of that beautiful resort, I shut down the van and looked at Annie.

"Please tell me what's going on. Look at me, Annie. What's happening to me? What's happening to you?"

The sleep seemed to have done her some good. She smiled, wide awake now, and said, "I'll tell you at dinner. I'm hungry as hell. Get us a room, any number will do."

I did as she asked and drove us around to our room. Annie grabbed her back-pack, climbed out of the van. "Take a shower, Mitch. Then leave me alone for a bit. I want to dress for dinner."

I was so happy to see her alive again, and seemingly in good spirits, that I didn't question her further. I took a quick shower, put on clean clothes, and went to take a walk on the beach. Annie was sitting on one of the beds as I opened the door to leave. "Are you sure you're alright? Don't you want me to wash your back?" I asked.

She laughed. "That probably wouldn't be a good idea. I wouldn't be able to resist you. I need a little time alone. Give me an hour and I promise you'll understand."

The sun was beginning to set as I walked around Smathers beach. I don't wear a watch, but could tell by that sinking sun that an hour had passed. When I entered the room Annie was standing in front of the mirror. She turned as I walked in, a tube of bright red lipstick in her hand.

She was wearing a black cocktail dress, black stockings, and shiny black pumps. Her eyelids were powdered dark blue with shadow and her lashes were full of mascara. The gray in her hair all derived from the same spot, which made her look exotic. She looked like a beautiful woman of forty or so, dressed to the nines and in full war-paint. She was wearing a necklace of pearls, which looked real, but then real ones always seem fake to me. To say I was shocked would be laughable. I walked in and stood next to her, looking into that mirror. We could have been mother and son. I started to say something, but she put a finger to my lips. "At dinner," she said. "Let's go."

The dining room at the La Concha was exquisite. Fortunately, in Key West, even at the finest restaurants, there are no dress requirements. I was in jeans and a tee. We sat at the linen clothed table and Annie ordered a martini. "It's just a prop," she told me, "like the dress. Do you see that young man standing at the bar?" she asked. I looked and immediately noticed the guy she was talking about. Everything from his Italian loafers to his Rolex Oyster watch screamed *Money*. "He's been designing software for computers since he was seventeen, Mitch. He flew down here in his own jet. He thinks he has it all, but he's pissing away his youth. He doesn't deserve it."

"You gave me your youth, didn't you, Annie?" I asked, holding her hand across the table.

"No, I didn't. What I gave to you I stole from someone else, someone like him," she said, nodding her head toward the bar. Then she laughed. "I haven't been this old in a very long time. You truly are a Hippie Prince and that's something special, something you were born to be. You kept hold of your soul through all those years; through fear and hardship and loneliness. Think how your spirit will soar with another young life to live!"

"You're going to leave me now, aren't you?" I said, and I couldn't help crying. I loved her with all my heart.

"There are others like you, you know, though they're few and far between. And I'll steal for them what I've stolen for you. Look at him, Mitch," she said pointing toward the bar. "He doesn't deserve his youth. He doesn't need it."

Annie picked up her martini and stood. "I'm a pretty fast chick, sonny boy, and I don't much care for being old. Do you like poetry, Mitch?"

"You know I do, Annie. I know you know."

"Then write me a poem and always keep it with you—to remember me by."

"How could I ever forget you?" I said, sobbing into my hands. "Who are you, Annie? Please, tell me who you are before you go," I pleaded, looking up at her one last time.

"I am Anna Bell Lee, but don't use that name in your poem. It's been done. Stay young, my prince—I've purloining to do!"

I watched as Annie walked to the bar. Before long she left with the rich, young stranger. Suddenly I felt very happy. Good God, I was young again, and soon my Annie would be young again, too. I thought about eating some oysters, but wasn't hungry. I went back to the room. Annie's things were gone.

There was lots of work in Key West, but I wouldn't stay there long. It was cold in Maine that time of year, but I was young and strong and, for some reason, the wilderness beckoned. There, in that unsullied place, I would see Annie again, in everything growing, in the bubbling springs; a greater thief than time, more giving than life itself. And there I would write her poem, and keep it with me, always.

Her power binds the daisy to its chain (she'll free
your mind).
Buckskin bangles dangle down her hugged hips.
With candy-slick lips she smiled, and I melted away
like years of memory.
Hippie Princess held me with petal-lashed eyes,
and the acid-trip of my love swelled,
burst psychedelic from my heart's wound (all that time)
and sailed through Peter Max skies.
It is love she craves/gives away.
She silks the May pole, stays in the groove, groks.
She is freak-out lovely, daughter of Earth
and soul of all love sung blue.
Always easy, never shy, she is loose now
and stealing time from the diamond sky. ✳

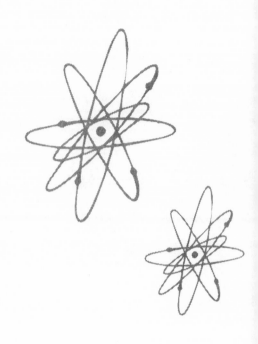

Detective White at the Magic Mirror, with Moonstone... Live!

H.F. GIBBARD

HIPPIES ARE THE BANE OF OUR CIVILIZATION. A stinking, drug-infested, disease-ridden plague on decent people everywhere. There's not a right-thinking person in this country who disagrees with me. Even if they won't say it out loud.

I'm under strict discipline now. On a short leash. But every once in a while, when the moon is full and the crowd gets rowdy and some damn fool gets out of line... I do like to get me some satisfaction on those freaks. I still do.

As a teenager, I looked into the big blue Kansas skies and saw the bombers flying overhead on their way to Germany. I decided I was going to be an airline pilot someday. After my accident, though... well, that just didn't work out. I ended up a cop in Oklahoma City. Worked for the department all through the '50s and '60s. Made my way up from patrol to detective.

The fifties were better, believe you me. Starting about '64 or

'65 we got a continuous stream of freaks passing through here. Breaking the laws, committing petty crimes, trashing things up. Burrowing into the crumbling old parts of downtown like crabs on a whore.

There was one thing that drew 'em down there. Barry Spear's place in the old Bingham Mattress Factory warehouse. The Magic Mirror—rock 'n' roll club, he called it. A glorified juke joint playing glorified nigrah music, I called it.

Spear brought all the so-called acts through there, through his club. Janis Joplin. Jimi Hendrix. Jefferson Airplane. He made money, buckets of it. I couldn't just shut him down, of course. His ACLU lawyers would've been on me like flies on shit. Pounding the table and yelling about their precious First Amendment rights to depravity. But I could bring a few officers down to the club on Saturday nights, to keep order.

Sometimes—this'll shock you—the officers spotted criminal acts going on at the Magic Mirror: long-haired freaky people shooting up dope or snorting illegal substances. Underage drinking or public nudity or gals giving blow jobs in the john… You think I'm kidding, right? Well, mister, if you were never down there then you just don't know.

I made sure my officers enforced the law. I gave 'em my permission to use the amount of force necessary to keep order. I didn't hold to this Earl Warren coddle-the-criminal stuff. More than one hippie pervert got his head busted in by my officers, wound up at the county hospital chained to a cot.

The docs down there had my permission to shave the kids' heads, if it helped with the treatment. And there wasn't a judge in town that would listen to any nonsense about police brutality. Not one. At least, that's what I thought.

Until June of '68, when Barry Spear found himself some candy-assed liberal judge to issue a restraining order. Against me! Telling me to stay away from the Magic Mirror. Keeping me from doing my job!

It made the *Daily Oklahoman*. Embarrassed the hell out of me. Just let those damn freaks break the law with impunity, infect the good kids of my town with their sex and drugs and whatever else until, until—

Anyway, I knew that order was wrong. That judge had been smoking the same stuff those hippies were. I went straight to my captain and told him that. He laid a hand on my shoulder and told me he was sorry and sure it was wrong but the city attorney was working on an appeal. Could take weeks, months, maybe, before they straightened this thing out. In the meantime, I had to stay away from the Magic Mirror. Me and all the officers in the department. Spear was hiring private security to watch over the place.

Bullshit!

They served the injunction on me on a Wednesday. Saturday night, the Magic Mirror opened for business as usual. A one-night-only engagement of a San Francisco band called Moonstone. I could only imagine. Drinking and drugging and pagan revelry. Homosexuals. Group sex. While the cat was away, the mice would play.

I stewed about it after work Friday night, drinking alone at DT's Lounge. I pounded one scotch after another. I couldn't have drunk like that if I'd still been married to Joyce, you know. She'd have had my hide. But I was alone that night, and I was getting drunk, feeling tighter and righter all the time.

They were treating me like *I* was the criminal. Me! What a pile of crap! I was just doing my job! Protecting the good people of this town from all the burglars and murderers and rapists that got shat into the world by their ghetto mamas. I'd been a damn good cop for the past what, fourteen years? Fifteen?

Before that, I'd been ready to ship out overseas. To protect my country during the Big One. Trained as a paratroop before my accident. But I was ready to go. I would have gone, but I had my accident, and then the war ended… but I didn't fight them damn Nazi bastards for nothing, so the worthless kids could drug themselves into oblivi—

I must have been talking out loud to myself. Yelling, because Smitty came over and told me to shut up and that I was cut off and to get the hell out if I couldn't hold my liquor. I said I was sorry and I stumbled out down the street. At first I contemplated a trip to a dive bar over on Stanley Avenue to finish up my bender, but then I just thought to hell with it and I took a cab home.

It was in the cab that the idea came to me. Just before I nodded off. Damn, it was a good idea.

That restraining order, that piece of paper, what the hell did it say? It said Detective David White couldn't come within one hundred feet of the Magic Mirror. All right. But what if Detective White wasn't there? What if it was somebody else? Somebody just as damn freaky looking as all the other hippies in the joint? An unofficial undercover officer…?

Moonstone only performs under a full moon, you know. Brings out all the really freaky folk. Vampires and Satanists and night creatures. That's why they need their very special security, who travels with the band. More about that later.

I went down to the Goodwill and outfitted myself. Flannel shirt, elephant bell jeans, scruffy jean jacket. A headband and leather boots. Topped it off with a big black wig. I looked at myself in the mirror and I laughed out loud. I looked like a class A freak-job.

The Magic Mirror was in an old brick mattress factory. The hippies had painted the walls purple and orange. I paid the cover and headed for the beat-up wooden bar in back to get a beer. The band was up on stage, setting up, doing a sound check.

The roadies were young, bearded, wiry-looking guys in psychedelic T-shirts and velvet pants. They came and went, checking everything out. Blasting ugly sounds that hurt my eardrums. Then they left, and the stage was empty except for dust and their equipment and cigarette smoke that swirled in the blue lights.

After a while the band drifted in and took their places, one at a time. The drummer was this big ugly dude with a barrel chest and a huge slashing scar down his face. Lead guitar was rail-thin, with blond straight hair parted down the middle and granny glasses—looked queer to me. I couldn't make out the bass player's face through all the hair. Keyboard player had short hair, and an earring.

So far I wasn't much impressed with Moonstone. I took my seat in a folding chair on the front row and waited. Felt my boots stick and un-stick from the floor.

Just before the music started, *she* came into the room. Yep. That's right. Mariana Molavi. I saw her for the very first time that night. Didn't know who she was back then, believe it or not.

Mariana looked as pale as death, with long white hair that flowed down her black backless gown. Was she moving, or did the room move around her? I couldn't tell. In her gown, she seemed to float. Her long thin arms hung at her sides and I could see the bluish veins running down them. She moved, unhurried, toward the stage.

She was flanked by two big bruisers, their faces hidden under black monk cowls. Security. They took up positions on either side of the crowd, their arms folded in the loose sleeves of their black monk costumes. Freaky.

Mariana mounted the stage. The crowd got quiet. She swayed a little, in front of the microphone. I could see her face better now, silver pale, with night-black eyebrows. She licked her scarlet red lips and I thought she was going to say something for a minute, but she didn't.

It was her eyes that caught my attention. They were wide and black, with a depth to them that was more animal than human. As she turned her head, the stage lights flashed off of them. I'd seen that kind of flash before, night fishing, when the moonrise suddenly struck a deep prairie pond. But never on a woman.

She stared out over the audience, saying nothing. Barry came on stage and introduced the band. Mariana's face stayed calm, attentive, through the applause. I wondered if she was drugged up. No. She looked alert, detached, as though she were studying the audience from some other dimension.

All at once, it started. A steady bass beat, like a heartbeat, with quiet little guitar sounds whirling around it like eddying wind currents. After a minute, the audience started to clap in time to the beat. Some of them stomped their feet. A few whistled.

The beat grew louder, then faster. The guitar riffs accelerated. The wind currents became a thunderstorm. Lightning flashed. Thunder boomed! Mariana hissed into the mike and it was like I felt the rain fall on me. She began to moan, writhing, and darkness filled the room as her hair spun under the lights. The strobe lights came on. Her body became the storm, violent, turbulent... Wilder, louder, a frenzy of sound and movement and flashing stuttering light—

It ended. The performers froze on the stage. Then the audience was leaping to its feet, applauding, whistling, calling out. Calling out to her. I jumped up with them.

The applause gradually died. We sat down. The bass beat started up again. That's when I heard it for the very first time. That guitar riff. The famous one. The one that launches their signature tune, "Pindar."

The audience recognized it. Applauded and whistled.

The album version runs for fifteen minutes. Live, on stage, sometimes I've heard them go on for twenty, twenty-five, more. Time doesn't seem to matter, once they get started.

What is "Pindar"? Hell, I can't explain it. It's just different. Damn it, I can't tell you how.

My dad's second wife was a Catholic. She took me to mass sometimes. "Pindar"'s like the organ music I heard, like the Latin chanting they had back then. Not slow, exactly, not ancient, really, but... You just get this *sense* through the drumming and the bass beat and the deep low chanting that the music stands for something deeper than you know.

Look. "Pindar," that song, it's like it knows about all the suffering in the world. It sings it all out at once, belts it out from the belly of the universe. And then, just when you're ready to pack it in, to slit your wrists and be done with it, it offers relief.

The relief of becoming what you really are, who you really are, who you were sent here to be, whether you wanted to come here or not. Who you have to be, in spite of everything. The wailing Mariana does—it's like the sounds of birth, of new birth, of release from everything you never really wanted to be. The transformation into... But now I'm choking up, damn it, telling you about it. Excuse me.

It can make you feel awful at first, that song. Make your guts twist. Like you're a kid and been called to the principal's office, or to the dentist, or your dad is staring down at you with fury in his eyes for something you did, or maybe just for something you are. The words are simple and Mariana sings them quietly but then she jerks from time to time like
they're being torn out of her and they get down inside you and those words they twist and they turn.

I had to get up from my seat. I didn't know where I was going. I just had to move. Before I knew it I was standing by the stage, face to face with one of the security guards. Looking down into the darkness of his cowl, all I saw was orange. Orange glowing eyes set deep in the blackness.

He growled at me. The voice wasn't human. But I can't forget the words: "Let it come. Become what you are."

Then I was running away, toward the restroom. The music followed me. I slammed into the door and stumbled into a stall. The puke hurled from my guts into the stool, splashing onto the filthy tile floor.

I was falling, falling, and my pulled on the cords but the wind had caught my chute and I couldn't control it anymore. I tried to steer and then the tree loomed up below me, a big mass of green and black and I threw my arms in front of my face, but I hit it without control. I felt a crunch and something in my leg snap and my bowels loosed.

Oh, god, Sarge. Oh, god, Dad. I screwed the pooch. I screwed it and now I'm hanging here in this tree with shit and piss going down my broken leg and I've failed and I'm going to die...

I was breathing hard, and sobbing. I reached down and tried

to undo my belt to let my crapped up pants down but my hands wouldn't work. My fingers were covered in thick gray hair and sharp claws were growing out of them, and I couldn't undo my pants.

I was sobbing and I tore my belt off and hurled it under the stalls. I heard some guy yell "What the fuck, dude?" Then I ripped them all off me, the shirt and the peace sign and the pants and the wig and everything, tearing them to tatters.

I left my gun and my badge somewhere in the rag pile. I wanted to be naked now, naked with power, with sheer animal muscle will…

I slammed my way out of the bathroom and headed for the stage. The power, an angry crying thing inside me, drove. I couldn't control it even if I wanted to. Waves of heat ran down my hairy arms, my legs…

All at once I threw back my head and howled.

The music halted. I heard the snare drum hiss from the echo of my howl. Then I heard the screaming. They were running away from me. All the hippies. The freaks and their little chicks, with their leather fringe purses and short skirts and go-go boots. They were all shrieking now, with their little girlish shrieks. I howled again, just to hear their screams again.

I saw a well-turned calf go by and I followed the gal, not to screw but to bite, to consume, to eat that girl alive with a power that radiated from my loins and ended at the sharp tips of my canine teeth and the knife-like claws on my fingertips.

I had nearly caught up with her when a shadow loomed up between us. I heard the claws on my feet clacking on the concrete floor as I slid to a halt. I crouched and growled, tensing my body, feeling the muscles knot.

Mariana lifted her hand, palm out toward me. Light flowed from the hand, a powerful, unearthly light. I felt something slam into my forehead. The light blinded me and I blacked out for a second, then my whole world spun around twice. The force knocked me to my knees.

I knelt and looked up into the face of Mariana. The face of

the Mistress. I knew it was she who had loosed me. Loosed me to serve her. Light was streaming from her face. I was crying. I couldn't stop crying.

Her eyes were sad. Her mouth opened and she spoke to me.

"To serve," she said, and her hand extended to stroke my furry forehead, "and to protect."

That's when I saw it. My life. My whole future in an instant. The light faded. A second later, the two monks were on either side of me. They each had a hand on my shoulder, steadying me. The hands were hairy and clawed. Just like mine.

The one on the right, the one with the big orange eyes, leaned over and growled in my ear. "Welcome, brother," he said.

That was five years ago. I've been touring with Moonstone ever since.

Sure, a lot of guys on the force do private security when they retire. Sit at a desk somewhere in a federal building or an office tower or a bus station. But I bet none of them has a gig like mine.

No paperwork. No surveillance monitors. No giving directions to the john.

I just work when the moon is full. Put on my big black cowl instead of a uniform. Watch for the rowdies who approach the stage with broken bottles and bad attitudes.

And you don't want to act up when I'm on duty. That would be a big mistake. A few of them freaks have found out how much of a mistake, over the years.

Like I said, I'm on a short leash. Mariana says I can't kill or cripple 'em. We want the fans to come back, after all. But I'm allowed to get the job done. When they get out of hand, I get the job done.

I like to say it's the best job in the world. The best damn job I've ever had, anyway. Because you see, thanks to Moonstone, to Mariana, to the Mistress, I've finally become what I always wanted to be.

One mean, howlin' son-of-a-bitch in a big black robe, keeping the bad guys in line. ✳

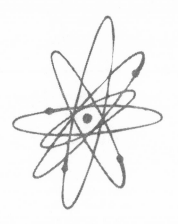

Rob Roy's Last Night in Northeast Philadelphia

MATTHUE ROTH

DARK BLUE LIGHTS, a skating pond warmed over, miniature golf and the Super Scoop Ice Cream Shoppe with strollers clattered in a line down the block. A low, throbbing disco hit from the next house over, red and yellow of McDonald's from down the block, and the loud grate of transmissions against pavement on the road. This is Frankford Avenue at night: there are no taxis in this part of town because nobody ever leaves this part of town, and every man on the street has at least three tattoos, and every woman has black leggings and socks pulled over them. After dark the socks go underneath, and the men are still wearing tattoos. The men's shirts never change: they always have roofers' names on them, and they are all a size too small.

Amy and Tasha and I are sitting on the patio outside Joshua's house, waiting for him like three prom dates on the edge of our plastic deck chairs. Joshua's father sits on the steps with the other Northeast men. They are talking about hoagies. His mother is in the kitchen, and she just made lemonade, and now she's deciding if she should serve it to us or not.

Joshua catapults down the stairs and grabs his sparkle spider necklace from a table in the living room. Then he runs back upstairs, and downstairs again. He glances at us through the screen door and says, "Shit!" Then he runs back inside.

Amy is reading what I'm writing over my shoulder. I just asked her why she was doing that, and she said—as a lesson to me, 'cause *she* thinks of herself as a writer and I don't—"Write that down if you're thinking it. You're not supposed to say it out loud, cause if you do, you'll lose it forever."

I look at her, exasperated. I thought I was supposed to be the muscle in our operation.

"I'm gonna train you to be a writer, Rob Roy," Amy says, "even if it's the last thing I do."

So now we're at a club: Tasha is the only one not wearing black, but she *is* black, so she gets away with it. Everyone's eyes glaze over her, and she dances madly across the floor. Amy is staring at my head, which we just shaved. She's nervous about the job she did, and also I am starting to suspect that she likes me, and I can feel myself sinking into myself.

I spot this girl from the Sister Machine Gun concert last weekend who was a friend of my friend Splike, and I remember how I tried to talk to her in a whir of a second at that show. I remember that she said something that was a quote from an Ani Difranco song, which seemed so iconoclastic that I fell in love with her on the spot. I want to go up to her and talk to her again, but I don't, and my gaze moves, and I flush red because I don't want Amy to be jealous or anything.

Not like she should.

In the industrial noise of the club, I feel quiet and lost. I realize that I'm swaying with the bass and so I stop.

"Hey, punkboy, you look haunted," says Amy and plants herself at my elbow. My face heats up because I don't want it to look like we're going out, and I tense up because I'm uncomfortable. This club is my place, and I wonder how me-looking-like-this looks to everyone else, all my friends who know me as me-with-out-a-girl-on-my-arm.

It's weird because, although it's my place, Joshua's band is performing, and really, he's more like the emcee tonight. Tonight, the dancing kids are here to see him, and I consider this: my friends are his fans? Not really. They're not close enough to be my friends, and they don't know anything about Joshua's band except that they play good songs... but nevertheless, they are here. I look at the black clothes and white faces and don't recognize anyone. For the first time at Vampire Nite, I feel a little lost.

"So, this is my scene," I tell Amy, as though saying it makes it so.

"Um. Fun place you got here," she says, twirling a hanging thread of pale white Christmas lights that dangles from the ceiling. We stop in front of a wall with Munch's *The Vampire* done up as a full-wall mural.

"Not really. Mostly it's just pretentious kids gnawing on each other. They take a lot of E and they think it makes them dance better."

"So that's why you come here every week."

I flinch. Everybody thinks I'm a monster drug addict—being two hundred pounds and wearing only black and having a shaved head will do that to you in Northeast Philly—but Amy knows as well as I do that I've never done drugs. It's like my Achilles heel. Only not.

"'Cause I need an excuse to flame out and dress this way is why I come here every week," I say, running my hand across the fresh baldness of my head.

"Does it really feel all right?"

"It feels naked," I say—which it does. "I feel good, it feels good, I mean. Sort of different. Sexxy with two 'x's. I feel like I should be reinventing myself."

"Fucking adolescent."

"You mean, *non*-fucking adolescent," I say and hold my hands up with the X's on them, and I feel like my saying I'm straight-edge is a barrier, like I'm spelling out to Amy that she can't have sex with me, but after I say it I realize that I've brought up sex as a conversation piece. Shit.

"Um, yeah," Amy says. I see the pack of clove cigarettes that she just took out, and I see she's worried that she's offending me.

"It's fine," I say. "I mean, it's not like nobody else is smoking…"

"Are you sure you don't mind?"

"I don't mind."

So she lights up, and I hear the paper crackle as it flows into her lungs. I imagine being inside her body like that, and I get cold shivers as a response from inside my body that I interpret as fear and lust. I feel myself backing into the crowd, my body starting to convulse with the beat like a… shit, what are they called?

"Mexican jumping beans," says Amy. "That's what these kids look like. They're not moshing, they're bouncing."

I gape. Is God telling me something?

By the stage, Joshua is setting up the trap kit like a model kit, fitting metal bars and drum stands together. He picks up a cymbal and his gaze gets caught by the crowd, too. He stares out into the sea of faces, and for a second I think he's looking for me but I know he's probably just stoned. As soon as I think that, his eyes flash on me and he twists his faces into a grimace. I stick out my tongue at him back.

"What the hell was that?" asks Amy, oblivious.

"That," I say, "was Sex Goddess of the Western Hemisphere, Joshua Lipman."

"Oh, Jesus. I can't believe he's doing this. A concert. I mean, the first time they practiced was, what, last Tuesday? They still suck."

"What's their name again?" I ask.

"I forget. Like, Christ Slugfest, something like that. No. Something about Christ."

"Oh, God," I say, shaking my head.

"Christian Death? Naah."

A pit was congealing on the floor. I saw Tasha jump into it, and for a second everyone else in the pit froze—there were no other girls there—until she ran straight into an big angry-looking fat guy and she kept going, and everyone else started back up.

"At least he's doing something productive, you know?" I said, shrugging. Joshua being productive meant Joshua Without Acid, which was a good thing, because Joshua With Acid meant conspiracy theories, alien abductions, and attempts to beat me up. And here I should note in all fairness that I am six-foot-one and Josh is five-foot-four, and we're both built like you'd think we would be, and I have been trying really hard to be a pacifist.

Amy, who is reading what I'm writing, mutters "Yeah, a pacifist Satanist." I shrug, since I'm not really a Satanist. I just give equal time to the establishment, is all.

Having Amy around makes me nervous again, so I go off and find my friend Splike, the man who is in charge of renting out this club and producing shows like this every other Saturday during the summer.

"So sometimes you get Sister Machine Gun," he says to somebody, "and sometimes you get Christbait Sucking. I can't get fucking Nine Inch Nails every fucking week. If you can, I'll hire you, but I'm sorry and I don't do refunds."

"That sucks," says a kid, this glam-goth in a Morrissey shirt.

"I thought they were called Christ Hates Fucking," said one of the girls with him.

"Management's rules," says Splike, who I'm pretty sure *is* the management—for tonight at any rate. He's young and huge, bigger than me, even, and he has a goatee and this bleached-white hair that sets you apart from him and below him.

He sees me and walks over, laughs, and rubs my head appreciatively. "What happened? Your hair get sucked by Christ or something?"

"I thought Joshua's band's name was Dead Christ Slugfest," I say.

"Whatever. Joshua better be fuckin' incredible or else there's gonna be a ton of angry customers," he says. "It's not easy to convince this many alternative kids to come to the Northeast. This whole every-other-week thing has got to end, you know?"

"Not good?"

"No one remembers. There's all these rave kids outside, and last week all these metal and goth kids showed up for the rave, and no one can remember which weekend is which and everyone's getting screwed over and I'm barely breaking even. Maybe not even barely tonight."

One of Splike's huge hands flashes out and grabs the shoulder of a kid walking by.

"Hey, Splike," the kid says. "Problem?"

"What's your band called?"

"Beats me. Christ Beats Children, maybe?"

"Right," grunts Splike, and lets the kid run off.

Then he turns to me and grunts in a more candid and helpless fashion. "What the hell kind of business am I running?"

I laugh, more nervous than I want to sound.

Like an Addams Family portrait or something, a coterie sprung up around Splike, half a dozen kids who all looked the cool, silent type—the kid who's cooler than anyone else in the room and who you desperately want to talk to you. One of them stares at me, unimpressed, and says "I *am* a work in progress." I realized it was from an Ani Difranco song, which would have seemed lame to quote except at the time it didn't, and I smiled and said hello, and though I got introduced to everyone else, all I remember is her whose name is Sara and she has long black hair that sort of float along with her as she moves.

"Oh. That's, um, that's Ani—"

Sara reaches up to put a finger over my mouth. "Don't say it," she whispers, aside, to me. "People will think we're too hopelessly not goth."

She smiles.

Amy, meanwhile, is lost in the crowd. The music has gelled the crowd from a pit into a swimming stream, and she finds

Tasha and sways to the beat. "Is this dancing?" Amy says.

Tasha, hurt, begins the speech about how these clubs aren't regular, these people aren't regular, and Amy begins to look even more pained.

"Let's go outside," Amy says.

Outside is a pastiche of Northeast night: those men in too-tight shirts coming and going, scattered kids milling about in twos and threes and packs. The 7-Eleven across the street has cars screech up and grab Slurpees like canned goods before a hurricane. The adolescent traffic stood by the pay phone outside, waiting for calls, or pretending to wait for calls. The boys are on one end and the girls are on the other, kids our age are just drifting all around the parking lot.

"Shit," Amy says, "there are so many kids out tonight. I feel like I don't know anybody here, inside, anywhere, you know?"

"Welcome to the suburbs, punko," Tasha offers.

"We're still in the city. You can still see the skyline down Frankford Avenue. It's grey and purple before sunset and yellow-on-black after, it's like magic pens or something, you know?"

"This is the suburbs, Amy. Look around. I mean—listen. There's no noise."

"And everyone is white," I add.

"Suburbs," contends Tasha.

"Shit, girl, I don't know. All I did was grow up here. And I got out the first chance I got."

"You still got the accent, though."

"What?" Amy is suddenly hushed.

"I was kidding."

"Were you?"

"Do I?"

"No, Amy. I'm sorry. I swear. I speak more like a Northeast girl than you do."

"I realized just last year how hard I was consciously trying to get rid of it," Amy said. "Did you ever notice? I started over-compensating like crazy. Until I was pronouncing my 'T's more than you do, more than my teachers did. By May, I sounded

Canadian, the way I was all 'oot and aboot' just so I wouldn't say 'warter' the way that I was brought up saying it."

"Say it again."

"Warter."

"Why did you want to lose the accent?"

"'Cause. It's a Northeast accent."

"So?" said Tasha.

"So I don't know."

They sit there, watching the kids at 7-Eleven, going in and out, waiting for kids they don't know to come up, talk, flirt, fight, hook up, go out.

Tasha fidgets with her studded leather bracelet, the one that gleams in the moonlight like a vampire's skin.

"You ready to come back in, Amy?"

Amy weighs her options. She looks at the kids by the 7-Eleven, the kids by the club. "Sure," she says, trying to sound more than half-hearted about it.

In a few minutes I walk up to Amy, and she screeches like a viper, grabs me by the shoulders, spins my head around, "Oh my god—"

"It's just Sharpie," I say.

There are coils and paisley swirls around the back, over the top, in black marker where my hair should be. If you tilt my head one way, it says "Sara" in thousands of little twirling shapes, but you have to be looking for it. And in another way it has an anarchy sign. Sara wanted to draw a bird inside the paisley, too, but we thought it would be too obvious.

"Fuck, Rob Roy, do you realize what the fuck your fucking head fucking looks like?"

"It's aesthetic. Um. I thought it was."

"Oh my fucking *god*, Rob Roy, you are so going to die. How many weeks are elections in?"

"My father doesn't need to bring me on the campaign trail—"

"—well, *duh*, not *now*, with your hair getting all Satanic—"

"—I'm just giving equal time to—"

"—and you look like a total *tool*—"

"—You always have to bring up my father—"
"And I think it looks ugly."
"Did I ask you?"
"Fuck you." And she leaves.
"Dag," says Splike from behind me.
I turn around. He is sipping his beer and smiling.

Tasha watches the people from on top of the club. The concrete
floor pulses with the music downstairs, the same way that a
7-Eleven at night pulses with the electronic hum of phospho-
rescent light. It's only twilight, so there's only a few people out
there dancing so far, and Tasha is not paying attention to them
anyway. I am looking at her, and as I come over she smiles but
doesn't look at me.

"What's up, Rob Roy? Why are you following me around?"

"'Cause I lust after you. What do you want me to say, Tasha?
It's cause you're the coolest person in the whole club and if I
hang out with you, the cool kids will think I'm cool, too."

"Yeah, right. Right on both counts," says Tasha, smiling. She
lifts the Coke out of my hand. "I thought you were straight
edge, punk."

"I still do caffeine, you crazy kid. If I should ever go off that…
well, here's me, and here's high school. Note how far apart my
hands are now."

She laughs, and I realize that I like the way she laughs the way
I like orange sherbet.

"This is my barrio," I tell her, looking out on what she's staring at. "Two more years, and I am so off to college. I will never
see this landfill again."

"Yes you will."

"No, really. I won't."

"Now, Rob Roy," said Tasha. "Who knows more about your

life: you or me?"

"Amy."

"The truth comes out."

Silence falls upon us. The moshers keep moshing, and we both keep taking sips of our Coke from the same can.

"Not now," Tasha says. "Right now I don't think she want to know so much about your life, Rob Roy."

I start to protest in that way that's so I'm-asking-for-it. She silences me with a glance.

"You want me to ask you why you did that to your head?"

"I didn't do it—"

"Don't give me that crap. You got it done, so you done it."

"So I like it, you know? I think it looks neat. Don't you think it's neat?"

"Yeah. Real neat."

"You're not lying well, Tash."

"I like it. I think it looks cool. But I hate the reason why you did it. I think you did it cause it puts Amy on the other side of the fence."

"No I didn't—"

"Well, it still does."

She looks at me, raises an eyebrow.

I nod.

"So I'm looking out on Frankford tonight, and there are no problems. I'm looking at the white trash kids in jeeps at the 7-Eleven, and I'm just watching their white trash drama unfold, you know?"

"Yeah. It's so Raymond Carver, all those redneck kids smoking their Marlboros, it's like the fucking *Wonder Years* or something."

"I liked *Wonder Years*."

"I didn't. All those suburban kids telling me what my childhood is supposed to be like in retrospect from thirty years later: 'These are the best times in your life, so live them this way.' It was so damn oppressive. I remember worrying what my life would be like if I didn't get a girlfriend like that girl on the show. The one Fred Savage was never going out with, but, like, they were always hooking up—"

"They weren't always hooking up. They didn't have sex 'til the last episode."

"Like, his whole life was destiny or something. There was this new dimension of real life that wasn't like TV because problems didn't get worked out in half an hour. But all his problems were the problems that adolescents are supposed to have, so he didn't have to solve them, you know?"

"I don't get it," says Tasha, her gaze flickering back to the crowd out front.

"Never mind."

I realized that we were supposed to be talking about Tasha, not just about me. I felt guilty, walking over her fantasies like I did. It must be different for boys to watch Every Typical Boy Show on prime time.

"You know what I'm thinking?" said Tasha.

"What?"

"How much I'd like to just walk over to one of those groups of guys over there, behind the 7-Eleven, and just start talking. And it would all be nice and innocent, and they'd look at my V-neck and try to see down my shirt, and I'd giggle at their jokes, and we'd just drive around for a while, and they'd give me a ride home instead of me waiting forever for the bus."

I looked at her. I'd never heard Tasha talk like this before.

"We'd just chill, and maybe smoke up, but it would be nice and innocent. There's so many kids around here, you know? I never realized."

"Yeah," I said, "but they're all Gs."

She snorted through her nose.

"I mean, you're black; maybe they'd revere you as the Real Nigga or something."

"No way. I'm not on TV, and I talk too white, anyway. They'd never go for it."

"Not yet you're not on TV."

"Wish I was white," said Tasha, suddenly soft.

"What?"

She turns a little pale.

"Shit, why?" I said. "You're a black-girl goth. You get freedom not to wear the same smelly fishnets that everyone else here is."

"Even the boys."

"Especially the boys."

The floor stands still, and then there are a few sonic bursts of crackle.

We look at each other, fearful.

Joshua is coming on.

The crowd is sizeable, even if they're not paying attention. With Dead Christ Children or whoever playing, Splike didn't expect fifty kids to show up when they got three hundred for Sunshine Blind last month.

"Whatever," Splike says to Tasha behind me. "All that matters is that somebody's giving the kids guitars and a beat. People just want to dance, you know?"

"Yeah, but they do that for free," Tasha says. "These kids are paying five bucks for the name."

And then there is a static

that makes everyone turn around

—noise—

"Fuck," some kid whispers.

The static cuts out. Everyone is still.

"Fuckin' blow your *brains out*!" screams Joshua, and the music cuts in just when he turns from whisper to yell.

The drums crash in, loud and fast.

"We are Christ Bait Rising," Joshua says, his voice echoing in family packs over the sound system. "Worship us!"

I groan.

The bassist nervously steps up to the second microphone.

"Or just dance," he says.

Joshua is screaming like a man possessed. The cacophony

grates like sheep on steroids, and the audience erupts in into a twisting limbering mass, a G.G. Allin piece of limbs and art, their heads a wave of rhythm.

"*Let go!*" Joshua yells. He is. For all his nihilism, Joshua is always calm. Seeing him like this is frightening and I can't take my eyes off him: he is riding the anger, using it. He builds crescendos with the music and lets them go with his left hand in the air. Tasha was right: everyone is into his act, and they don't care whether he looks like Marilyn Manson or Abba, as long as the music is harsh enough to dance to.

Standing by the bar, where the music is not so loud, I see that girl Sara glide by. Michelangelo is on her breath, and I tug her sleeve as she passes by. "You've already cost me one friend tonight," I tell her. "Wanna see what we can do about the rest?"

"What?"

"My head. Overnight, I've become too avant-garde for my best friend."

"It's not art, Rob Roy. It's just your head."

"Everything is art," I yell back into Sara's ear.

"Then all music is art rock," she says back, into a normal voice, into my ear. I can hear her fine. I feel sheepish for yelling.

"What are you doing after this?"

"Dancing."

"Moshing?"

"Dancing."

Sara tugs on my sleeve, and tells me she'll see me later, not dismissive but hopeful, and I touch her elbow lightly as she passes on.

Splike comes up to me, all grins.

"She likes you, you know."

"What?" Astonished. "Sara, you mean?"

"No. The pretty chick in black who yelled at you."

"Amy?"

"The cute one."

Amy who has a round circle-y face and piercing hazel eyes set back far into her skull and hair that goes straight down to her shoulders and lets loose a little curl. She is the one who you'd call cute when you know she isn't pretty or beautiful. I don't know where she is right now. I know that I'm not going to let her read this, now—but I think I knew that all along: she's making me write it (still, now, even though I don't want to talk to her) but it's mine.

Whatever.

"Whatever."

"I know these things."

"Thanks for coming out tonight," says Joshua, the first time his voice is normal since the beginning of the show. "This will be our last song. I will kill myself after it is over." And he takes out a gun.

No one says anything.

"Um, our encore will be an instrumental," the bass player says.

"Life on the farm is kind of *laid back*!" Joshua screams. He is staring straight at me with the "I told you I would do a John Denver cover, muthafucka" look. He is jumping up and down. His shirt is off. The band is working its way into an orgasmic frenzy and the pit is tumbling gnashing clawing itself like a mule, a pile of meat and leather two and three goths tall. Convulsing. It strikes and strikes again. The rage is relentless, and the floor is gravitating toward it, even Amy moves to it, thrashing some hardcore kids in Misfits shirts. Splike is looking half nervous, half impassioned, as he stands at the back with his hands on the bar, watching. The music should have ended, it seems, but they transformed the fiddle solo into some ungodly thing, two-guitar interplay, a woman yelling sampled, Joshua roaring nothings.

"Yeah, I got those cakes on the motherfuckin' griddle…"

This is too weird for words, but the kids are loving it.

"Hey, Rob Roy," comes a voice to my shoulder.

Sara is standing there, by me, and taking in the crowd with her eyes. "This is bad," she says.

"Oh, it's always like this," I tell her. "bruises and blisters and bones broken."

"No, I know it's usually just friendly. But look at the kids in the crowd, I think it's…"

What is weird is not just Joshua kicking the hardcore groove to "Thank God I'm a Country Boy," but the kids, who are as goth as your average TV talk show host. They muted it tonight, but they got that whiteboy rapper look engraved into their souls, the bad facial hair, the b-boy cuts, the jeans with a crotch down to their knees for God knows what reason.

The guitars cut out, suddenly, to a bass solo, and Joshua crouches down, pulsing with the beat, sunk into his knees. He plays with the spikes on his shoes, waiting, probably to jump up maniacally, and now —when you can hear things—someone shouts, "Fuckin' punks!"

And things erupt.

"Oh, yeah," Joshua says on the stage, and the guitars break back in, but they don't realize what's going on for a second. In that second there is blood flying, blood landing, and all kinds of bad shit is going down.

This kid I was talking to a minute ago is lying against a wall, and two of his teeth are just hanging onto the wall. Goths and Mayfair kids are attacking each other like wolves. You can feel the pent-up hate spilling out like afterbirth.

I look for Splike. He's already in the pit prying kids apart. To the Gs, he's just another dork in black, though, and not even an adult. There are three kids on him, and they're just about match-ing him. Sara is by the door, calling the cops over from the 7-Eleven, and the melee has cleared away to most people standing by the walls, watching the few remaining kids have it out.

"God, Sara, what happened?" I ask when the sprinkler system comes on.

And the fights start again.

"We should get out of here," she says. Frantically I'm looking for Amy.

"Hey, whiteboy, come on!" Someone grabs me and hustles me to the door. Sara is running with us, ducking under the tables and bars. I can feel the drawings on my head melting like icepops, running down my face with the water. The door is narrow, and there aren't many people left in the club, at all. Outside there is a circle surrounding the club; kids of both species stand and watch us all come crawling out. Inside is a chaos of battles, and we scramble to get outside the circle, away from the action and away from everyone.

"Tasha," I say, recognizing my savior.

"Hell, yes," she says, smiling kamikazily.

"God—thanks, I guess. Where's Amy?"

"She's backstage, with Joshua, I think. He was going to sock it to some Gs, and I was just gonna sit back and laugh until things got really severe, but Amy talked him out of it. Said if he wasn't gonna save his guitar from certain death she'd do it herself, and keep it. I shudder to think what was going on back there now."

"You think they're okay?"

"Sho'nuff. You think those wiggers can find their way through the backstage labyrinth?"

I shrug. She's probably right.

We're sitting in front of the 7-Eleven, nursing Slurpees and watching the police haul kids out of the club, wondering who they're gonna blame it on, how the newspapers are gonna read it, what my parents are gonna say. They'll probably attribute it to eyeliner and baby powder, and stick me in my room for a week. And I will slide off the roof down into the hollyhocks and verbena out back every night, and go running with my friends under the big blue moon.

Tasha's on one side of me, Sara on the other, and I realize they probably don't know each other.

"This is my friend Sara," I say to Tasha.

"I know," she says. She swigs her Slurpee.

"You already met?"

"One of my friends tried to set us up," Tasha says.

"Like, on a date?"

"Like to get married. He figured we were the only two bisexual people he'd ever known, so we had to be perfect for each other, you know?"

"Was it Jake Slater?"

"You know it," says Tasha.

"Wait. Hold on, you know Jacob Slater?" Sara says.

"We're in school together. He's the one who asked all the masturbation questions in Health last year. That's basically all I know about him."

"Is that how you know Tasha?"

"Tasha and me? No, we're, like—I don't know, she's my main man, or something."

"You don't got a lot of men, then, I guess."

"No, she and me and Joshua and Amy… we're, like, I don't know, we click with each other."

"Wait, you mean Amy di Novio?"

"You know her too?"

"Oh, yeah."

So Tasha has cleared out of there, gone over to see if she can get back into the club. The night is like Chernobyl by then. The girls in tight shirts are all cleared out of the 7-Eleven, and the crowds are dying down, and there's a dim red glow of morning in the sky.

"Oh, yeah what?"

"What?"

"Like that 'Oh, yeah' was, 'Oh, yeah, I had sex with her last night.' Or 'Oh, yeah, we're mortal enemies and if you see her I have some cyanide for her.'"

"No, it's an Oh, yeah, ages ago we were best friends and we only have truly serious conversations about once a season, but when we do it's like in the *Dark Crystal* and we absorb each other's memories. It's this really intense, separated friendship we have going."

Life feels like a Cole Porter song in the background, and out of the club comes the band: Joshua carrying a suitcase, and Amy holding his hand.

"God." he declares, sinking down beside me. "It's this whole fucking capitalist state. Fucking wiggers. Fucking b-boy homey-

g snoopity doggity dog fuckin whiteboys think they fucking
wanna rule the fucking world, fucking intolerant fuckers."

"Fuck fuck fuck," I say, handing him a Slurpee.

"But, oh, those hoes can do that Daisy Dukes thang," he says.
I slap him.

"I'm just being observational, fuckhead."

"Go get drunk, Joshua."

"Okay."

So Joshua is gone, me staring after him, when Amy starts
walking away. I tug her pant leg and she pulls me along, and I
croak "What?" She puts her hand over my mouth and catches
my phlegm and points to Tasha and Sara, quietly necking on the
corner.

Inadvertent sigh.

"What's that for?" she says.

"I don't know. I'm just thinking. I've just been thinking."

We walk, silently. She stares at me for almost over an hour
and we wind up in the Country Club Diner, which couldn't be
less like a country club, eating Belgian waffles and apple slices.
Everything is so quiet. I hear the tink of her fork against the
plate, look around at the empty tables, and wonder why a place
that only old people eat at is open twenty-four hours on week-
ends.

"So."

"Yes?" She looks up from her waffle.

"Was Joshua really gonna kill himself after that song?"

"You didn't know?"

"My guess is those b-boys were hired thugs to break it up
early. What do you think?"

"I think there won't be any more Vampire Nites at that club
for a long, long time."

I nod.

"But with Joshua, I don't even know. We spent a lot of time in
that room. He showed me the gun, showed me the bullets in the
chamber. *Ich luge*, right?"

"Real bullets?"

"Performance art, man. Crazy things, kids."

"He wouldn't have. He hates the world too much to let it win like that."

"I don't know, Rob Roy. Sometimes you caricature things too much."

"What do you mean?"

"I mean, for such an ACLU punk, you see things as pretty black or white."

"'My father, the Congressman, part two ...'"

"No, seriously. I don't know. You're so judgmental, you stuff things into compartments. Black. White. Life. Frankford. Art. Joshua."

She takes an apple slice, peels off the skin, chews. Swallows.

"Me," she says tinily.

"What?"

"Everything I do with you: it's just like, Hi, Amy, how are you, fine, you have a crush on me, whatever, you'll deal. You're as bad as Joshua with his own politics. You know what I think. What do you think?"

"God, Amy, I had no idea—"

"Yes you did, Rob Roy, you're such a *man*—and I know how much that stings you because to you, 'man' means those kids tonight, and those forty-something working-class guys with tight construction company shirts who come home and rape their wives every night. You put things into compartments, everything except you."

"So what does this mean?"

"This means I'm telling you I like you, okay? I think I'm going to go home now and go to sleep. I want to feel my blanket on my cheeks."

"I'll walk you."

"No. I want you to be alone right now," she says and leaves.

"Are you still writing?" she says, coming back in and counting out change and a tip, leaving it on her side despite my "Don't worry about it"s.

"Yes," I say.

"Good," she tells me and leaves again. ❋

Lullaby for a Dead Girl

AUBREY DAVIS

SHE CAME BACK. Three months and six days later, she came back. Dan just stared at her from where he sat on the couch in the dimly lit, smoke-fogged back room of the bar, the needle still in his hand. All he could think was that he wasn't dreaming, and he wasn't high yet, so he shouldn't be seeing her here, now.

She drifted out of the doorway—walked, really, it just seemed like she *should* drift, like a ghost—and the curtain they had in place of a door swung shut behind her. Huge dark marks circled her eyes like an excess of makeup, and she looked extraordinarily pale in the tiny black dress she wore. They'd buried her wearing white.

Slowly, carefully, Dan set the needle aside, on top of an amp. His hands shook, and he couldn't decide if it was because he needed a hit, or because of her: whether he was scared of her or wanted to touch her. He remembered how she felt, smooth and sweet, like some perfect drug.

"You shouldn't be here, Becks," he said at last, his voice rough. He'd strained something, singing earlier tonight, and didn't much care anymore.

Becky giggled, the same high, soft laugh she'd always had, dark eyes bright above the blue-purple-black circles that made her look so very tired. It was a little too high and sharp, in this tiny room. It cut through the thick air and died quickly. Her smile lingered.

"Why not?"

There were some words you shouldn't ever have to say. Words it didn't make *sense* to say, and Dan found himself wishing he had taken that hit, wondering if he could reach over, grab the needle and shoot up right now, because then it wouldn't matter if it made sense.

"Because you're dead."

The smile vanished, and she looked pale, gaunt, almost like she looked when he'd found her in the bathroom that night, track marks on her arms and a needle on the floor. Less peaceful, though. "What makes you say that?" With her head tilted to one side the way it was, she looked like a lost child, or some strange, fragile bird, like a strong wind might snap her in two.

"Well..." he searched for the right words, failed utterly to locate them, and settled on the obvious, "you died."

The fragile, birdlike look vanished as quickly as the smile before it had. Her lower lip stuck out in a petulant pout, irritation flickering over thin features. "You're always so *literal*, Daniel," she said, playful scorn and affection lacing her tone.

When Becky stepped forward, just a step or two, Dan fought the impulse to stand and back away until his back hit the grimy wall, fumble for the door, and run home, or maybe lock the door behind him. She wasn't real; she was a ghost, or a monster...

Something brought his attention to her feet, small, pale as the rest of her, bare. Who went barefoot in New York City? And on the heels of that question, another followed—how had she even gotten here?

"Daniel?" she asked, leaning forward a little, and his eyes flickered back up to her face. No one had called him Daniel since she died.

"It is literal, Becks. You ODed. We buried you. It doesn't get much less metaphorical than that."

He should have asked. Why and how she came back, what she

wanted, whether or not she was a hallucination. Instead, bypassing all questions, he reached for the needle he'd set down, slid it into his forearm, since he'd even forgotten to take off the tourniquet when she walked in, and depressed the plunger with his thumb. If the smack didn't make things clearer, it would at least make them seem so.

Becky rolled her eyes at him. "And there you go, right from talking about my accident to shooting up. Real smart, Danny-boy."

And abruptly she was in his lap, arms twined around his neck like creeping vines. She didn't *feel* dead. She didn't even feel cold. And she smelled like violets and mothballs, a little too sweet, cloying. Slowly, he wrapped his arms around her, feeling oddly that he ought to be clinging desperately to her, but... it seemed like only yesterday they'd been backstage after one of his gigs, just like this, high and kissing messily, screwing like simple contact was all that mattered in the world.

"How long's it been?"

"Three months." And six days, he added silently. Maybe seven; it was probably past midnight.

"Did you miss me?" Becky asked, and before he could answer, added, "Can we go home? I don't remember the way."

Dan's lips flickered into a hesitant smile. He neglected to ask how she found him but couldn't find home, five blocks from the bar. It didn't seem to matter that much.

"Yeah. 'Course." He hesitated, thinking she could hardly walk home barefoot, then shifted so he could fish his car keys out of his pocket and set them on the amp, right beside the empty needle. One of his bandmates would find them, take care of the equipment, and he could explain later. Somehow.

Becky in his arms, he rose slowly to his feet, her arms tightening around his neck. If anyone he knew noticed him leaving, they didn't say anything. Maybe they were just glad to see him leaving with a woman for the first time since Becky died. Dan walked through the midnight patchwork streets of the East Village, stretches of shadow and isolated pools of light, surrounded by the smell of violets.

The phone rang while Becky slept. Dan carefully eased his arm out from under her and rolled out of bed, then dove for the phone before the insistent ringing woke her. He picked up the phone then glanced back to the bed. Becky shifted a little, but didn't wake. With a relieved sigh, he turned his attention back to the phone. "Do you know what time it is?" he demanded before realizing he had no idea who was on the other end.

"Four-nineteen in the morning. Since when does that matter to you? You're usually up past dawn." Zachary. One of Dan's bandmates. His best friend, in point of fact, but he really didn't need best friend concern right now. Dan sighed as Zachary went on, "More importantly, that girl you left with?"

Dan glanced to the bed where Becky lay, sprawled with charming gracelessness, the blanket half covering her, bare thighs pale in the moonlight. She was all black and white, hair and skin, tangle of tattoos down her right arm she'd done herself, dark smudges of track marks on her other arm that hadn't faded with months in the grave. She was beautiful, a rock star's goddess, shining in the dark apartment, on a beaten-up mattress, the paint on the walls chipped and peeling, golden streetlight and silver moonlight mingling through the window. "What about her?"

"Looked an awful lot like Rebecca," Zachary said, too casually.

"Yeah, I guess. Any reason you called, or are you just feeling observant?"

"Well, it's not exactly moving on, is it? We talked about this, man."

His eyes still on Becky, Dan hesitated before answering softly, "I don't need to move on."

"What?"

"She came back. I know it sounds crazy, but… it's Becky."

"You're really losing it," Zachary said after a long silence. "Do you want me to come over there?"

"No, no, it's fine, I'll talk to you about it later." Becky shifted on the bed, sleepily rubbing at her forehead without opening her eyes. "Listen, did you find my keys?"

"Yeah, I got your car, but-"

"Great. I'll talk to you later, I gotta go." He heard Zachary start to say something else, but hung up before he could actually hear it. He was pretty sure he didn't want to anyway, something about being crazy, not coping, some shit like that.

"Who was that?" Becky asked as she propped herself up on her elbows. Dan smiled faintly and walked back to the bed.

"Zachary. Just wanted to check up on me." He let her grip his wrist gently and pull him into bed beside her. Lying next to her, he rested his hand on her side—warm, soft, his thumb gliding over the sharp angle of her hip. He kept thinking he'd blink and she'd vanish.

"Oh." She kissed his cheek, then the line of his jaw. "Tell him 'hi' for me."

"I already hung up, Becks."

She lifted her head, a frown creasing her forehead. "Right."

Dan brushed sex-mussed hair from her face, tilting his head to meet her eye. "Are you okay?"

"Yeah. For someone in my situation, I'm actually remarkably perky."

"Your situation?"

Becky gave him the level, silently mocking look she managed so very well. "You know. I died."

He sighed, letting his hand fall. "Sorry. I didn't mean to…"

"Don't worry about it, babe," she murmured, and laid her head against his chest. "Sing for me? Anything."

He wrote a lullaby for her long ago, in the days when she'd wake up from nightmares two or three times a night, when she couldn't sleep without him next to her. He wondered if she'd had nightmares in the grave. Wondering if it would be the same now, he sang her lullaby, though the words seemed to have changed since the day he wrote them.

"Hushabye, my dearest one, there's no need to cry…"

"Told you I'm not crazy," Dan said, his eyes on his guitar as he tuned it. Zachary ripped a sheet of paper out of his notebook, balled it up, and tossed it at Dan's head. It bounced off without a glance up or a comment from Dan.

"No. I think you're still crazy."

"What?" Dan finally looked up to meet Zachary's eyes, hands frozen on the guitar. "You saw her back at my place. She's real."

Zachary tucked his feet up under him on the couch. "And I don't think you're questioning enough just how that happens."

"You get a miracle, you try not to question it much," Dan said. He looked back down at the guitar and went back to tuning; every note that came from the instrument sounded sour.

"Sorry, I didn't know there was etiquette for these things."

There was a pause and a rhythmic tapping. Dan glanced up briefly to see Zachary's head lowered over the notebook, only the top of his head visible, dyed hair, brown and blond. He kept tapping his pen against the notebook until, abruptly, he looked up. Dan dropped his eyes.

"You know, you're better at this songwriting thing than I am."

"Yeah, well—" He paused to play a few notes, frowned, shook his head, and went back to tuning. "Not exactly, since Becky died. It's called writer's block." Writer's block, ever since the death of his muse. Well, it made sense, at least. Maybe the reverse would work.

"Well, she's back now, so you should be able to write again. Might as well make use of this freak of na—I mean, miracle."

Dan looked up sharply. The movement jarred the guitar and his fingers slipped on the strings, producing a discordant sound that made both Dan and Zachary flinch.

"Christ," Zachary said, "you're sure you should be doing this for a living? Here, give me that."

"You play keyboard," he retorted.

"I know how to tune a guitar. Give it."

Dan sighed and handed it over, rolling his eyes. "You can try, but there's something wrong with it. Piece of shit."

Ignoring him, Zachary set the notebook and pen aside, settled the guitar in front of him, and started to tune it. After a minute or two, he stopped and played the opening to one of their songs, note perfect. "Something wrong with it, huh?"

Dan frowned, staring at the guitar then at Zachary. "You know what? Shut up. Just, whatever you're going to say… shut up."

Zachary shrugged and offered the guitar back. "I told you. You're losing it."

Dan took the guitar, and tried to play a few short chords. They all came out sour.

When Dan got home, he didn't see Becky at first, just heard the tinny sounds from the old Casio keyboard coming from the bedroom. The keyboard was Becky's to start with, and Dan had put it away after she died. He guessed she'd found it.

He set his guitar down on the couch and walked slowly toward the bedroom, not sure if he wanted to interrupt the music. It didn't sound like Becky's music—the music Becky used to play was soft and sad and lyrical. This sounded just as competent, but more nuanced, less sad and more longing, a difference hard to pinpoint but certainly there.

"Becks?" he ventured cautiously as he reached the door of the bedroom. She'd set up the Casio and a chair by the window, and sat with her back to him, facing the window. When he spoke, she stopped playing and looked up from the keyboard—not at him, just out the window. Unable to see her face, just the back of her head, it struck Dan as odd that her hair was plain black, no color to it. She always used to dye it in streaks, red, blue, purple. Pink was her favorite.

"Hey, baby," she said, though all of her attention seemed to be fixed on some passerby on the street outside, five floors below.

Dan stepped into the room, taking a few slow steps toward her, resting his hands on her shoulders when he reached her. "What're you up to?"

Becky leaned back and rested her head against his stomach, tipping her chair back far enough that she could look up at him. "Trying to remember how to play. I think I've gotten a little rusty."

She played something that showed a passing resemblance to "Lullaby of Broadway", and of course it wouldn't be perfect, played on a Casio keyboard, but Becky's version held echoes of the rumbles in subway tunnels, the wail of sirens, and Dan couldn't imagine how she'd gotten that out of the old keyboard. He found it both beautiful and profoundly unsettling.

"It sounds fine," he said simply, because he couldn't put words to what he really felt about it. "Better than anything I'm managing today. This keeps up, I'm going to have to get a job in a coffee shop or something just to pay the rent."

Becky frowned and turned around in her chair. "What?"

He gave a careless shrug and took her wrist gently to pull her to her feet. "I don't know. Think I'm just having a bad day, but it's making me play like shit." He pulled her closer, and leaned down to kiss her lightly. "It doesn't really matter."

She was silent for a moment, her dark eyes flickering with something he couldn't put his finger on. Abruptly, she said, "You know, I'm thinking of getting a new tattoo. On my left arm, since I don't have anything there. I mean, I'd have to have someone else do it, even if I had all my stuff, because I can't get a straight line with my right hand to save my life, but..."

She looked up at Dan, and he smiled uncertainly, trying to track the thoughts that had led from music to this. "Or maybe we could give you a new tattoo. Would Chinese characters be too trite?"

Before he had the chance to answer, Becky rocked up on her tiptoes to kiss him, harder and deeper than the first kiss. The overwhelming smell of violets surrounded him, with the underlying hint of dead things, of things locked away in dusty attics for years, untouched. But her mouth was so warm on his, one of her hands curled in his hair, the other playing with the bottom of his shirt, that it was worth overlooking.

Dan didn't recognize the sound that woke him. He'd long ago learned to sleep through traffic, sirens, neighbors fucking downstairs—a required ability for any New Yorker. This was different. It was an unearthly keening, soft but high-pitched, a sound that reached into him and somehow ripped away something precious. Maybe it wasn't the sound so much as the feeling of loss he couldn't sleep through.

He opened his eyes to see Becky leaning over him, her face close to his, her moon-pale skin seeming to glow with a light of its own. She started back as soon as she saw he was awake. Her slightly parted lips closed quickly, and with that, the sound ended.

Dan sat up, blinking blearily, glanced to the glowing red clock beside the bed, then back to Becky. "What the hell? It's four in the morning." He didn't ask what she was doing or why. He found he couldn't bring himself to. You don't question miracles.

"I was just..." She sat back on her heels on the bed, looking just a little guilty, like a child with her hand caught in the cookie jar. "I was just watching you sleep. I didn't mean to wake you up."

She tucked a bit of her hair behind her ear, though it quickly fell back to brush along the line of her jaw. Dan stared at her for several long seconds, searching for words.

"There was a sound..." he said slowly, knowing it sounded stupid.

"Weird dreams, Daniel?" Her voice was calm, arch, and strangely distant. "You did seem a little restless."

"I guess."

He fell silent, the only sound above the distant noise of a car down the street his breathing, and Becky's, much faster than normal. Dan frowned and caught her eye. Her eyes looked flat and dark, black with no whites at all.

He blinked and they returned to normal, just the pupils dilated, and that wasn't strange at all, almost comforting in its familiarity in a strange way. Dan had seen her high a hundred times before. Before she died, he'd almost forgotten what she looked like without the widened pupils and lazy addict's smile.

Dan glanced automatically to her arm—the left, because she never shot up on the right. She didn't like to mark up her tattoos. There weren't any new track marks there, and he didn't even know where she'd have gotten smack. But he knew the look of Becky high, she never cared enough to hide that she used… and come to think of it, Dan felt like he'd just come down too hard from a high, tired and sick and a little shaky, and most of all, empty.

"You gonna go back to sleep?" he asked at last, gently. She looked so fragile, sitting there on the bed wearing one of his much too large shirts to sleep, he couldn't be anything but gentle. Even though, fragile or not, familiar or not, the look in her eyes had really begun to unsettle him.

Becky crawled back across the bed to curl against him, her small body pressed tight against his side, her head on his shoulder. He could feel her heartbeat, that close, practically racing. His own pulse, loud in his ears, seemed unnaturally slow by comparison.

"Okay. First things first." Zachary sprawled on the couch, his feet resting on Dan's lap. It wasn't like there weren't other places to sit, even in Zachary's tiny apartment, but Dan didn't move. "Are you sure you weren't dreaming?"

"Well… No."

Most people in the world, at least to Dan's knowledge, couldn't raise just one eyebrow. Zachary was one of the few who could, and he managed it with the perfect arch of mixed questioning and condescension. It would make the most self-confident person in the world squirm in their seat. "You're so very helpful," he drawled, prodding Dan in the side with one bare foot.

"What do you want? I just woke up!"

"Fine. Assuming Becky's mere existence isn't some kind of shared delusion—which, frankly, is more believable than the alternative..."

"Z," Dan warned softly.

"*Assuming that*, I don't see why this couldn't be real, too." He paused and considered.

"Yeah I've really got nothing."

"You're so very helpful," Dan echoed, wishing he could match Zachary's scornful tone. It just didn't sound the same.

Zachary sighed and the almost ever-present smile slipped from his face like it was suddenly ashamed to be seen there. The last time Dan saw Zachary not smiling was when Becky died. "Look, Danny, I don't know what to tell you. This is all just a little too weird."

"Oh, come on—"

"No, just listen, okay? How do you know it's even Becky?"

Dan shoved his legs off his lap even as he asked, "What the hell are you talking about?"

"Dan. She came back *from the dead*," Zachary said, expression unwavering.

For a moment, Dan said nothing, unable to find an answer except that... it was Becky. And he loved her.

"So?"

"Did it ever cross your mind that that's not normal?" Zachary sat up slowly, leaning forward. "People who die are supposed to stay that way, in case you've forgotten. And when they don't, you're supposed to stake them or shoot them with silver or something, not just *accept* it. How do you know it's not someone—some*thing*—pretending to be her? It's just as likely. More likely, when you think about it. Just for a second, forget you're you and it's Becky. Think about it."

Dan wilted. "I'd know. If she weren't Becky, I'd know."

Zachary looked down and pushed his glasses up his nose. "Dan, she called me 'Zach' the first time I saw her. She knows I hate that name."

"She forgot a lot of stuff. She couldn't remember the way home when she first got back."

"And how do you think this helps your case?"

"I would know."

"If you say so."

Becky always seemed like she belonged in places like this, tiny East Village clubs where the air was thick with music and smoke, seen through the pleasant haze of heroin. He met her in a club just like this, though which one long ago faded from memory. She always seemed to come more alive in places like this, a little more of a glow about her face, an extra brightness in her eyes. Dan was glad to see it, his eyes following her around the dance floor. It seemed to him like every eye in the room ought to be following her, too. How could they not, when she shone like that?

"We could be doing other things with our time," Zachary said, frowning into his beer.

Becky insisted on him coming along, said it would be just like old times. Zachary had yet to be convinced.

Dan spared him a brief sideways glance. "Like what?"

"Searching for your lost talent, for one," he muttered, his voice distorted by the glass as he lifted it to his mouth.

On the dance floor, Becky sidled up to some blond girl with short hair streaked just like hers used to be, dancing so close their hips and breasts brushed against each other. Dan couldn't even bring himself to be jealous. She was laughing and smiling. She was alive and would come back to him.

"It's not like that's anything new," he answered at last, distracted.

"You sucking at writing isn't new, no." Zachary slid his glass back and forth across the table, watching the trails of condensation. "You not being able to play at all, though. That's new."

Dan sighed in frustration, though he doubted Zachary noticed. He had to raise his voice just to be heard over the music. "You're starting on this again?"

"Have you noticed this only started when she showed up? I mean, if anything, you'd think she'd *help*..."

"Will you just cut it out?" He didn't look at Zachary, keeping his eyes fixed on some point across the bar. He'd lost track of Becky at some point. "She's your best friend besides me; will you give her a break?"

"Becky was," Zachary said darkly into his beer. "I'm just not sure it's her anymore."

"Z, I swear to God—"

"Hey, Dan," Becky said, suddenly beside him. He fell silent. "Zach."

Zachary gave a curtly polite nod and took a drink, Dan was sure, to avoid having to speak.

"Daniel, would you like to dance?" Becky leaned into kiss his ear. He didn't have to turn to see the grin. He could hear it in her voice.

"God, yes," he answered, already rising to his feet and downing what was left of his Scotch as he did. They left Zachary behind, as he pointedly avoided looking at either of them. Dan wondered if maybe he should feel a little guilty, but Becky took his hand and he forgot it.

Time moved differently in New York than it did anywhere else in the world. Dan was often convinced that it moved so fast most of the time to save up for moments like this. Moments like this, time dilated, stretched out like a lazy cat in a patch of sunlight, and everything seemed so much more real. And every moment was filled with Becky. Her eyes. Her smile. Her scent of violets and mothballs, mixed with sweat and smoke. It ran together in a bright, colorful blur, few individual moments standing out.

They danced. It couldn't have been hours, though it felt like it. At some point, Becky pulled him into the bathroom with kisses and a much-too-sweet smile. They touched, and kissed, leaning into every contact, for minutes that stretched to life-times.

Becky bit her lip, and her eyes seemed to darken. Dan pretended he didn't see, pretended it was just the darkness in the room and the drugs. Dan looked at anything else, the way her fingers balled into the fabric of his shirt, or the tumble of color-ful tattoos that ran down her right arm from elbow to fingertips. Anything to convince him Zachary was wrong, it was still and always would be Becky.

She whimpered softly as she came, clenching around him. The high-pitched sound made something twist a little painfully in his chest. It left him feeling empty. They walked back out with rumpled clothes and mussed hair, to a knowing, disapproving look from Zachary that Dan did his best to ignore.

"What the hell were you thinking?" Dan growled into the phone, gripping it so tightly he expected to hear plastic crack. All he heard, though, was Zachary's voice on the other end of the line.

"Well, let me see, I was thinking that we have a band on the assumption that we actually perform every now and then, that playing gigs is good because it means we have money; that a gig at CBGB's would be good for us… What the hell's the matter with you?"

Dan almost laughed. What the hell was the wrong with him? He wished he knew. "You can't just schedule a gig without talking to me. I'm the frontman, or have you forgotten?"

"Yeah, keep this up and see how long that lasts." He hung up, leaving Dan holding the phone, trying to remember when Zachary had ever taken that tone, with him or anyone else.

He slammed down the phone at last, glowering at nothing in particular. Zachary expected him to play a gig when he could barely coax a simple tune out of his guitar? And they thought they could *replace* him…? He practically was the band.

Not if I can't play, though. He shoved that thought violently to the back of his head and turned away. Becky stood in the doorway to the bedroom, watching him with such perfect stillness he had to wonder how long she'd been standing there.

"What's wrong?"

"Nothing," Dan lied, rubbing tiredly at his forehead, but then he looked back at her and couldn't make himself leave it at that. "Zachary scheduled something without bothering to tell me. Jackass knows I've been having… problems."

He walked to the window and leaned heavily against the wall next to it, beside where Becky had set up her keyboard, staring outside. It had to be Zachary, of all people, and he wouldn't be arguing nearly this much if Becky weren't around, or if he hadn't gotten the lunatic idea that Becky wasn't Becky. He heard Becky move into the room, the squeak of the bedsprings as she sat down, but didn't turn until she said, "Well, I can't blame him."

He turned to stare at her. He could deal with Zachary and Becky turning on him. One at a time. "What?"

She sat on the very end of the bed, legs folded up under her, dark eyes critical and fixed on his face. They didn't even seem like eyes anymore, just dark pits with something unfathomable at the distant bottom. "Really, what've you done for him? You haven't written a single lyric since I died. You can't even *play* music now, let alone write it. It's not his fault if he doesn't want to be dragged down by you."

The world dropped out from underneath him. She didn't even look angry. She had this faint smile, like she was teasing, except… this couldn't be teasing, she knew what was too far.

Maybe Zachary... No.

"Did I do something I'm not aware of to piss you off, or...?"

"No, Daniel," she sighed, more bored than annoyed.

Her expression didn't change as she swung her feet out from underneath her, stood, and stepped toward him. She'd been so fragile when she first came back, it had seemed like he ought to be able to see through her. Now Becky looked nothing like a ghost. There was no mistaking that she walked firmly on the ground. She looked more solid than Dan felt.

"You just... There's so much music in you and you won't even *use* it." The strange phrasing gave Dan pause, and he couldn't find an answer as she placed herself directly in front of him, small hand resting on the center of his chest. "It's stupid."

She hadn't been around. She was used to him writing and playing all the time, like he used to before. Of course she didn't understand, and it made sense. "I can't use it! There's such a thing as writer's block, Becks, and I can't just... flip on a switch and... You know?"

"Oh, that's eloquent, Danny-boy. You want to write a song with that? It'd be great, instant hit..." Her faint smirk turned into a mocking sneer. "You don't use it. You're not *going* to use it. You might as well let someone else."

Becky leaned in to kiss him, and without thinking Dan held his breath, responding to the almost subliminal, high-pitched hum that issued from her. Her kiss was so soft he could barely feel her lips, like the brush of a moth's wings against his skin. Her hand curled in his shirt, balling up the fabric, and something in the center of his chest ached, right where he guessed his heart would be. But she was kissing him, she couldn't be that upset with him, whatever it was, and he wouldn't lose her again. Dan let out his breath, and parted his lips to return the kiss.

The hum, the keening, rose a little in pitch and volume, and his heart gave a new twist. It felt like it might any moment be ripped from his chest, and a part of him didn't care. Becky pressed closer to him, tangled her fingers in his hair, tight enough that it hurt, but he hardly noticed. If she just kept kissing him...

Music whirled through his mind, notes and chords and the perfect words for them, and if he could just pin one of them down it would fix everything. He let them slip by.

She bit his lip and he jerked back, though there wasn't far to go with the wall behind him. His head hit the dirty plaster, hard, and leftover music circled in confused spirals in his head, both his own songs, and songs he knew, songs he'd heard.

Becky narrowed her eyes, chin tilted up to look him in the eye. She was so tiny... so why did he feel like she could break him if she wanted, if she just raised a hand?

"Becky?"

"Stop it, Daniel," she snapped, sounding like a petulant child, upset that he wasn't playing fair. It seemed like any moment she'd stomp her foot or something. She leaned forward, brushing her fingers over the keys nevertheless, with a deep, resonant sound more like a grand piano than a Casio, and then a few strains of something achingly familiar, something gone before he could fully register or recognize it. "I need it. I don't want to die again. Just let me..."

If she kissed him again, if he let her, she'd kill him. He didn't know how, it didn't matter how, but he knew, just like he knew the color of the sky, the map of Manhattan, or the necessity of oxygen. And maybe he should let her. Much as his chest hurt as she leaned in, much as his head spun as her lips touched his, it would go away. And didn't she deserve it? She'd come back, after all.

His head whirled while music streamed away, painting his mind brilliant streaks of rapidly disappearing color. His knees buckled, and he leaned back against the wall, Becky following him. He wasn't using that music. It was easy to let her take it. All he had to do was... nothing.

Dan reached out with one hand, groping for support before he fell, and his fingers hit the keyboard. Becky must have turned it on with whatever she did, because a couple tinny, discordant notes rose from it, nothing like perfect, just a few chance sounds from a crappy old keyboard. Those few notes were enough, a memory of songs written and songs played. Music and color exploded in his head as he grasped for it like a drowning man, and Becky reeled back, eyes wide.

"Danny, what're you *doing*?"

"I can't…" He shook his head, and tried to ignore that stricken look in her eyes. "It's mine, Becks. I love you, but… I need it. I'm not ready to die, either."

Turning slowly to face the window, he set his fingers on the keyboard. The music was right there. All he had to do was use it. His fingers traced over the keys, careful and deliberate, and the song he played was far from perfect, but it was his. His head cleared, the music became clearer, surer.

When he turned around, she was gone.

A summer night, with the occasional warm breeze making its way through the canyons of steel and brick that made up the city, shouldn't have felt like the dead of winter. It wasn't the weather, perfectly pleasant, or anything about the actual appearance of the city, because Dan knew it was just in his head. It was only the way things seemed to him, but it was almost real enough that he felt the cold.

Zachary glanced sideways at him as they walked through Tompkins, in and out of patches of golden light from street lights, between the shouts of some junkie somewhere in the park, the wail of sirens along St. Mark's. Dan noticed, but pretended not to. He would want to say something about Becky, ask where she'd gone, what had happened, questions Dan couldn't answer and wouldn't even if he could. He never questioned her return. Her departure was no different.

He tensed as he heard Zachary draw breath to ask a question. "So."

Dan closed his eyes.

"Why the hell are you wearing that stupid leather jacket? It's like eighty-five degrees out here."

He opened his eyes again and looked over at Zachary. All the questions still hovered in his eyes, but they could both ignore them.

"The jacket looks good on me."

"Yeah, until you melt. You look good without the jacket, too, you know."

"I'm not the Wicked Witch of the West, Z. I'm not gonna melt. I get hot, I'll take it off."

"Oh, stripping for the crowd now? Have we reached that level? Really, Dan, you're not *that* bad a singer. I think you can keep your clothes on."

"You mean you don't want to see me stripping?"

"God, no…"

In the back of Dan's mind, a stray bit of music shook itself loose and came spiraling to the front of his thoughts, like a falling leaf. An old song, a familiar song, his lullaby for Becky.

Winter's passed away again, as the world sings… ❋

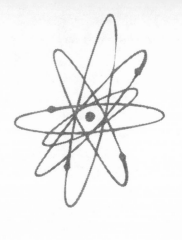

The Wriggling Death

HAROLD GROSS

THE SCREEN DOOR SWINGS TOWARD THE JAMB with a creak and slams closed as my youngest, my last of the litter, leaves for the final time. Night smells puff back in and surround me with the green life of summer. I have imparted the last of my wisdom to her. The wisdom of 244 full-turned seasons, 1500 or more cycles of the moons and over 100 seasons of the Wriggling Death. Until now. But who's counting anyway?

The box on my lap begins to weigh heavily. My legacy to my sister, passed from my mother to me and, within the night, to her. I used to use it to hold my guitar picks, to my mother's horror and my sister's jealousy. Even after I stopped performing, I held onto it. But no longer.

Chalen will arrive soon. Against all custom she is returning to say good-bye. Of course the Season is over. The chance of encountering a Wriggling Death is vanishingly small in these hot dry months. And ours was, had been, a special relationship. All over now, or soon to be.

The box. It is a beautiful dark wood. The finish reflects the dim lighting I've come to appreciate as my eyes have become more sensitive. I can see my wrinkled face and sticky looking eyes, but not too well. That is a kindness tonight. I am not reminded of the life I had to leave, that Chalen stepped into, which was only right. The lid is held closed by a single silk ribbon. Red, still Chalen's favorite color after all these years. My feet, my legs, my hips all ache as I lever myself out of the chair and go to the mantle. I want the box to be by our pictures for her. She should see it all as one.

The carpet threatens my balance, but for all my frailty my determination is stronger. At least for a few more hours. I am becoming as single minded as a Wriggling Death now, can't seem to shake my mind from the coming oblivion. Well, I can make my peace soon. Soon as Chalen arrives. We've unfinished conversations that need to be voiced. Unsettled business that needs be completed.

Chalen and I were the only two in our litter not including the males, but they were never counted anyway. It was a small collection of sibs to be sure, and our mother's only litter before her death not too many years later. We were always the odd ones out at school. It was hard to rise in the order of things when there were only two of you. The boys were always bigger until later. Even now, in my humped and brittle state I look at them and wonder why so many of us found them frightening at that age. Only a few years later they would all just be silent servants.

The mantle is higher than I remember and raising the ribboned box is a difficult process, slow and full of trepidation. If it should fall all would be lost. I owe Chalen so much, such a long history together.

I set it by a picture of the two of us standing outside our childhood home; the hedges in front and our mother on the porch and, just barely in frame, the Female moon rising above the roof ahead of her male pursuer. Our friend Trowlane took the snapshot. He was a year younger than us and not quite mature yet, else we would never have been allowed near him during the Season. Chalen wears purple overalls that set off her black hair. My own blonde hair glints against blue overalls. We had just returned from building a stage in the woods. The three of us had performed our songs to an unappreciative forest for hours. Our mother was upset, but too weak at that point to yell at us, and she refused to go beyond the foul smelling boundary of her protective garden. We knew that and had taken advantage. Our bright smiles were not long lived after that picture--we were bathed in our mother's displeasure the rest of the evening.

I remember noticing the hair on Trowlane's arms that day. It glinted and flashed as his muscles flexed while he pretended to strum his air guitar and move logs where we pointed as if they were amplifiers and lighting. I still thought of him as a female then despite the physical differences. Immature males are so much more able and interesting than mature males and perhaps that explains my lack of differentiation. But why my mother hadn't yet spoken to us about sex and its consequences I cannot say. I told my girls, from all three litters, when they were much younger than I was that day.

I look again at the picture. Despite the pain, a smile pulls at the desiccated corners of my mouth. I don't mean to sound as if I have not found joy in my life, work, or in my children. I have. I might have selected this path on my own eventually. The fact that I had little choice does not preclude me from finding joy; I only question it at times.

Next to the childhood photo, the realization of those forest pretendings, a picture of Chalen and I outside our first gig at a small tea house at the edge of the city. Our arms around each other and the necks of our guitars slung around and up above our heads. It was the beginning of our Odyssey. Soon after we began our tours, Chalen playing and me singing as front. We never added to the band, only hiring studio backs for each engagement. It was our chemistry and music that lighted the stage. All else was as meaningless as some of the lyrics I sang. But I sang them with gusto! The memory pulls the edges of my mouth up in an unexpected smile.

There are other pictures on the mantle; my daughters. All twelve. The eldest group of 4 still young, only 22. On their own. The youngest litter only scant years less than the first at 18. That was all I was to have before my body sped past its fertile stage and traveled on into its deterioration. I've actually outlasted most. This thanks to my mother. Her books and journals were full of herbal remedies and tonics to stave off the effects of the Death. I've bequeathed them to my youngest for her help here this evening.

The rocker seems so far away as I come back to my surroundings. The couch is much closer. Though I know I will regret it when I try to get up from its soft cushions, I shuffle over toward it. Besides Chalen will be here soon, she can help me up before she leaves.

The cushions are hotter than the wood of the chair and no air flows through the doweled back, but it is soft. With little of my own cushioning, it feels good. As I settle I see my glass of iced, mint tea glinting on the table by the rocker. Bother. Well that too will have to wait for Chalen.

I can see the pictures and the box from my place on the couch. I think of Trowlane again. How only days later Chalen and I and he were back at the stage. We were playing... I don't even recall anymore, some silly song about cleaning up our little portion of the woods. Trowlane had been snappish and nasty all afternoon. He kept grabbing us and pushing. Finally, Chalen and I had enough. We sent him home. Males are so annoying at times. Soon after he left we lost interest in playing anyway. Without someone to play the male to order about, it wasn't any fun. Trowlane was good for that part and neither Chalen nor myself were about to play at being a male.

The day was hot and motes of pollen and dead grass and leaves sparkled all about. It made the air thick and loamy. It was wonderful. The uneven path stretched off toward home through several more copses of trees. We moved silently as we could, stalking imaginary nemeses. As we got around the first bend we heard sounds to our right. A thrashing and moaning. At first we thought it was animal in trouble and cautiously edged toward the bushy area. We knew better than to startle an injured creature, but we also had enough compassion in us then to want to help. Silly during the Season, but we didn't know that then; we were young and naive.

As we peered through the bushes we could see Trowlane's reddish hair. He was tossing his head back and forth as he moaned. Now we weren't sure if what we'd come upon was trouble or if something stranger was going on. Even more cautiously than before we edged around to his side and stole another peek.

Trowlane's pants were down about his ankles and he was pulling at his penis with increasing speed. His eyes were closed and a grimace of, what we were sure had to be pain, pulled at the sides of his mouth. Suddenly, and with a final cry, his eyes opened wide and his penis popped off in his hand and then it fell writhing to the leaf covered earth. It all crystallized for us in that moment. You remember those moments when you cross from innocence into adulthood. You expect it to happen by degree, not by one quick leap. That day, however, we both leapt into adulthood as Trowlane's hideous, wriggling member began to gain motility and travel toward us.

After another infinite moment of hesitation we saw Trowlane slump back against the log he'd used as a back rest and smile in release. His eyes were hazy and unfocused as his hands dropped to his side. We saw nothing else as our wits and survival came to us in a mad rush. We turned and fled toward home all the while hearing the shuffle of the leaves as the Wriggling Death pursued us to the very edge of our mother's house.

It didn't get us that day. Those hedges we hated so much deterred it. More of our mother's herbal legacy. As we stood in shock and crying within our fortress of hedges our mother came to the gate and smashed the hideous organ with a shovel. It was then she finally talked to us about sex, not the reproductive rape of the Wriggling Death, but of the love of a willing female partner. The perpetual support that endless life together could bring… if. "If" you avoided the Wriggling Death. Once impregnated, the slide toward death would begin. Sometimes you had many years, as I have, or sometimes only a few as did our mother.

We buried her only months later.

Our lives went on. Many years of joy were before us. We

finished school and moved on to performances and friends and lovers. Many wonderful years. Many wonderful audiences and successes hearing our songs broadcast and copied. Being recognized at restaurants and in clubs. More myself than Chalen; the front person is always recognized first. I never realized how that must have felt to her.

Then, only twenty-two years ago—my, time does fly—Chalen and I were seized by a strange nostalgia. No, that isn't right. It was the end of an avoidance. With only two of us to celebrate our First Century we opted for something small and private rather than the typical multi-litter grand party. Instead we went home. We still owned the house. Even made sure it was kept in one piece. Trowlane was our first grounds keeper, though many had filled the position since. Male life is so brief. Neither of us had been back to the house in 60 years at least, but we had a need and we went. The hedges had died back some, but the house itself was as we remembered it in the hot end-of-Season sun. We spent a week reliving old memories and honoring our mother. The nights were spent on the porch sipping tea and talking. Then we remembered our forest stage.

It was still only early evening; we had time for a quick look. Just to see if we could find it again. And find it we did, or at least the copse of trees we thought was it. We even both winced as we passed the bushy dell where we discovered Trowlane ushering himself into manhood. By then night was coming in that slow languid way of late-Season; almost as if several veils were being dropped one upon another to slowly absorb the light, but not quite put it out.

After finding the dell, we walked homeward in a more subdued fashion. After only a few steps, the contemplative silence was broken by the rustling of leaves behind us. We stopped in our tracks. We'd outrun Deaths all our lives and, in high Season, had even gone off into the desert to protect ourselves. More than enough females were willing to accept them into themselves and breed for as long as their accelerated aging would allow. There were always those that wanted to bear young. But that wasn't

Chalen or myself, thank you. We had our voices and our music and our fans. That was enough.

Something about that sound in that place, though, froze us. Then, as we listened more carefully, we could hear that there were more on both sides of us boxing us in. We began to run toward the house and the hedges. Sanctuary.

The air burned in our lungs as we tore the final 200 yards through the woods, through the clearing, and into our childhood yard. We stopped just on the other side of the hedges. Bent over and panting, covered in sweat and dust, we laughed through desperate attempts to make our breathing normal again. We saw the first of the Deaths break from the woods and start toward us. Then another and another. Fifteen in all were angling through the dust toward the house. We edged back out of habit but knew we were safe behind the hedges. Chalen ran to the porch for the broom we had brought out to clean up on our first night. She returned ready to do battle as the helpless things crowded at the odorous wall trying to get to their quarry.

They squirmed over each other blindly, confused, looking for the smell that was their goal now masked by the herbal barrier. We neared them. We'd seen them in classes before, trapped in glass observation booths, but never really in the wild. They were…disgusting, blind things single-mindedly trying to shove their way forward. Chalen began to swat them, managing to crush two before it all went horribly wrong. The hedges were old. Very old and not as well kept as when our mother had tended them. The Deaths knew we were there and suddenly leapt forward. Chalen screamed and backed up, tripping. I grabbed her and pulled her to her feet, but the Deaths were right there.

I will never know, probably not even after tonight, if she meant to throw me down as a decoy or only was so frightened that she acted on impulse. Before I could save myself, I was on the ground swatting at the beasts. Their warm skin suddenly moistening as they sensed opportunity. I heard the door to the house slam shut somewhere, but I was occupied trying to swat Deaths. Fortunately I was wearing pants. I pulled myself into a ball as our teachers had taught us, then rolled toward the front door. The Deaths clung like slugs to my body, three more dying as I rolled onward, my shirt wet and muddied with their blood.

I hit the stairs with my shoulder and then quickly sprang up and dashed for the door. My sister was staring out at me with wide, frightened eyes. Glazed. I pounded on the door, but she wouldn't open it, I broke the glass that ran alongside the door but I couldn't get to the handle as she kept swatting my hands away.

And then I felt it. A cold, quickly-slithering, pulsing, trail up my leg. I abandoned the window and pounded at my inner thigh, but I was too late. Suddenly I felt the shock of being violated by the creature. It pulsed two or three times inside me before ejecting its load of genetic messages and sealing itself permanently between my legs. The other Deaths, the ten or so that were left, were easily destroyed as they tried to crawl to Chalen through the broken glass. Their ichor dripped through the boards of the porch and pooled in the dirt below. I sat with my back to the door crying for hours before Chalen finally let me in.

We tried to go on. To perform together, but with the swelling of my first litter, and the rapid aging of my voice, Chalen took over the lead vocals. And, soon, she suggested I step away as she'd found someone to replace me. No one wanted to see an old breeder with a raspy voice. At least not anyone with credits to spend. I know she was right, and the spotlight treated her well. She'd waited so long to be there, and her new partner filled in the background admirably as she played. I only watched them once, I couldn't bear it more than that.

I shift on the couch and try to improve the circulation that is slowing to my legs. As I roll my hip, I can feel the base of my Death in me, sealing me off from my most intimate pleasures and forcing my poor body on toward final putrescence. But that is done with. That is done. I have had my litters. And whether I would have chosen this eventually or not, I am here.

I hear Chalen on the steps. Her young stride bounding up them quickly. I haven't even been down those steps in the last year. Thank goodness my neighbors and girls have been willing to help me. I do not want any males about, cheap labor or not. The door swings open and the raven-haired beauty with whom I'd spent so much of my life, and so many of my dreams, walks in. I hold her soft unwrinkled hand in mine. She tries to keep her eyes bright and happy, but I can see the horror. This is good. I have her pour the tea my youngest daughter set to steep in the kitchen. A special herbal blend that will relax us both.

The tea feels warm in my limbs and weighs my head on my neck. I can see Chalen too feels its effect. I ask her to get me the box from the mantle. She hesitates to stare at the picture and smiles wistfully. She does not hear the scraping in the box. I am quite sure she will not be able to run once she opens it. I have always wanted her to have everything I did. Now she will. ✳

Drunk, Penniless, and Fucked in Amsterdam

LEE JOHNSON

I LOOKED DOWN INTO MY GLASS and examined the chaotic patterns left by the froth. The band begun to play a horrible cover of "Number of the Beast," and I let my head hang. Were these bands getting worse, or was I just losing patience?

I headed across the dark pub to the bar and ordered a Guinness. I deserved it. I sat back down and continued listening to the foul excuse for a cover that spurted out of the PA system. My notepad barely had anything written on it, and in a strange call-back to my college days, I'd doodled pictures of turtles all the way down the side.

"Journalist?" said a tall man, wearing a scruffy jacket, behind me.

I started. "Er, yes, technically, I'm reviewing this for *Sandman* magazine. We do local unsigned gigs around Sheffield, Manchester, Hull, and York."

"What do you think?" He offered a grin.

"It's poor. The cover they just played was off-timed and un-interesting. They didn't make the song their own. And the songs which are their own are quite dull as well." I tried to smile politely, and the man took a seat next to me.

"I agree."

"Are you one of the band member's parents?"

He let out a gruff, croaky laugh. "God, no."

This soothed me. "To be honest, I really don't know what I'm going to say. I could just lay into them, but what's the point? I should try to see their merits as well. Objective journalism, and all that."

"Indeed." He paused and sipped from his bottle of Stella. "Always looking for answers, eh?"

"Aren't we all?" I put a Lucky Strike into my mouth and raised my lighter.

"Do you not think there are some people who have found them?"

I blew out some smoke and looked straight at him. What the fuck is he on about? I thought. "Not really. People find things they believe are the answers. Like Christians, hiding in the myth of God."

"How do you know God doesn't exist?" he asked.

"How do you know I exist?"

He locked eyes with me for a second then fell back into his chair and laughed. The band's noise continued unnoticed and he sprang forward again. "I know where you can find them."

"What?"

"The answers."

He looked serious. I examined his face for a hint of a smile, but there wasn't one.

"What the fuck are you on about?"

"You need to travel to find them. It is a secret, but you can learn. You seem to be the right type."

I took a sip of my Guinness. "What type is that?"

"Journalists are almost all the same. They love drink." He pointed to my empty pints. "Lots of them smoke. And various other things." He gave that grin again, passing something under the table.

I looked into my hand and found a small bag of white powder. "I don't really do cocaine," I protested.

"Drugs, though?" He arched his eyebrows. "Of course. I've seen you—The Corporation—the rock and metal club on Milton Street."

"Who the hell are you?" I managed to get out at normal volume, though I couldn't discern whether I had been energized by fear or hate.

"I know you're ready to learn these things," he said, ignoring my question. "And you only have to do one thing: go to Amsterdam."

"Now?"

"Anytime." He grinned and sipped his Stella. "The Secret is there. All you need to do is walk through the Red Light District. You'll find it. Keep your eyes open, and you will see. The gleam is everywhere. Follow it. You will find what you're looking for."

I took a second to let it sink in. "Why Amsterdam? What the fuck does it look like?" I couldn't control my anger; I am a journalist, damn it. What was I listening to?

"You will know it when you see it. Now"—he pointed at me—"there is nothing left to ask. And nothing else you need to know."

As his empty Stella hit the table, he took off out of the door. Silence descended. It took me several minutes to realise that the strange man had not paid his bar tab.

"Now then," I said into the phone to my friend Craig, "you useless ginger, what are you up to for your birthday?"

"I don't know."

"We should go to Amsterdam," I suggested. The idea had being playing in my mind.

"Hmm," he said. I could almost hear Craig stroking his chin.

"What's the good word, Craig?"

"I think it's a plan! And I assume my black slave shall be joining me?" he asked.

"Why else would I have asked? But I can only be a slave to someone with a soul, and you know full well ginger people don't have those."

"Got big cocks, though," Craig said.

"And black people don't?" I teased.

"*You* don't, redneck," he said, getting a little confusing.

"Shut up, porch monkey," I said.

He laughed. "I'll get it booked and ask around. See you later, mate."

The phone went dead and I stared at my ceiling. Why won't that conversation with the stranger in the bar leave my head?

My friends and I scanned the crowded bar and chuckled. The England match was on, and we sat outside, basking in the warm Amsterdam sun, sipping our Budweisers, slightly stoned.

Most of them insisted on watching the football; I hadn't realised that we'd come on holiday during the World Cup until Craig had already bought the tickets. Sitting in a pub watching the football is pretty much the same wherever you go: people shouting advice no one hears, followed by collective responses to fouls, goals, and possible goals.

I'd been looking around feverishly for the Secret all holiday, to no avail. I cursed myself for believing the shit I'd been fed in the pub about "answers." All I saw was people being happy. Of course they're fucking happy—look where they are. In fact, I thought, look where *I* am. To hell with pub conversations.

We were laughing because we'd all noticed something about Adrian. The four of us—Craig, Hudson, Fester, and I—seemed to be hatching the same plan, not speaking a word to one another. I looked over to Craig, who's mechanical cogs you could see working. The same with Hudson and Fester, you knew it: Hudson's distracted stare and Fester's twisted grin.

We all sat in our usual corner in the club, me feeling the effects of my two bottles of wine and the few pints of Carlsberg I'd had. Adrian was on the floor, back against the wall, and everybody else was in a circle in front of him. The DJ played "Halo" by Soil, a song Craig and I had gotten into the habit singing together. We screamed along with the song and head banged like bastards, but Adrian kept attracting my attention.

"What's up with him?"

"I think he's just pissed," Craig said, not really looking around.

"Really?" I thought back. "He's only had about six pints." I looked at him, trying to work out if he was drunk of just tired.

"Must be a lightweight," Craig said. Then, after a pause, "I thought he could drink, actually."

"Aye, me too." I turned to Adrian and extended a hand. "Fancy a dance, sailor?"

"No, I'm alright, thanks, Lee." He slurred his words heavily. "Bit pissed."

"Oh, right," I said. I'd had a bit of fun with him earlier, my own drinking game: drinking for every pinched harmonic while listening to Black Label Society. I put my iPod on to shuffle all my Black Label Society and put an earphone in Adrian's ear. So maybe it was my fault. I wandered back to the bar and sipped my beer. The bar maid came up and I asked her for a glass of water.

"Here you go, Adrian." I passed him the water.

"Cheers," he mumbled, still pressed against the dark wall of the club in his bright colored short sleeved shirt, his skinny arm holding the glass.

"Are you thinking what I'm thinking, Lee?" Craig asked.

"I'm not sure, you perverted ginger bell-end." I laughed. "Is it to do with Adrian being a light-weight, by any chance?"

Craig laughed and Fester joined in. "Let's get him pissed then make him fuck a hooker."

"Pissed and stoned," Craig corrected.

Adrian looked up, suddenly alert. "Are we gonna play some black jack?"

We looked at each other. He didn't seem to have heard our plans. I spoke up. "Yeah, but we should get some spliffs first."

Hudson had been serving as the black-jack dealer up to this point on our holiday, playing casino rules (stick at seventeen, twist before, with his own hand) and had made quite a bit of money. "You play, my friends!" he shouted, in his foreign croupier voice he'd been putting on throughout the holiday. "You, smoke-a-spliff, bet big!"

After a short game, we went down to Funny People, which had quickly become our favorite coffee shop. We were staying just on the edge of the Red Light District, and we passed several sex shops on the way. I looked across, seeing the happy people pointing at prostitutes and wandering into sex shops. They all seemed to glow with happiness and laughed freely. I love European life, I thought.

"We should get some porn," Adrian said, as he'd been doing all holiday.

"No." Craig glanced to him. "Let's get stoned, play some cards, then we can come out and look around the Red Light District." Fester let out a giggle.

We all had a couple of pre-rolled joints each then headed out towards our hotel.

It was a shit room, truth be told: five beds, a little floor space, and a little bathroom barely big enough for one person. The carpets and bed sheets were a horrible beige color, and by this point we'd settled in, so it was also covered with clothes, the ash-trays spilled over, and it stank of weed.

We arrived and crowded around Hudson's bed, or Tony's table, and played some cards 'til we were all slightly poorer, then we told Adrian we were going out. My iPod had been playing throughout the holiday through a makeshift speaker we desperately made from a discarded bottle. The metal music seemed to rally us all, to keep us in the spirit of getting drunk and being idiots. Adrian was completely drunk, made obvious by his reckless betting, and Craig saw the opportunity to casually introduce the idea.

"We're going shopping," he said.

Adrian seemed to have resigned himself to the idea. We paraded up and down the sides of the canal, trying to help him choose a girl. I was stoned and slightly tipsy, speaking in a high-pitched like Latka, Andy Kaufman's character from *Taxi*, and intent on doing good deeds. These included smiling at prostitutes to make them feel pretty, and attempting to bring merriment into the lives of passersby.

"Stop it, now, Lee," Hudson said. "You're being silly."

Still in the Latka voice, I insisted, "I am doing good!"

"Perhaps. But those big black drug dealers want to beat you up."

"But I will make-a them laugh!"

I caught the serious tone in his voice then realised that I actually would get beaten up. I began to speak normally, still trying to do good deeds on the sly. All of a sudden, we'd stopped. I looked around rapidly, trying to work out what was going on, and certain passers by were laughing.

I saw Adrian and the others had stopped still, in front of a girl. She smiled from behind the window, trying to catch eyes with one of us. A man beside us turned to his friends. "Wow! I wouldn't mind that!" His friends agreed, so he continued, "Who's up for fucking her with me?" He had the same glow, the gleam of pure joy.

Adrian stood still, debating. It struck me that no one had put pressure on him to actually do it yet. It'd just been a series of off-hand jokes. He looked at her, then to the floor, shifting his feet a little. His arms were tightly folded as he looked back to the prostitute. She was wearing a green bikini and had shoulder-length blond hair and prominent eyes. I saw them catch eyes and smiled to myself.

"If you do one today Adrian, I'll do one tomorrow, for my twenty-first," Craig announced, glancing around, as if surveying the scene. "And I'll put fifteen euros in."

Adrian cast him a glance, lingering for a second, before Hudson joined in: "I'll put ten in, Adrian. You might as well."

"I'll put ten in," Fester said.

They all looked at me.

"I have about enough for a little bit of food tomorrow and a few spliffs. I can't put any in. Sorry." My response was honest.

Craig regrouped quickest. "So what'll it cost you? Fifteen euros. About £10. It'll be fun, and it would technically make you the most decadent one on the holiday." He looked to Adrian. "'Til tomorrow, at least."

Hudson added, "If you don't, I'll put gay porn on your bed, take a picture, and tell everyone."

We all laughed but Adrian. He looked like a puppy whose food had just been taken away. He looked at the girl again, still smiling at him from straight across the booming street.

"Alright," he said.

He emptied his pockets, gave all the stuff to us, and took fifteen euros out of his wallet. Everyone paid up and he walked up to the window. The girl smiled and opened her glass door.

The fifteen minutes seemed to take forever.

People came up to us and laughed when they heard what was going on, all happy and gleaming. I reflected on the conversation that brought us there. I saw the gleam. I could see it—but it was just happiness. What's the *big* Secret? I wondered. I couldn't ask the others. They knew nothing of the conversation. How could I tell them? It'd just been pitched to them as a lad's holiday.

We were having a nice conversation with some Americans when Adrian emerged, saying only, "I'd prefer it if we left now."

We walked back, the group buzzing. We quizzed him on the details then moved on with the holiday. Something occurred to us all at the same time: Had any of us seen him even with a girl before?

Adrian was quiet and reserved for the rest of the night.

That night I lay awake while everyone else slept. Adrian groaned a little bit. He began to talk. "It's not fair."

He was asleep; I'd heard them all snoring. It was only me awake.

Hudson, an avid sleep talker, asked, "What isn't?"

"You've all been picking on me."
"Shut up, Adrian. You fucked a hooker."
He groaned again.

Adrian remained quiet most of the day. Craig made good on his promise of a walk out with Fester and I, but he had returned to the pub disgusted, vowing to shower for half an hour to try to make himself clean again.

I walked with Adrian to the bank machine. "When Craig came back," Adrian said, "he was so disgusted. I know I didn't appear to feel that way afterwards, but I did. I felt it, but I didn't show it."

I lectured him. He needed it. He'd lost his glow. People's vices often haunt them like this. I don't know where the speech came from, but I got it out. The truth of the matter is that if it makes you happy, truly happy in yourself, what difference does it make what "it" is? Adrian's problem lay deep within his knowledge of himself, or lack thereof. He hadn't taken the time to explore his nooks and crannies. He hadn't taken the pill, he hadn't had drunken nights where he made a tit of himself. He just sat quietly, his back to whatever lurked behind the wall. So, thrust into the city of freedom, did he turn loose on it? No. It turned loose on him.

I looked around as we walked through the Red Light District again. Was it all a waste? I saw the gleam. The happiness. But no secrets revealed themselves to me. But wait. Did they?

That lecture I gave Adrian had came out of nowhere. What did I say? *He hasn't taken the pill.* What did that mean? He hasn't behaved recklessly. I considered where I was. The people around me were happy for one reason: Amsterdam is one place where their decadence is celebrated. They were happy because they celebrate themselves. Is that where the gleam leads? I thought about my life and smiled. And at the moment, I, too, had a glow.

I thought back to the man at the gig—he'd probably seen it all. Sadness. Depression. Perhaps I was the last straw, and he thought he could show me what I'd lost, and how to find it again. I needed a lesson, and Adrian and I learned one together.

Back in the room, Craig said, "Lee. Mushrooms." We ate half a pack each, the strongest ones they had. When they descended into our stomachs, we went outside to enjoy our last night's wander around Sin City, smiling broadly, pupils the size of pennies. ✳

Burnin' Love

By Rhonda Eudaly

"WHAT HAPPENED TO THE ELVIS TRACKS?"

Frank didn't look up from the bar he wiped down. He simply pointed at the machine with the "Out of order" sign on it.

"What does that mean?"

"It means they've all been corrupted from overuse. You guys and your need to sing Elvis has worn them out beyond recovery or repair." He continued to wipe.

"What're you doing about it?"

"I've ordered not only new track files, but the whole new up-graded system so they won't corrupt the data files anymore. It's been delayed because we're all in the same boat. It's going to take a while to get the new tech in."

"But what're we supposed to do?" The petulant whine had a strangely familiar sibilance.

Frank finally looked up at the six-foot tall, bipedal reptilioid wearing the white spangled jumpsuit. He sighed and shook his head. If the *Homo-Saurians* hadn't been so good for his business, he would've packed up and fled with most of the other humans from New San Diego.

But the odd passion for karaoke bioengineered into the *Homo-Saurus* species had saved Frank's failing bar. He owed them enough to stay behind when most other humans aban-

doned their terraformed colony to the burgeoning Sauri population.

Besides, who knew the indigenous lizards those early scien-
tists had tinkered with to create a bigger, better beast of burden
would turn out to be on the edge of sentience? With only a
handful of generations, some quirk of technology, and some
geek's sense of humor, *Homo-Saurus* was now a living, thinking,
singing, hunka-hunka burnin' new species.

"I have a catalog of over two million songs from over fifty
member planets covering two hundred years." Frank sighed.
"Pick something else."

Dino, the Saurus in question, hissed in shocked surprise
bordering on horror. His jewel-toned eyes whirled red with
agitation. Frank often wondered why, during all the genetic
tinkering, they hadn't been given more normal eyes, like blue
or something. After all these years, he still found them strange.
"Don't blaspheme, Frank. There is no one, *nothing*, that can
replace the King!"

"No, of course not. But I could introduce you to another
whole group of performers who were almost as popular as Elvis
in their own ways and times…" Frank held up a hand to stop
Dino's outraged protest. "Give me a moment! They were called
'Lounge Lizards.' One was even called 'Dino.' It's a similar
style—"

Dino waved him off and stalked toward the exit. "You've been
around us long enough, Frank, to know it's the King or nothing!"

Frank tried not to cry as he saw his nightly profits walk out
the door in a huff. "Well, that's it. Dino was our last hope. We
might as well shut down now."

"You think?" Maggie said with sarcasm from behind the
swinging kitchen doors.

Frank glared at his only employee—his sister—and slapped
the bar with his towel. "I hope whoever bioengineered that
karaoke gene is dead and buried. I'd hate to go to jail for killing
someone who's already dead."

"Why would you do that?"

"You're kidding, right? This whole give-me-Elvis-or-give-me-death thing is costing me money. A lot of money!"

"You should've had backups."

"Funny, Maggie. You know I had backups. I had backups of the backups. We would've been out of business six months ago if I hadn't."

"Then why didn't you order new tracks back then?"

Frank resisted the urge to take out his frustration with the whole situation by strangling his younger sister, but the temptation made his fingers tingle. "I did! The Sauri Proliferation has all the sources for tracks backlogged almost to infinity. It's the demand all at once. And before you ask, yes, I'm harassing all my sources. No one has access to any Elvis tracks. Not for the old tech, anyway."

A loud crash broke the oppressive silence of the empty bar. Loud, angry voices followed the crash. Frank and Maggie exchanged frightened looks. As one, they jumped from behind the bar and raced to the front window.

"What the...?"

A mob of staggering, slobbering, shouting, inebriated Sauri, all dressed in various stages of Elvis, stomped out of the bar across the street. A drunk Sauri had slammed into a parked air-car at the curb. As they watched, the spangled Sauri bashed into the aluminum/titanium frame once more.

". . . to practice? Festival's coming up! Must pay proper homage..." The words were somewhat slurred but clearly audible. "It's a conspiracy!"

"Aw, crap." Frank turned from the window.

"What is it?" Maggie asked.

"They're talking conspiracy." Frank pulled Maggie away from the door. "Come on, we've gotta get out of here."

"Why?"

"Haven't you figured it out?" Frank asked in exasperation as he propelled her toward the back room. "Conspiracy is Sauri code for 'break anything within reach.' Get out through the back before they decide to break you."

"What're you going to do?"

He didn't like the worried look in Maggie's eyes. Frank was Maggie's only family since their parents died, and rioting Sauri were something to be worried about. The normally musically minded species became more violent and destructive than old Earth dinosaurs.

"I saw Dino on the edge of the crowd. I'm going try to find out what the problem is."

"Be careful."

He waited until he heard the back door slam before going back to peek out of the front windows. The crowd outside was getting uglier, but a quick scan revealed Dino to be still on the fringes, looking uncertain.

Frank knew he had to capitalize on the confusion before it was too late. So far, the Sauri were concentrating on the breakables across the street—tough luck to his chief competition and any other club on the street. Fifty-ninth Street hadn't been a happening bar scene place when Frank set up his bar, but now he was one of the many and trendy. Frank slipped out the front door and darted over to Dino, sticking close to deep purple shadows. He didn't want to draw undue attention to himself just yet.

"Dino!" Frank tugged on the Sauri's sleeve.

Dino whipped around. "You shouldn't be out here, Frank!"

"Duh, Dino, but we've got to stop this before it gets out of hand."

The Sauri looked back at the enraged mob moving down the street. "Too late."

"Come back to my place," Frank urged, "and let's see what we can do. I'll even break out the good stuff."

They darted back across the street and into Frank's bar. Frank made sure he threw the locks and engaged the security system the moment they were inside. Dino had already settled at the bar by the time Frank turned around. He poured a drink for Dino. Then with a mental shrug, he poured one for himself.

"What seems to be the problem?"

Dino sighed. "Elvis is dead."

Frank refrained from mentioning that Elvis had actually been dead for centuries. "You're going to have to walk me through it, Dino."

"It's only two weeks to the Great Festival, and there's no music. No one has Elvis! The music is dead."

Frank set his glass down and swallowed hard, which wasn't easy considering his mouth suddenly felt like someone had stuffed a wool sock in it. "What's going to happen now?"

An explosion outside answered the man's question.

"They're going to destroy New San Diego because you can't find Elvis karaoke tracks? How single-mindedly insane are you animals? You have to know we're going to get more tracks. Or you could learn to play…"

"We cannot play the instruments. It's not just physical limitations, it's tradition! The King didn't—"

"In the beginning Elvis played his own guitar… but that's not the point! The point is"—there was another crashing boom—"it's insane to destroy a city over karaoke!"

Dino looked briefly embarrassed. "Humans have done equally idiotic things in their history."

Another explosion rattled the windows. Frank put down his glass. "Come on. We're going to put a stop to this before it gets any worse."

"How?"

Frank didn't answer the question, mostly because he wasn't sure. The niggle of an idea formed in the back of his brain. He only hoped Dino would follow his lead.

"We'll go to my place first," Frank said finally.

They slipped out the back door and climbed into Frank's battered, aging aircar. The aircar already looked like it had been through a Sauri riot. It shuddered up onto its airjets and coughed into gear as Frank finessed it forward and up to speed.

Frank took the next corner at full speed, airjets screaming in protest. If all went well, they'd be in his building's underground parking lot before anyone knew they'd been on the streets. The idea was starting to root and bloom, but he still didn't want to say anything. Dino followed him into his apartment.

"Who's the best singer among you?" he asked the reptile as he fumbled with the lock.

Dino's scaled head crest fluffed up in pride. "I am."

"Seriously? Or are you just saying that?"

"You asked. I answered. I have had a featured role in the Festival for the last five years." Dino's crest rose higher and his voice took on a distant, old-Earth accent. "Thank you. Thank you very much."

Frank tried very hard not to roll his eyes at the inevitable lip curl accompanying the quote. The Elvis thing was sometimes a bit much to take. He should've been used to it by now, but sometimes…

"Would you like to share what's going on in that mammalian brain of yours, Frank?"

He ignored the question as he rooted through his bedroom closet. "Aha!"

"Aha, what?"

Frank backed out of the closet clutching a hard plastic case the size of a weekender suitcase but with an odd shape. He couldn't help the huge grin on his face as he set the case down on his bed and approached the dresser. He pulled open the underwear drawer and pawed through the socks and shorts.

"Would this be considered 'Too Much Information,' Frank?"

"Under other circumstances, maybe." Frank yanked his hands out of the drawer as if something bit him and shoved small plastic chips into his pocket. "That's it! We're in the Milk Bath now, Dino. Let's go."

"Go where?" Frank heard the irritation in the Sauri's voice. Dino was starting to lose his cool, which was difficult for a cold-blooded reptiliod. "Don't make me hurt you, Frank. Where are we going?"

"To save New San Diego." Frank hefted the case and headed for the door.

"Why does that sound more ominous than encouraging?"

"Because you're a pessimist instead of an optimist." Frank paused at the door. "Look, Dino, I have a plan, and I really need your help. I just don't want to talk about it yet, in case it falls apart. Will you, please, just trust me?"

"What's in it for me?"

Frank grinned. "Now that's more like it, Dino. What's in it for you? The performance of a life time and an open tab for a year. Whatever you want, old pal, but only if this works out."

"Why?"

"Because if it doesn't, there won't be a New San Diego left— much less a Frank's Place. Now come on. Time's running out."

By the time they made their way to the city park, flames were clearly visible in the skyline around them. The blue violet night turned ugly brown where sky and flames met. City noises were drowned out by screams of people and emergency vehicle sirens.

"I can't believe how quickly your people went berserk," Frank said as they set the case down on an improvised, open-air stage in the middle of the park.

"*Us?*" Dino shook his head. "That wasn't something innate in my species until your people messed with us. Now will you tell this brilliant plan of yours?"

"Music."

"Be more specific, human."

Frank opened the box, pulled out a wad of cables, and started manipulating them into the stage's built-in karaoke system. "Music."

"What good will that do if all the Elvis is gone?"

Frank smiled. "Not completely gone."

"Don't toy with me."

"I'm not. Before this goes any further, promise me one thing."

"What?"

"Once we're out of this mess, and you're the big hero and all, you'll do me one favor."

"Anything. Just let's do something. I hear a mob coming."

"Promise me you listen, just once, to Dean Martin."

"I promise! Anything! Frank, whatever magic you think you have up your sleeve, now would be a good time to pull it out. That's definitely a mob coming."

Frank looked to see an angry group of Sauri approaching. Half of them wore white spangled jumpsuits and capes, like Dino. The other half sported blue suede shoes to represent the King.

"Power up the machine," Frank said.

Frank hunched over the case. He had to hurry now, but there was still so much that could go wrong. He wasn't sure he could pull off what he was about to ask Dino to do. It had been so long… he'd not even attempted such a thing in years. Not since the accident that had killed his and Maggie's parents. He wasn't even sure he could remember how it was done, or if the equipment would work after so long. But there was an ancient Earth proverb that insisted some things were like riding a bicycle. Frank wasn't sure what a bicycle was, but he was counting on the idea a person didn't forget once-learned skills.

"Frank? They're getting closer."

Frank stood, shoved a microphone into Dino's hand, and power up the stage system.

"What do you want me to do?"

"Sing, Dino, sing! Sing like the world depends on it! Right now, brother, it does."

"There's no music!"

"That's what you think!" Frank knelt quickly and stood again with a vintage Earth, six-string Fender Stratocaster. He did his best to empty his mind and let muscle memory and need do the rest. The first chords were hesitant and weak. Then the opening riffs of "Burning Love" poured out of the instrument and Frank's fingertips with greater confidence.

"You know Elvis?"

"Just sing, Dino!"

Dino sang.

The roar of the unruly crowd shifted from hysterical anger to hysterical enthusiasm as they realized what was happening. The long dead king of rock 'n' roll wove magic once more.

"Wow, music does soothe the savage breast."

Frank jumped and turned his head. He tried not to falter on the guitar. "Maggie!" He saw his sister standing beside him, grinning wickedly. "What're you doing here?"

"Backup. What else?" She held up a small, handmade percussion instrument and fell into beat with her brother.

Frank tried not to feel a pang of guilt. Maggie had been forced to leave her full drum kit behind when they'd immigrated to New San Diego in the first colony ships. The kit had put them over the weight limit, but his guitar had been allowed. He'd always felt bad about that.

"I thought I knew what you were up to, and Elvis isn't the same without the rhythm section. And I still want to know how you pulled this off." Maggie had to shout to be heard.

"Made him promise to listen to some other musicians."

"Our Great-great-... Great-to-the-whatever-power-grandpa Sinatra would be proud."

"The Chairman of the Board belongs on the same stage as the king of rock 'n' roll. It's just the right thing to do."

Frank looked at the audience. 'Lounge lizard' was about to take on a whole new meaning in the universe, and his bar would be right in the middle of it. He and Maggie would be set for life. He didn't think his ancestor would mind in the least. ✹

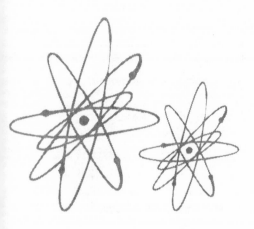

LoveFM

SARAH HILLARY

JOHNNY SHOULD HAVE TOLD HER—would have told her—
that Elvis was his first love. But the time was never right.

That song had been playing all summer as they lay on the
beach, love's jetsam, her long hair roped with sand, his skin
grainy with goose-bumps: "Love me tender, love me long; take
me to your heart…" and then that last line about dreams coming true, sung so beautifully Johnny felt his heart break each
time he heard it. She got sick of it in the end. "Dumb song,"
she said, and reached a sandy hand to switch the radio off. It
was a vintage Roberts radio, contemporary to the King, finished
in Ferrari Yellow leather. Johnny had told her he didn't want it
touched.

The trailer park was the lousiest, most godforsaken spot Johnny'd
ever seen.

It might've been a shanty-town but for the gaudy ghetto
touches: neon signage on the biggest of the trailers, gold paint
peeling from the window-frames, stars and stripes slung in fray-
ing swags everywhere. Mired ankle-deep in garbage, the place

stank of petrol, cooking fat and waste. The trailers were packed
cheek by jowl, hundreds of them, set up from the dust on
cracked concrete stilts or sinking into pits of mud and worse.

The ranks of dirty-white boxes gave the place a mausoleum
air. Strung between two posts, a banner was sagging in the wind,
denoting the name of the park, "Graceland 2," above a scabby
daub of Elvis with a half-eaten hamburger in both fists.

Propped against one post were the remains of a wooden
Indian, stolen from outside a tobacco store some place, his face
and torso peppered with buck-shot. Bullets had removed his
nose and broadened his mouth from ear to ear, leaving shards of
wood hanging like loose teeth.

Johnny shivered despite the damp heat curdling the air
around him. He had the feeling he was inside a dream, but one
so real he'd wake with the taste of petrol in his mouth and the
stain of neon on his skin. He wasn't sure how he'd got here. The
last thing he recalled with clarity was driving his beat-up Buick
away from the beach, away from her...

There'd been days of driving, tires choked with desert, windows caking up so bad he'd had to stop and clean them every
few hours. He remembered the heat and the car radio—*You've
lost that lovin' feelin'*—the road ahead bubbling like a swamp.
Then the trailer park had shimmered into view, dazzling him.

He'd stopped the car and walked, stumbling in the potholes,
his legs stiff from sitting so long behind the wheel, a bottle of
Coca Cola hanging from the numb fingers of one hand.

The park was deserted; the only sound the snagging of the
wind shifting the flags and the faded image of Elvis. The sun
made a blaze of the trailers, crazing every ugly angle, lifting a
smog of fumes that turned the air to treacle.

Johnny took a slug of cola, grimacing as the metallic-sugar
taste found his tonsils. What was that slogan? *Life tastes good.*
Life.

He scrubbed the back of a hand across his eyes, tired beyond
belief. The stars and stripes billowed and boomed about him,
their red-white-and-blue exaggerated to crimson, silver and sap-

phire. Like her eyes.

Passing the remains of the Indian chief, he entered the trailer park. He expected a dog to run up barking, or a kid. His boots were muffled by the thick dust, making him another non-sound in the place, an extra layer of emptiness. He approached the nearest trailer and peered through the grimy window at an unmade bed, film posters on the wall—*Full Metal Jacket, Jaws*—empty beer bottles spilling like bowling pins in all directions. The next trailer was the same, and the next. No people, but plenty of signs of recent life: plates of food left out on tables were attracting flies. In one trailer, a TV was tuned to the shopping channel, its volume turned down low.

After passing a dozen trailers, he reached the largest, a palace by comparison, with plastic awning set around its roof like the icing crust on a wedding cake. One side was defaced by a sprawling picture of Disneyland, all sickly-pink turrets and phony sunshine. It was the same box as the others, just larger and gaudier, with beaded curtains at the windows and a scarlet neon sign that winked at him: a Smith and Wesson. From the muzzle, the word "Bang!" flashed on and off, on and off. The place had the sweet-meat smell of barbecued ribs.

Feeling nauseous, he leaned against the side of the trailer, remembering the way her fringe curled on her forehead, cradling it like a hand. He felt his gorge rise and thought he might puke, but the feeling passed. "The things we do for love," he muttered when he got his breath back.

The dry beat of the sun on his head urged him to get inside. It had beaten like that on the beach, drumming down on his body and hers. He swung up the short flight of stairs to the front door of the trailer.

It was unlocked, opening onto a dim space striped with colour by the bead curtain, stretching back into a darkened right-angle where he could just see a couch. He blinked, waiting for his eyes to adjust to the change in light, and heard music. The tinny sound of loud speakers was stripping the sentiment from the song, "Love Me Tender," reducing it to a ringtone, raucous with feedback: "When at last my dreams come true, darling, this I know: happiness will follow you, everywhere you go."

The tune looped back on itself, starting over: "Love me tender..."

Sitting on the couch, propped by plush cushions in every shade of pink, was the King.

In a white jumpsuit, its belt and bib a riot of rhinestones, his face half-hidden by mirror-framed glasses and his hair coiffed and brilliantined—who else could it be but Elvis?

The song rumbled on and the King joined in, a live performance from beyond the grave: "Love me tender, love me sweet, never let me go..."

That's when Johnny saw her. Dancing. A slow, hip-slinking dance, her skin stained strawberry by the lighting. Her face was turned towards the couch, her back to him. She looked drunk; the slutty moves only needed a pole. It didn't seem decent, dancing like that in front of the King.

"You have made my life complete, and I love you so." A hand, flashy with rings, waved in his direction.

The King. It really was. Which could only mean—

Elvis raised a hand and plucked the glasses from his skull, the dying ember of his eyes glinting across the trashy expanse of trailer. He dropped his gaze to the girl. "Shake those tail feathers, baby."

The music squawked on and the girl kept dancing, her limbs sinuous, sinful. The red tip of Elvis' tongue tapped his upper lip, keeping time.

"What—what's she doing here?" Johnny managed to ask at last.

Elvis put a finger up, hushing him.

The girl danced her way back, away from the King and towards Johnny, turning at the last minute and draping her chin over his right shoulder, chest to chest with him, her face hidden in his shoulder.

Johnny could smell her hair, the salt that still clung to it and another scent, rusty, russet, beneath. His skin itched all over with the memory of what he'd done.

He stared across the lurid space of the trailer at Elvis. "Am I dreaming?"

"You want me to pinch you?"

"Oh," Johnny said. "Oh, no. This can't be right. You're Elvis. You should be in heaven."

"We reap what we sow." The King looked at him, rhinestones winking. "Where should you be, sonny?"

The girl lifted her head, the long hair parting like a curtain on her face. Johnny could see the imprint of the radio dials across her forehead, a rank of bruised and bloody indents. From one crimson socket, the ruins of a sapphire eye, silvered by the antennae of the Roberts radio, gazed on him with unquiet reproach.

"Welcome to hell," drawled Elvis.

Hell. It was almost worth it, to be sitting in the same room with the King. ✳

Paying Tribute

Lyn C. A. Gardner

THE CROWD RAGED IN THE PIT below the stage, screaming and shoving, an assault of praise. Young girls stretched out
their arms, wiggling and squealing as they always had, but the
girls today looked so skinny, in their white tank tops and mid-
riff shirts, their retro-flowered jeans that hugged starved bellies,
tanned shoulders partly obscured by long, curling hair. Boys in
baggy jeans and crew-cuts mingled with men whose curls had
gone gray, sporting faded T-shirts from the band's early days.
Blankets and deck chairs covered the muddy field, while younger
fans wormed their way around section fences to stand on the hill
for a better view.

Just another reunion concert. Who isn't doing it these days?
Tony thought with a certain amused shame, a certain scornful
pride. He stood behind the stage, watching roadies hustle back
and forth as they removed the opening act's equipment, ducking
as they crossed the stage as if to avoid the fans' eyes. They needed
to: they all bore that same dirty, disheveled look—long greasy
hair, ratty black T-shirts, stained jeans. It was getting hard to
tell the roadies from the bands. When Tony Simpatico had been
at the top of the charts, the rock and roll gods had dressed as
though they were worthy of that adulation.

Pete Henley walked up beside him, touched his elbow. "How

are you feeling?" Pete asked, pitching his voice above the crowd.

Tony shrugged, staring toward the dressing room. "What about him?"

Pete hugged him suddenly, so tightly that tears of pain rose to Tony's eyes. "Don't worry about him. You don't have to worry about any of it anymore. How many times have we gone over this, practiced every song you know? He studied your moves and your style for years before we ever found him. He's going to be fine. You chose him, Tony. The perfect man for the job."

Tony ducked his head, embarrassed. The painkillers and incessant headaches left him on a roller coaster of emotion these days. Only a few months ago they'd been saying it was only a matter of time, that all they could do was make him comfortable. The tumor was benign, but it would still kill him, lodged in his brain. But now the fans were giving him back the life he'd poured out for them: a crack neurosurgeon who loved the band had contacted him, told him he had one chance, a long shot, but he couldn't plan on singing anytime soon. A chance at life—for which he'd have to give up his life, this overbooked reunion tour that he'd seen as his farewell—singing until he could sing no more.

Patting Pete's shoulder, Tony walked to the dressing room. Young Anthony sat in front of the mirrored counter, sequins flashing from a white pantsuit with low-cut chest and wide cuffs. Through the open collar, a hematite medallion glinted darkly in its nesting place. Tony felt uneasy, looking over the kid's shoulder into the mirror, seeing that long dark hair, square jaw, and eagle-hooked nose right below his own. If Tony were thirty years younger, they would be virtually identical. Now Tony's hair was lighter with all the gray, and his face had grown heavy with lines he could not ignore, his eyes hollow where the other's flashed fire.

Anthony smiled nervously and stood, meeting him eye to eye, height for height. Tony swallowed back nausea, dizziness, as their eyes struck, the young man's eager, cocky—his own.

"Ready?" he asked quietly.

"Mr. Simpatico, you'll never know what this means to me— I've dreamed of this all my life…"

"So did I," Tony said quietly, his eyes searching the other's face. The young Anthony Syracuse had chosen his stage name for its similarity to Tony's and its reminder of Tony's birthplace. He'd been uncanny at the front of that Heart Attack tribute band. "I know you've played me before—"

"I built my career replicating your sound. But it was nothing like this," the young man finished. "Never with the real Heart Attack. Never to this great a crowd—never with any illusion that it's real. Not just size, the expectation—"

Tony nodded. "It all happens in the first few minutes. You'll either cave into yourself, or you'll learn how to channel the energy of the crowd, until you blow twenty feet high. But you've got it a little tougher than we did. Even when you're most in the groove, you've got to remember—"

"I'm you," the young man said, and smiled.

The operation was an unqualified success. Even the doctors were amazed at how rapidly Tony recovered, how clear his sight was, how his memory returned with leaps and bounds. Six months of therapy, radiation and steroids bringing him back to who he was. He'd moved in with Ma before the surgery; she'd helped keep track of the endless doctor's appointments, making notes about everything and taping them all over the house so he wouldn't forget. When he returned from the hospital, she kept him away from TV and loud music, made lemonade, cooked him breakfast in bed, and fussed over him as if he were still a little boy.

But as his health returned, so did his energy, his old restlessness. Hours in the basement with his acoustic guitar had proven that his voice—and his songwriter's inspiration—once again had what it takes. His old songs ran through his head without warning, fresh and new as if he'd written them only hours before,

making his spine sing. The new songs that had poured forth
since he'd left the hospital felt just as vibrant, back to his classic
style. It was as though in removing the tumor, they'd cut away all
the age, the scars of bitterness and disappointment, the cynical
thickening of his skin, anything that had grown old and rot-
ten—all that had been holding him back. Soon it would be time
to step out that front door to take his life back.

"How ya doin', Syracuse?" he said to the old, cracked mirror,
grinning at himself through the murk.

From upstairs, Ma's voice echoed down the well: "Tony,
dinner's ready!"

He turned toward the door; fluid and slow as water, the reflection did the same. Both opened mouths slowly with the old
words, "Coming, Ma!"

At the table, he ducked his head, patient while she said grace.
Then he asked, "Ma, have there been any calls?"

"No, sweetie. Please tell me you didn't have another fight with
Marissa. I was so hoping everything would work out this time."

"You just want grandchildren," Tony began, the old retort
springing to his lips. Then he realized what he'd said. "Ma? Marissa and I haven't seen each other in over a year."

She looked up at him unhappily. Misery winked the cheeks
behind her spectacles as plainly as a shout. Mutely, she lifted the
bowl of waxed beans toward him. Ever since he was a kid, she'd
grown them herself, harvested them, canned them. These looked
different, too uniform. Machine-cut. He set them in the center
of the table and stood, not wanting to face the truth in her eyes.

"Sorry, Ma. I'll be in the study. I've got to make a call," he
apologized.

He didn't answer when she called after him, "Tony? You
haven't eaten your supper!"

With the study door closed, his hand hesitated on the heavy
receiver of the old rotary phone. After all the trouble she'd taken
to help him remember, Ma wouldn't just forget if Pete had
called. Darkness brought on an odd feeling. He forced it aside
and dialed a number he knew by heart.

When Pete picked up, Tony cut in, "I'm fit as a fiddle. When do you want me back?"

A long pause. Tony heard rustling papers, the tap of a pen. "I'm glad to
hear it," Pete said at last.

"What's the matter?"

"I've got a lot of commitments right now, Tony. I'll get back to you."

"Well, don't wait too long. I might just snap up a better offer," he joked.

"Really? That's great, Tony."

"What? Pete, I didn't mean—Heart Attack is my life—"

But Pete had hung up.

Tony couldn't sleep that night. He stayed up putting his songs in order, polishing demos, putting lyrics and melodies in their final form. By the time he went upstairs for a glass of water, the sun was already peeking through the blinds.

He dozed in the old black leather armchair, listening to Ma puttering about the kitchen. Whenever he cracked his eyes, the morning sun slipped delicately into the thick, cut glass of the curio cabinets to his left, where among the china dogs and miniature porcelain slippers ranged all the souvenirs Ma had saved from his career: framed photos, a cap with the band's logo, T-shirts, albums, set lists, and ticket stubs, bearing autographs in every place they could, like some miniature Rock and Roll Hall of Fame. The photo albums on the lower shelf now contained more news clippings than family photos.

Ma hummed to the crackling of pancakes on the griddle. Barks punctuated the rumble of the lawn mower across the street: the soothing sounds of Saturday morning. At some point while he dozed, Ma had draped one of Pop's old sweaters over him; the wool scratched his bare arms as he turned in the reclining chair where Pop had found comfort in his last days. Tony put his back to the locked curio cases, watching lazily as the sun slid up the cool, pink plaster walls of the house his parents had built themselves.

The linoleum creaked above the kitchen stairs. Ma smiled to see he was awake. "Breakfast, Tony?" she asked, drying her hands on a flowered towel. He smiled back, feeling rested despite the weariness still heavy behind his eyes. He took a seat across from her at the yellow Formica, and she switched on the boxy old wooden radio on the counter.

Her ear for music news was still keen. Tony recognized Stan Kemelman's DJ patter. The talk show was familiar: coverage of local acts, not all of it positive. Reunion bands took a hard rap, pegged as musicians whose talent had drained away, surviving on the last dregs of stale glory, bitterness masked by the heavy lacing of nostalgia.

Stan Kemelman said, with characteristic cheer, "As the Tony Simpatico of modern rock—"

"Pardon me. Not 'the' Tony Simpatico."

Tony recognized that voice. Years ago, he'd heard such a tenor played back on endless tapes during the maze of composition, before time had dropped it into a lower register.

"What would you prefer to be called? Anthony?"

"I *am* Tony Simpatico."

Tony set down his milk, his throat tight.

"And how long have you been with Heart Attack?"

"Figuratively, or literally?"

"How about a little of both?"

In the background, someone had begun to spin "Calling All Dreamers," the only hit on their last three albums. Pete's guitar work sounded more ornate than it had in years, a complexity they'd left by the wayside as times changed. Then the vocals: and ice shot down his spine. The style was subtly new, but the voice was his—from thirty years ago.

The band had re-recorded the song without him.

Anthony was saying, "You've heard how I got my start. I joined my cousin's band when I was fifteen. When that didn't go anywhere, I struck out on my own. By the time I was nineteen, I realized there's no room for solo acts these days unless you're already a name. But pick an outrageous concept and do it big, everybody's gonna notice. So my buddies and I got together and decided we'd tap into the heartbeat of the times. We'd tap so hard we'd cause a heart attack!"

"You little shit," Tony muttered. "That's my life, that's my line—"

Across the table, Ma dropped her spoon. Tony apologized, but she shook her head, her eyes as wide and bewildered as they'd been the night before.

Stan chuckled. "You're speaking of Tony Simpatico, of course, but ladies and gentlemen, the story of young Anthony Syracuse is remarkably similar. When his self-titled album took a dive and his label dropped him at the tender age of nineteen, he decided to tap into the reunion craze, with a difference. Since the originals were no longer performing, he and his friends took up the mantle of their heroes to become Your Second Heart Attack. Anthony, when Tony and Pete and Chas and the rest dug themselves out of the grave, what effect did that have on your business?"

The voice was low, suave, calm. "I'd rather not discuss that. The past exists only in your head. The present is real: Heart Attack is alive and pumping."

Tony's hand trembled on the volume. That cornball gimmick with their name was exactly what another brash young rocker had done at twenty-four, when they'd begun to climb their first real groundswell of popularity.

"We'll leave you with this. During the opening week of the new tour, fans were stunned to see Tony walk into the spotlight, straight out of the past, for a set that hasn't rocked this hard since 1977. I've said it before, most reunion bands are a dish best served cold, straight out of the original vinyl jackets. But this is no reunion—this is classic Heart Attack as fresh as when we first heard them by the pool on FM radio."

The backing song grew louder, till "Calling All Dreamers" filled the speakers and Tony's heart ached for a voice that had been his and his alone, before the slow changes over the years— waking to phlegm and loose cords that buzzed so low he had to practice hours each day just to keep his voice tight enough to perform. Long before the tumor, he'd been dying slowly, piece by piece.

Now the voice was young and powerful again, strong and soulful—his no longer.

"That was classic Heart Attack, folks! And if you didn't get the chance to see them the first time, they'll be playing live at the amphitheater on the 18th. Believe me, they sound just as good as they did thirty years ago—maybe even better! Tony, tell us about the new album."

"It's amazing to watch everything come together the way it has. I've always wanted to do another record, ever since the band broke up five years ago. Since Heart Attack got back together, we've been on fire with inspiration. The songs are flying in on the wings of our dreams!"

"You cut the album in just two days, is that right?"

"We couldn't have done it without our fans. We owe them so much—their energy and belief really keep us going. They've never let us down, even in the lean years. We especially want to thank everyone who's been to our concerts these last six months, cheering us on. You really pumped us up. We couldn't do this without you!"

The lean years, Tony thought numbly. My years.

"Well, here's an album that really shows why we all stay in this business, despite all the hassles, the heartaches—the heart attacks!"

Stan spun the record. Opening chords—power and soul. Tony listened as the words poured out—words he'd first set to the page six months ago, when he came back from the hospital, alone and hurting, thinking his best years were behind him.

"Forgotten Man."

Calls to Pete went unreturned. Ma watched anxiously as he tried to reach Stan Kemelman, or Heart Attack's manager. Finally he kissed Ma on the cheek and left, telling her not to worry.

It wasn't hard to pick up the tour—he'd helped arrange it. As he stood on the hill above the amphitheater, the breeze felt strange on his shorn skull. He wandered through the crowd, protected by the anonymity of an ancient Heart Attack shirt, the faces of the band so abstract no one would recognize him with his younger double glamorous on the stage. The crowd swelled, thick as blades of grass, waving in a wind of their own emotion. Security guards at every stairwell kept them moving. They flowed through the channel like slow syrup, face after face the same. No one seemed to notice his. A few eyes lingered; but no one touched his arm and asked, "Are you—?"

"Are you ready? To step into yesterday?" Anthony's tenor boomed as he gripped the microphone with both hands. He shot a glance at Pete, electric-quick: and the band pounded into motion, one instant beat. The audience surged to its feet. Girls screamed, so young they'd never seen anyone sing these songs but Anthony.

The lights revolved like Catherine wheels, purple spraying in veils from heaven, white misting the night like snow. Anthony danced before them in his shimmering white suit, stretching his hand to reaching fans. He nodded to Pete, who smiled faintly and stepped forward to burn down the night with his guitar while Anthony bent over the microphone like a lover, stroking it till the crowd screamed.

Tony pushed his way through the crowd. They closed ranks behind him as though he'd never been. Individual faces shone up at him in the pallor of the safety lights, bright with a reverence reserved for heroes, or for miracles—as though none of them had expected to see this again, and it was better than they'd believed.

Tony let the flow carry him to the base of the stage, then fought to the backstage entrance. Two guards waited, arms crossed above the locked gate.

"I'm here to see Pete Henley."

"You got a pass, buddy?"

He had never needed one. "Don't you remember me?"

The one on the left frowned, but the one on the right leaned over to whisper in his ear. A moment later, the surly one grunted, "You a relative of the lead? You're not on the guest list. Let's have your ID."

They didn't recognize him: they would think he was a fake. While they fumbled with his wallet, he craned to catch some sight of the roadies, the bus driver, anyone who might vouch for him. A slim black shape passed behind the stage, crossing toward the tour bus. "Jeanne!" he called desperately. "Jeanne Willet!"

A cigarette glowed in the darkness as the figure turned toward him. She strode into the lights by the fence, slim, her moussed black hair looking bigger than the rest of her. The opening act.

"What can I do for you boys?" she said, one hand hooked in the pocket of skintight leather pants that laced up the front.

"Man says he needs to see Pete Henley. No pass, no appointment," the bald one grunted.

"He's with me. Let him by," she said, with a tight little smile. They looked unhappy, but they complied. Tony snatched his wallet back from the big man's hand.

Jeanne took his elbow and led him back while the band thumped on. She didn't pause until she'd got him in the lounge and closed the door. She pulled up a stool and an ashtray and sat down by the bar, leaning against it with one elbow while she hooked the high heels of her wrinkled suede boots on the rungs of the stool.

"Spill it, Tony man," she said as she ground out the stub, her eyes twinkling. "What are you doing back here? Please say you're a scout now. I need to get back on a label."

"Jeanne, I'm sorry—" He stopped when he saw her slow smile, the laughter half-hidden by long, black lashes. "You know I'd sign you in a heartbeat."

"We has-beens got to stick together," she said, patting his knee, her long nails glossy black. She lit a new cigarette, tilted her head back, and blew smoke at the ceiling, watching it dissipate. "That's my career up there."

"What do you think of my substitute?"

She arched a brow. "The kid? He's okay. It would be interesting to see the two of you together."

"I'll be happy to oblige. I need to talk to him anyway."

Her waif's smile lingered like a ghost in the smoke, as they sat and waited for the set to end. Jeanne said, "You know, I had a girl approach me once.

That time I broke my ankle. She looked as good as I used to, once upon a time. Offered to go on for me. But I saw the way she smiled. That flower face. It would have been a sucker punch. If I'd let her have her way, she would have stolen my fans. Better to hobble across the stage and know their hearts are still mine."

The last chords sounded, ripples dying into the wave of cheers. Jeanne stood. "Be right back," she said, leaving Tony alone at the bar, facing the mirror, his face sallow and tired, almost gray in the weak light. The skin sagged below his eyes. Too many lines, too many gray hairs. He held his glass loosely and rattled the ice, unable to look away.

Jeanne returned, mouth wry, eyes amused, her hand resting easily in the young man's. Pete trailed behind.

"How's business, Pops?" Anthony asked with a smirk. Jeanne released his hand and he floated smoothly to Tony's side. Jeanne mimed holding a camera, framing the picture, bending her knees to capture the perfect angle: "Say cheese."

"Cheese," they both said on cue—the same lilt of amusement, the same timbre. The hairs rose along the back of Tony's neck. Jeanne adjusted the pose, turning them parallel to the mirror, close enough that their shoulders touched.

It was like looking at the reflection in a vanity table, two mirrors facing a third: twin images, side by side, doubled and tripled, smaller and smaller into eternity. One man dressed in white, the other in black, with a hole in his head that seemed to funnel straight into the man who had replaced him in so many minds. Looking at his younger twin, that mass of springing curls, that album-perfect face, Tony had the sudden crazy notion that maybe his soul had skipped like a stone into the more likely host, the one that looked most like home.

"So, what are you doing with yourself these days, Tony?" Pete said, his voice too loud. "Writing any songs?"

Tony said steadily, "Well, I was. But young Anthony here seems to have finished them all for me."

Anthony smiled beatifically, revealing teeth that were straight but nicotine-stained, the left front tooth chipped from a bottle brawl.

Those are my teeth, Tony thought in shock.

Tony said, "What's going on here, Pete? The bouncers wouldn't let me in. They claimed they didn't recognize me. I don't suppose you told them to keep me out."

"'Claim'? Why would they recognize a nobody like you?" Anthony said.

Tony stiffened, but he held onto his temper and spoke to Pete. "I'm not so sure this is a good idea anymore. I'm getting better, and I'm going to come back. If you keep billing him as me—"

"We need the publicity, Tony. Surely you realize that. It's almost impossible to climb out of a slump like the one we were in. No one's going to pay good money to see a lead who's just a clone. But to see you the way you were thirty years ago—"

"He isn't me."

Pete said, "You know, Tony, Heart Attack sounds better now than it has in years. You used to sing like Orpheus. Now you sound like Dylan on a bad day."

"That was the tumor."

Pete continued, "If you hadn't dropped out when you did, we'd have called it a day."

Tony knew it had been bad, at the end: he'd tried to close his ears to just how bad. While they were practicing for the reunion tour, he was giving himself raging migraines every night just to sing at all. He clung to the truth: "But they're my songs, Pete. How did you get my songs?"

"Do you really think anyone cares? This is the sound they all loved. This is their youth. How many of them actually love you, do you think? How many have even noticed you're gone? Face it, Tony. It was never about you. Only about your image and our sound."

Tony thought about the fans on the hill and was silent.

Anthony said with a contemptuous smile, "I don't even have to do anything. You don't belong here anymore."

There was an odd look on Pete's face. "We have a contract, Tony. We're not leaving you out in the cold. You're getting a cut from these performances, too. If it's the medical bills—well, just give me a call." He drew something from a satchel and placed it in Tony's hand: *Long Drive Home* by Heart Attack. The new album, every song one of his, right on down the line. The byline was his and Pete's, the way they always split it.

Anthony left the room, flicking off the lights; Tony followed, a ghost in the mirror. As he heard the kid answering his band-mates' congratulations, he felt like the imposter.

Jeanne touched his shoulder. "Be careful, Tony." She gazed at him a long moment with her beautiful, dark eyes, as if to fix him clearly. "Don't let them forget you."

He tried to make it home, but the confrontation had drained him. He felt woozy, as though a great surge of energy had left him all in a rush. The doctors had warned him to take things easy; but he didn't have time to coddle himself. In an effort to wake up, he pulled out his cell phone. It was too late to be calling, but the problem ate at him like heartburn. Mitch had stepped in as Tony's agent when the band had gone separate ways. Though Tony's solo career never went far, Mitch had always been sympathetic when Tony called in the dark hours of doubt, rehearsing ancient wrongs. Now Mitch stifled a yawn. "Tony who?"

"Simpatico. You know, Anthony Smith? I was the lead singer

for Heart Attack?"

"Your voice—"

"The surgery," Tony said, hating how quickly he offered that excuse. "They've got me on so many hormones and steroids—you wouldn't believe."

"What can I do for you, Tony?" Mitch said. But his voice held an odd formality, as if he repeated the name to remind himself who Tony was.

"Have you heard anything about my replacement recording some of my songs? Anthony Syracuse and the new Heart Attack?"

Mitch seemed to perk up. "The greatest hits revisited? *Life After Your Heart Attack*? Now, that's a stroke of genius. As soon as I heard about the project, I thought, there's no better way to rope in a new generation, than to have a modern voice redo all the old hits! In just a few weeks, the fans will be able to hear everything they've enjoyed in concert, the way it was meant to be played!"

Tony felt as though he'd had the wind knocked out of him. All that emerged was a strangled sound.

"What's that, Tony? I can't hear you. You're breaking up."

"Who authorized this?" Tony bellowed.

But Mitch didn't answer. The phone crackled with static.

Tony pulled over, his hands shaking as he punched the keys for Mitch, then Ma, without result. The endless ring had a dead sound. At last he tossed the phone into the glove in disgust.

He stopped at a fleabag motel. The clerk took a long, frowning time with his driver's license and credit cards, declining each with a muttered apology and a suspicious glance. When the clerk refused to return the third card and picked up the phone, Tony fled.

Even if motels had somehow joined the mass hysteria, Anthony Syracuse couldn't fool an ATM. Tony left the Jag's windows open, the radio pumping out "classic rock," familiar songs that grounded him even as they relentlessly reinforced his age. He typed in his code. But the withdrawal screen didn't appear.

At the warning, Tony punched "cancel" and tried again. He'd gotten the PIN wrong the first time, that's all. But the ATM demanded he call customer service, and refused to release his card.

Tony drove in white-knuckled fury. His eyes crossed with weariness, till he saw two yellow lines—a double vision familiar from his illness. When he began to drift off despite the booming radio, he pulled over and shut his eyes.

When dawn came, he thought he'd slipped in time. The dash belonged to Ma's old clunker, a Buick '73 she'd nursed along for years. As he saw the faded blue of the wide, dusty dash, a chill seized him. He opened the glove—the Buick was still registered in her name.

Of course, the cell phone was gone.

He drove the rest of the way home without sleeping, his eyes dry and dull as paper. Emotion swelled in him as he stepped out to unlatch the wire gate, then drove up onto the two concrete strips in the front lawn. Through the elms, the pale morning sun glinted on the windows.

His key didn't work.

Tony pounded on the door. When it swung open, Jerry Kinsale, the next-door neighbor, stood staring down at him with red-rimmed eyes.

"Ma?" Fear closed Tony's throat.

Jerry scowled. "Mrs. Smith had no children."

Tony wanted to scream. "Had?"

Jerry saw the look and patted Tony's shoulder. "I guess we all thought of her as Ma."

"How—"

"It's a funny thing. The paper printed something about her son… the one who died, what, thirty-five years ago? But the paper showed photos of him alive—as if he was still young. Some band he used to play with after high school—Heart Attack— God, what a name. That's the way she died. 'Heart failure.' Everyone in town knows what did it. You don't know what it was like, burying that boy, all mangled from the car accident. He would have been about your age. Maybe you knew him?"

"Not very well."

"The rumor goes he'd had too much to drink, but it was snowing, and no one likes to say a bad word about a widow's only son. He lingered for hours, trapped in that car. Two of his friends died with him. Hey, mister, you all right? Maybe you'd better sit down."

"No, I'll be fine," Tony heard himself say, but the reflected sun doubled in his vision, crowned with starry rays like oncoming headlights, filtered through falling snow. He remembered that skid. He and his friends had almost died, and for what? They'd been going nowhere fast. If they'd disappeared that night, no one would have remembered them. That was the night he'd realized how short life was, and resolved to give all he had to making a name for himself in music.

"I have to go," he said, dazed.

"Where? One of my boys can take you. You don't look good. You're in no shape to drive, if you'll pardon me saying so."

But Ma's car stood waiting—his last connection to her. Somehow, she still stood by him, supporting his need to find someplace safe to stand. As long as he had the power, he wouldn't waste her gift. Even if, in the end, she hadn't remembered he was alive, and he'd wound up just another orphan—like Anthony Syracuse had been.

The old Syracuse stations hadn't forgotten. If he played the radio long enough, he was sure to hear his own voice. This time it came across with a kid's pure-throated innocence: "Better a Lie Than a Life Without You." Ma had loved that song. Tears slid down his cheeks as he remembered all the times he'd wanted to quit. After Pop died, he'd wanted to work, to support his Ma. She'd fought with him fiercely, demanded he honor his God-given talent, live for all of them. She'd had to give up school in the eighth grade when her mother died, and she wouldn't let him sacrifice his dreams.

Tony found a battered acoustic in a pawn shop and worked his way downstate, playing small bars and Mom and Pop restaurants, polishing his act on the road. Compared to his early days, Tony's voice was rough around the edges, but that sound was just right for the raw simplicity of his roots—the folk and blues on which he'd cut his teeth, mixed with acoustic songs he'd written before Heart Attack had ever formed. The money was just enough to keep him going, to reach New York before Heart Attack was scheduled to return to the studio to finish reshaping their golden hits between legs of their tour. At one time, Tony had been no stranger to this studio; now the men at the door just glared. He hid in an alley, waiting for his moment.

A limo pulled up, its sides painted with flowing reflections of buildings and gray sky. The chauffeur opened the doors. The narrow toes of powder-blue boots emerged, followed by silver bell-bottoms, a royal blue silk shirt with gold fleur-de-lis, a sky-blue scarf, and opaque silver glasses: but it wasn't Anthony Syracuse who stepped onto the pavement, it was Tony Simpatico, twenty-four years old, live and in the flesh.

Tony felt it, as deep as the age in his bones: If he finishes that record, I'm history.

The young Tony Simpatico crossed the threshold with lifted chin while his entourage fluttered around him. The rest of the band filed in without fanfare, their faces tight. Tony knew that look. He'd seen it before the band split up, when they'd muttered curses under every breath.

Tony followed in the wake of the band, lost among the crew. When the young pretender strutted down the hall to fix his hair, Tony followed. Lurking wasn't difficult. As old and rough as he looked, Tony didn't rate a second glance. When enough time had passed, he walked into the lavatory, as cool as if he owned the joint.

Inside the lounge, young Anthony kissed a slim, black-clad figure whose cloud of moussed black hair floated above their hidden faces. Tony froze as he recognized Jeanne Willet, surprised by the hurt that struck his heart. Had she sunk so low? Was this how she saved herself? Had she finally been taken in, like everyone else? Or was that a message in her eyes that widened at him over Anthony's shoulder?

At last Anthony broke it off. "Sorry, babe… some other time. I've got a record to make." He began to turn toward the door, but Jeanne pulled him back, frowning and rubbing at a spot on his face. Guided by her hands, he walked to the mirror to check himself for lipstick.

Tony put a finger to his lips. Jeanne hesitated; then, with a worried look, she nodded and stepped back. Tony crept up until the mirror caught him, his face floating like a ghost above Anthony's shoulder. Tony smiled: and Anthony blanched.

Tony said ironically, "Remember me? You've got something of mine. I want it back."

Anthony's lips curved in a cruel smile. "I have nothing that wasn't mine already."

Tony stalked closer. Jeanne crossed behind him in the mirror to the swinging door, her eyes asking if she should go for help. Deliberately, he looked away and focused on Anthony.

"How about this," Tony said. "We can be partners. You can help me perform. Heaven knows I'm not up to speed yet, and I might never be. I'll help you write. Just don't claim any of my songs. And stop trying to pretend you're me."

"Are you crazy?" Anthony smiled, a dangerous light in his eyes. "This way, I get to live forever. Everyone will remember me as the voice of Heart Attack, and I'll go down in history as the youngest aging rock star ever."

"Not if I put a stop to it."

"You can't kill me. I'm you."

"Kill you?" Tony gripped the boy's shoulders, the royal blue slick under his hands. "You talk about killing, now? Ma is dead because of you."

"What?" For a moment, Anthony looked frightened. But he was light on his feet. "I did nothing wrong. Nothing unethical. Fair use, my friend. Fame flows to the one who uses it. It's not

LYN C. A. GARDNER

my fault if people get in the way."

"The police might take a different view."

"She died of a heart attack. You've got nothing on me," Anthony spat.

"And here I thought you stole my songs by osmosis," Tony mocked.

In the mirror, his hands tightened around the other's throat. Below his, Anthony's eyes were implacable as stone. Blue eyes caught blue in silver: the world swung upside down. Whose hands were his? Whose scream?

"No!" The shout was endless, ricocheting and doubling inside him.

A hand held his shoulder. Jeanne's anxious voice reached him: "Remember who you are!"

The world reeled and fell in a sparkling streak like the light show behind his eyes. He pulled himself up by the sound of her calling his name.

Jeanne held him by the waist. He swayed so hard he wondered why they didn't fall. At his feet lay a boy gasping like a fish out of water—a boy in glitzy pants and a torn blue shirt. Thrift-store chic. A roadie? His mind reeled, and he groped for thought, for memory, through the fog. But this was a trick he'd practiced during the illness, and after a moment he said slowly, "Anthony. Get up."

The boy lifted his head, panting, looking at Tony with startled, frightened eyes. He could not be more than nineteen—the age when he'd sacrificed his own talent to Tony Simpatico's.

"Tony," the kid murmured, his face flushed.

"Pull yourself together. There are record producers out there, and you want to look your best."

The kid speed-combed his hair and rushed out the door. "Be true to yourself," Tony called after him.

The door swung back again a moment later. Pete walked in with two executives, who promptly sat in the plush blue chairs of the bathroom lounge. They looked indifferently at Tony and Jeanne, as though it was nothing new to see the two together.

Pete said casually, "So, Tony, you want to cut the record now?"

A moment of panic. Tony stared at Pete's bald spot. He felt Jeanne's hands pulling away. But he didn't let her go. He whispered a question in her ear. She looked nervous, but she nodded.

He said, "I don't think so, Pete. Let's let Heart Attack rest in its well-deserved grave."

As he and Jeanne walked down the hall, executives clamored to sign Tony's new project. He waved aside their questions with one short answer: he was linking his star to Jeanne's. Out in the lobby, the police were cuffing a young man suspected of hastening his mother's death for the insurance—the only way to fund his failing band, now that his label had pulled the plug.

As Tony helped her into the band's waiting limo, Jeanne asked, "Are you sure you want to do this? Luck as bad as mine might be contagious. When my fifth band bit the dust, they started calling me the black cat."

"Are you kidding? You're my lucky charm."

The grin brought out warm wrinkles around her eyes. "I'm glad you finally noticed."

He took her hand. "You knew me," he said quietly. He searched her face, hoping to surprise her secret.

"I hope to God I never forget my friends," she said simply.

"But you—and Anthony?"

She shrugged. "Someone had to keep an eye on him for you."

He wasn't sure at first that he believed her. "Is that all?"

She winked. He recognized that spark: trouble, with good humor to see it through. Her loyalty might be crafty, but she had Ma's strength. The look she gave him was better than words.

Her voice was husky: "We'd better get back out there before they have time to forget us."

He squeezed her hand and grinned. "Forget Black Cat & the Midnight Soul? Not likely."

They were on the stage in no time, their styles joined in a bluesy mix of folk-rock, funk, and soul—a sound that spoke of roots, of the old made new. The venues weren't always large, but cheers filled them all. When Anthony and Jeanne walked out on stage, fans laughed and whistled as if they'd pulled a good trick, a kitten from a hat. Onstage, they joked about Tony's voice, their age, and Jeanne Willet's black-cat luck, and they never played the same set twice. At home, they wrote songs that told the truth as if their lives depended on it.

And Tony opened each show with the same shout: "Hey, remember me?"

Jeanne's Cheshire grin and laughing eyes answered him every time. ✳

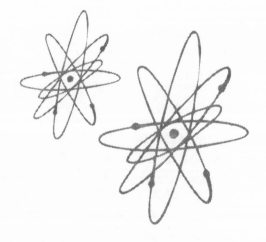

Subterranean Blues

Gillian Palmer

THE HOUSE DIDN'T LOOK LIKE VERY MUCH from the road, but Jen swore it was perfect. The second-floor apartment was in our price range, near enough to campus without being on it, and had the benefit of the original full bathroom. Most important to Jen's fabric softener sensitivities, it had basement laundry facilities.

The landlady didn't live on the premises, but she clearly cared about the upkeep; I'm still not entirely sure how she did it, but the house looked a lot more impressive on the inside. The landlady made sure we'd both be all right with a guy living on the first floor, and we went through with the lease.

Somewhere short of a week after we moved in, I came back after class to find Jen attempting to nap on the couch.

"What happened to you?"

"When you came in, was the stereo downstairs on?" she asked.

"Um, no. Should it have been?"

"Hell if I know. Only if it wasn't, I'd like to know who I get to kick for the really loud rock music what was going on when I got back this morning. I had a headache anyway, so I didn't really check the obvious source."

"Weird. Was the music any good, at least?"

Jen sighed. "Far as I was in any state to tell, it was all right.

Just too loud for the moment."

I shrugged. "Maybe the guy downstairs has a band. If we see him around we could ask."

We heard the music every few days after that, usually in the early evening. Jen went down to investigate one day.

"It's loudest near the basement. Here's the thing, though: there aren't extra cars or anything out front, there's not really even any sign of the guy downstairs, and… I'm not sure whether there's actually anyone *in* the basement."

"Well, did you go down and check?"

"Not as such."

"So this will forever remain a mystery?"

"Until I get around to investigating, it will, yes. For what it's worth, though, I didn't see any music equipment down there last time I did laundry."

"Well, I like it. And if it's a haunted-house sort of thing, there are definitely worse ghosts to have around. But still."

A couple of weeks after Jen's half-hearted investigation of the house's musical interludes, I came home to find a note on my desk:

Annie—I left some stuff in the dryer, and it should still be fairly wrinkle-free when you get back. If you could get it out for me, I'd really appreciate it. -Jen

She'd mentioned something about an interview after one of her classes; whether it was for an internship or a summer job, I couldn't quite remember. She was always busy. I wasn't sure when she'd found time to get things in the wash, never mind the dryer, but it was quite possible she'd come home during her lunch break. Either way, there was laundry in the dryer and someone had to remove it.

The music started up again when I was about halfway down the stairs to the first floor.

The first funny thing to catch my attention: even before I got the door to the basement open, the smells coming from around the edges were less like laundry detergent and more like pizza and pot. Maybe it was the second funny thing, in retrospect, since the apparently phantom music made for quite the mystery on its own.

The second (or third) funny thing... that would have to be walking into a fairly well-lit jam session instead of a dark, if inexplicably well-soundtracked, glorified laundry room.

One of the guitarists, a guy who looked about my age so far as I could tell behind all the hair, stopped as soon as he noticed me; the rest of the band followed suit after a few bars.

"Ronnie, what the hell'd you do that for? We were really on a roll, man. You cut out like that at our next gig, how are we supposed to—"

"Hold your damn fire. We've got company, and *I* didn't invite anyone over. Did you?"

"Well, no." The drummer shook his head, and they all turned to me, pretty clearly expecting an explanation.

"It wasn't my idea, okay? I was just trying to get my roommate's laundry."

"Laundry?" The guy who'd chewed out Ronnie for stopping treated me to a half-stoned and three-quarters-annoyed look. "Does this *look* like a damn laundromat to you?"

I sighed. "No, but it does look like the place I was aiming for, sort of. It's kind of confusing, but this sort of thing's happened to me before, it's..." I paused for a few seconds' mental math— trying to determine, based on the surroundings, how best to compare it—and then plunged ahead with it anyway. "Any of you guys read much Kurt Vonnegut?"

"Billy Pilgrim syndrome?" the drummer hazarded.

"Something like it, yeah. Except I think it's a bit more literal, and as far as I know, there are no aliens involved. I came down these stairs in 2007, and… what year *is* it at the moment, anyway?"

"Nineteen seventy-three." The drummer paused for a moment. "Have to say, I never thought a laundry service would be on the agenda for this place after we cleared out."

"There are apartments upstairs, and the landlady's nice enough to have an in-house washer and dryer." Apparently, my choice of explanation had left Confrontational Guy speechless for the time being. I was quite willing to call that a plus.

"It amounts to the same thing, in a way. Bit too quiet for the house as we know it. I'm Mark, by the way—the loudmouth's Brad, who already sort of introduced Ronnie."

"I'm Annie. You guys are pretty good."

That, unfortunately, started Brad talking again. It took me another hour or so to extricate myself from the conversation, go back upstairs (and into the right year), and try for the laundry again.

I had to restart the dryer for a few minutes, but I figured it was a small price to pay for sorting out the grand musical mystery.

Jen didn't believe my explanation at first, though after I pointed out the general lack of music equipment in the basement-as-laundry-room, she backed down. It didn't take long before I noticed a bit of a correlation between picking up the music in the house and ending up in the wrong year in the basement.

Brad, meanwhile, proved a little slower on the uptake. "You *again*? Why do you keep barging in on our practices?"

"I told you before, it's not exactly my idea. Maybe if you guys stopped playing loud enough to be heard *thirty years in the future*, I'd stop ending up here every time I try to get my laundry done. If it bothers you that much, stop sniping at me about it and try to stop the situation!"

I didn't feel like going back upstairs for another go just yet, so I just sat down on the bottom step and settled in to wait out the practice session.

After about ten minutes, the band called for a break, and Ronnie came over. "Sorry about that. Brad… he doesn't like his flow being interrupted very much."

"Why do you guys put up with him?"

"If it weren't for him," Ronnie said, "we wouldn't have anywhere to practice. I think that's one of the other things getting to him, even if he won't admit it. He's been set on becoming rock's next big thing since we were in seventh grade."

They were good, though I'd never heard the band's name before in my life, or anything they'd done. I made a mental note to ask Brandon, an old friend of mine, about it next time I talked to him. Brandon kept more of an eye on local music phenomena than I did, partly from his own interest and partly thanks to his summer internship at a concert venue just the other side of Cincinnati. If they were famous on a more local scale, he might know. "You guys stand a decent chance, I think," I said. "If you don't let Brad handle the PR."

"You think so?" Ronnie sighed. "I know we've got a few people who actively keep an eye out for our gigs, but so far that's pretty much our biggest claim to fame. We've tried recording things a few times, but it keeps falling through before we ever get to the studio."

"Since you mentioned it… I've been wondering if I might be able to record you guys. I'm not sure how much good it'll do you in the long run, since you'd have to wait for the technology to catch up, but in light of your problems with the official channels, it'd be better than nothing. And I've picked up enough about acoustics from one of my friends that it probably wouldn't sound horrible."

"You'd do that?"

"Sure. Just because your front man is lacking in social skills doesn't mean you and Mark should have to suffer him with no gain."

Ronnie grinned. "Thanks a lot. Even if it doesn't quite work out, it's a better plan than what we've got on our own."

"Cheaper, too."

Brandon called that evening, as luck would have it. Fortunately, by that point I'd managed to get my laundry done and folded.

"Question," I said as I tucked my clean shirts into a dresser drawer. "You ever heard of a band called Countersink?"

"No, can't say that I have," he replied after a few moments. "Why do you ask?"

"Oh, no particular reason. They're half haunting the house Jen and I are living in, is all."

"Only half? This your temporal whatsit acting up again?"

"A bit. And they keep having practices that we can hear, which I sometimes walk in on. But we can hear them upstairs all the time. We thought it was just the stereo of the guy downstairs, for a while. But it's not."

"Have you even seen your downstairs neighbor yet?"

"Nope." After living in the house for two months, we still had not met him.

"Well, I don't recognize the name. Are they any good?"

"Enough that I'm considering making a tape recording of them, despite the front man. The other two are pretty nice."

"As long as you're sure you're not gonna create any strange paradoxy things…"

I laughed into the phone. "Fairly sure, yeah. What's up on your end of town?"

"The usual, more or less. Southgate House called earlier and said they'd like me back next summer."

"Already? You must've really knocked their socks off. I'm not surprised, in light of how quickly you took over the theatre's sound board in high school."

"Hey, if they're gonna offer me something to do this early in the school year, I'll take it. It was a fun job, and besides, there were some rumors floating around that they might book Peterborough for next summer sometime."

"You sure you can get through that without dying of a fanboy heart attack?"

"Now you're just mocking me, aren't you?"

"Only the best for my friends."

I found a small, inexpensive tape recorder and fell into the habit of carrying it with me when I had to go to the basement. Better that, I figured, than being caught unawares and not being able to go back upstairs for it in time.

After a couple weeks, I finally walked into a rehearsal break rather than the laundry room. Brad, fortunately, wasn't in the room for the moment, but Mark and Ronnie were. They looked up expectantly at me from their couch.

"I've got something for recording," I announced. "The bad news is, I'm not sure how much practical use it'll be in 1973. I might have to take it back with me and wing it from there."

Mark raised an eyebrow. "What makes you say that?"

I pulled the tape recorder out of my sweatshirt pocket.

"Damn, that thing is tiny! They get smaller in the future, huh? We probably won't be able to get the tape to play on anything."

Ronnie shrugged. "It's better than nothing. And this way, we don't have to tell Brad."

"Good point. Last thing he needs is the encouragement."

"So how are we doing this? Will you actually get good sound if you leave that in your pocket?"

"Well, your amps are pretty good. Long as I don't put my hands over it, we should be okay. I don't know if I'll be able to play it back—that'll depend at least in part on whether your *dear* front man insists on hanging around. If I can, I will. Otherwise… we'll just have to take it on faith for the time being, I guess."

Mark grinned. "If all else fails, we'll send him after a pizza to get him out of the house. The best place uptown doesn't do deliveries."

I put the tape recorder back in my pocket and said, "You guys think you can act like nothing's out of the ordinary, like it's just another practice session? Aside from the time-traveling guest, of course."

"He's practically used to you showing up by now."

"He still doesn't like the implications," Ronnie added, "but he's dealing with you better, at least."

"Probably too much to hope he'll improve in the long run, isn't it?"

Brad came down the stairs just in time to overhear my last comment. "Who's improving in the long run?"

"Never you mind."

"Yeah, whatever. You two ready to get back to practice?"

Ronnie nodded. "I was hoping we could finally give 'Copper Thief' a try, if nobody's got any objections."

The band returned to its practice corner, and I sat down on a stool across from them, quietly turning on the tape recorder while they tuned.

Brandon came over a couple of days after I made the tape to help me digitize the music. Whatever else came of the recording, I wanted to have the stuff handy.

"Did you get to play this back for the band?" Brandon asked, making sure all of the wires connecting the stereo to my computer were doing what they needed to.

"No, unfortunately. We were trying to pull it off without the front man finding out. The other two tried sending him off for pizza, but he didn't want to leave the house, and I had to come back upstairs to the future. I mean, the present."

"Bummer."

I sighed. "No kidding. But I played it back as soon as I had a chance. It's a little muffled, but I got them, and it's still pretty good. Five or six whole songs and a few false starts."

"False starts are always entertaining. Is the software done installing yet?"

"Just about, yeah. Are you sure you're up to doing this today?" I asked.

"Shut up. I'm very nearly a professional. What're you going to do with this stuff once you have it in handy dandy MP3 format?"

"I can't decide whether it's worth trying to market the stuff when there's so little of it, and I have no idea where the band is now. Wouldn't do me much good to have people accusing me of setting up a hoax. At the very least, I'll have it to listen to."

"If you do decide to do something with it, I know some people who know people, thanks to the Southgate House thing. They'd be glad to pass it on."

"I don't doubt they would. Anyway, looks like this is ready to roll, so if you wouldn't mind making your electronics-inclined self useful…"

"Fine, fine. I see why you've been keeping me around." For all his fuss, Brandon was grinning as he sat down at the computer. Before long, he had the volume adjustments on the digitizing program sorted out and the tape playing.

"I have it set up to pick out breaks between songs automatically—that'll work for the first run. You were right, Annie, these guys are pretty good."

"What, do you not trust my musical judgment until you hear otherwise? You wound me."

After I got the recording, the music stopped spontaneously interrupting everything. I didn't even notice the silence for a couple of weeks, even though I was keeping a Walkman on hand just in case a rehearsal popped up. But the weeks kept passing by without any temporal anomalies from the basement.

The mystery behind the dry spell, as well as that of as well as the ongoing saga of the Invisible First-Floor Neighbor, finally came to a head just before Thanksgiving. Both answers sprang from me needing to do some laundry before I headed to my parents' for the family gathering.

I hummed while I pulled my stuff out of the drier. I knew I was indulging in a bad habit, but "Copper Thief" had been positively lodged in my head for a few days by that point, and I've found the best thing I can do in that situation is try to let the song out. It wasn't like there was anyone around to bother.

Except there was, in this case. Someone else picked up the harmony—a guy, no less. No one aside from Brandon and my roommate had heard the song, that I knew of. I paused, turned around to see who was there, and abruptly stopped.

"*Ronnie?*"

He stopped his own humming and gave me a sheepish smile. "Hi. You done with the washer?"

"Nearly. What are you *doing* here?"

"You're not the only one who's unstuck in time. My case seems to work in the opposite direction to yours."

"Yikes. My sympathies. This era is difficult enough for me, sometimes. And I'm from now."

"Thanks. I wouldn't say it's been entirely bad, though. Your landlady was… a good friend of mine, once. When she got over the initial shock of me being around, she said the first floor was mine whenever I was around to need it."

"We'd been wondering why our supposed neighbor was never around. And I guess this explains why there hasn't been a rehearsal to walk in on for a while now?"

"Yeah. I've never been stuck this long before. It's a little worrisome, to say the least."

"Well, I've never actually been stuck in the wrong time, but if I can help, I will. This can't be very easy."

"No kidding. Even Brad's probably noticed, by now." Ronnie sighed. "Thanks for the offer, even if nothing comes of it."

"No problem." I reminded myself that I had a load of laundry to get drying and pulled the last of my clothes out of the washer. "And now that's all yours."

"Thanks. How'd that tape of the band turn out, by the way?"

"Pretty good, actually. Still don't have it in any format you could take back and use immediately, but you've been recorded for posterity." I didn't bother mentioning the digitizing program—it only would've confused matters, and Brandon would be a better person to... wait.

When I updated Brandon on the situation, he had the same idea I had—see whether Ronnie would want to take advantage of Brandon's Southgate House connections and get a gig in while he was around. There were many rumors, as I think tend to crop up around historical buildings, that the place was haunted anyway, so if something came up in the middle of the show, most people would probably take it in stride.

Ronnie had his reservations about the idea, though, and neither of us could really blame him for not particularly wanting to research his own future. He did like the idea of trying to do something with the rehearsal tape, if circumstances allowed, so Brandon asked around and found out what information we would need to pull that off, assuming the actual band members were... unavailable for comment.

A few days after we'd done all but the 'where are they now?' leg work—having Ronnie around saved a lot of bother on such matters as who had written what—a drum solo cut through my efforts to make lunch. I grabbed the bowl of chips I'd set out, in case this excursion took a while, and headed downstairs. Ronnie was already by the door to the basement.

"Take it this is your cue, then."

"Guess so. Don't know why the hell Mark's playing on his own, unless it's some kind of 'kill the drummer' bet, but there you go. Are you coming along?"

"Weird as this may sound, it doesn't feel like I should this time. Might be the world's way of saying 'if the mayo's still out in three hours, your roommate will kill you.' So… tell Mark I said hi?"

"Yeah. Thank you *so* much for all your help. And if you can visit again, let us know how the recording efforts work out."

"I will. Good luck."

"Thanks." Ronnie opened the door to the basement, and then turned around before he started down the stairs. "Oh, and if you can get a hold of your landlady, you might want to ask her about the last of your research. She'll probably know some of it."

"I'll keep that in mind. Thanks."

A week after Ronnie got back home, we got music again—at very nearly two in the morning. I was in the middle of updating Brandon on instant messenger; Jen had been asleep for an hour, since she had somewhere to be fairly early in the morning.

"Annie? 's that your music?"

"No." Admittedly, I'd been playing the CD I'd burned off of the entire rehearsal—the copy we'd made to send to producers in hopes of getting it marketed only had the complete songs—quite a bit lately, but I hadn't felt like bothering with my headphones for the night. "I'll go take care of it, though."

"'k. Dunno why th' neighbor's playing stuff this late anyway." She retreated to her room, and I told Brandon I'd be a moment, got up, and headed for the stairs. I hadn't really had a chance to fill her in on the Invisible First-Floor Neighbor end points, and doing so wouldn't have worked out well at that time of night;

she wasn't awake enough to scoff properly.

Somewhat to my surprise, the basement stubbornly refused to be more interesting than a very dark, detergent-scented foundation level when I opened the door—even though the music definitely got louder. I briefly wondered if my temporal-disconnect problem would only act up if I tried to go down the stairs, but I didn't really have time to experiment, so I just stayed at the stop of the stairs until the song finished.

"Guys? I still think it's good and all, but my roommate needs to get to sleep sometime tonight. Any chance you could wait until tomorrow?"

After a few seconds, a pair of amps clicked off. ✳

Rock is Dead

CHLOE WALKER

They said rock was dead, until Scott Fletcher's ghost walked onstage. Thomas Hunter conducts a paranormal investigation.

TWENTY-SEVEN IS A BAD AGE for rock stars. Astrologically, it is the moment when Saturn returns to the place it occupied at birth. At twenty-seven, Saturn has an effect similar on someone's life similar to that of a stadium rock band on an expensive hotel room: it runs yelling down the corridor at 3:00 a.m. It smashes furniture. It orders room service until the bill reaches the thousands. It shoots up in the bathroom and tries to seduce the cleaning lady. It leaves the taps running until beer cans and cigarette packets float an inch above the sodden carpet. It throws the TV in the swimming pool.

If this is your life already, the unhinging powers of Saturn can be deadly.

Jim Morrison died at twenty-seven in his Paris bathtub, his years of excess delivering a heart attack. Brian Jones of the Rolling Stones drowned, and Nirvana's Kurt Cobain shot himself in the head. Janis Joplin died of a drug overdose, and Jimi Hendrix famously inhaled his own vomit in the back of an ambulance after taking eight, maybe nine, sleeping tablets. And a heart attack claimed Jimmy McCulloch of band-on-the-run Wings.

Then, on April 10, 2010, fans of stadium rock revivalists Vacate lost their lanky idol. Aged twenty-seven years, Scott Fletcher was found dead in a hotel bathroom in Norway. Fletcher died as he had live—the ultimate rock cliché, choked to death on his own spew. (It seems that Saturn is an AC/DC fan, too.) Rumor has it that paramedics couldn't wrench his last bottle of Jim Beam from his hand before zipping up the body bag.

To label someone a "rock god" implies immortality. It comes as a shock to learn that our idols have flesh as fragile as our own. When Cobain died in 1994, my mourning adolescent mind projected his image onto every crowd, letting me think for a second that my hero still breathed. There are those who still believe that Elvis Presley lives and that Jim Morrison is pulling beers in a South American bar. So when reports sprang up of Scott Fletcher sightings, it was chalked up to denial, a phase of mourning intensified by the media. But as sightings became more frequent, and large groups of people reported similar visions, it became clear that something about this celebrity demise was different. Fans claimed to have seen Scott Fletcher onstage, reunited with his band, describing with an almost religious fervor a surge of energy pulsing through their bodies and a kind of spiritual experience of the music. This was no garden-variety Elvis sighting.

In their early days, Vacate did little more than emulate their New Rock heroes, The Strokes and The Hives. Formed in high school, the band—singer David Li, guitarist Robert Gladwell, bassist Chris Jacobs, and drummer Steve Wainwright—played regularly in Melbourne. But things changed after Li met Fletcher at Work for the Dole.

Ringwood's forgotten boy, Fletcher was the son of a truck driver who taught him to love AC/DC and Cold Chisel. Fletcher started studied sound engineering at RMIT but dropped out, he once told Rolling Stone, because there were "too many techno wankers." "He was obnoxious," Li told the press just after Fletcher's death, "but he had a certain energy." Fletcher met the boys after a pub gig and became their roadie-slash-sound guy.

Soon after, Fletcher was promoted—to lead singer. The band discovered Fletcher's voice during sound checks, when he would sing Cold Chisel's "Khe Sanh." A residency at the Empress ended abruptly when the band was offered an album deal with EMI. Meanwhile, Fletcher schooled the others in the dying art of pub rock, which they fused with their existing sound.

After years of hard work, the band was touted as an overnight success. Their first album, *Vacate the Premises,* went gold, Australian fans responding to their balls-out rock ethic. They were filling stadiums, touring the world. Vacate became the biggest rock success story in over a decade.

Fletcher took to the star lifestyle like a Russian fish to vodka. Groupies were deflowered, hotel rooms set on fire, until the assault on his major organs finally took its toll.

Rock was dead until Vacate resurrected it. With the visionary leader gone, would it finally rest in peace? Vacate decided to continue performing and recording, thankfully foregoing any INXS-style reality TV antics. But like INXS after the suicide of Michael Hutchence, something wasn't right about the music.

The first mass sighting occurred at Vacate's first show after Fletcher's death. The band was on tour promoting their fourth album, *Body Heat.* But without Fletcher to give their sound the one-inch-punch quality the Sydney audience had paid to see, Vacate found themselves slipping into old habits: the posturing and choppy riffs of New Rock. The disappointment was palpable.

Then, at one concert, a series of lights exploded one by one, sending shards of glass onto the stage. After getting the go-ahead to continue, Vacate broke into the opening to their first hit, "Sonic Love Story."

To their surprise, the audience went wild.

Reports were mixed. Some fans said they only saw Scott Fletcher for a second. Others said he picked up his guitar and played out the song. Some say he was transparent; others swear he was alive and well. Some of the most fervent descriptions were from ticket holders in the back row. Every one described an almost transcendental experience. They had seen a rock god, and he had touched them.

Theories were bounced around the music press and the internet. Fans blogged obsessively, convinced of ghost sightings. Music critics were more cynical, and hoax theories emerged: Scott Fletcher had faked his own death. The record company had faked it to generate publicity. Tasteless promoters had hired a fake to impersonate the dead star.

The remaining band members fuelled speculation by avoiding the media. The ghost drew fans back to the concerts, creating havoc for promoters when it didn't appear.

When Vacate returned to Melbourne, recently I decided to investigate. They had brought rock back from the dead. Had Scott Fletcher come back, too?

The venue was crawling with security personnel in black t-shirts. After flashing my media pass, I walked up the corridor towards the dressing room. During one section of the cold, white corridor, I was alone. Music was playing in a room up ahead, a lone guitar mingling with the dust in the air. Creeping up and putting my ear against the door, I heard the intro to "Tight." I wrenched open the door and flung it open. The room was empty.

Someone was playing a trick on me.

When I found the band, I was struck by the sense of fatigue in the room. The loss of their leader was taking its toll. Li looked exhausted. Jacobs and Gladwell bickered over the rider. Wainwright, the only band member who claimed to have seen the ghost, looked on the verge of mental collapse. It was clear that Vacate were under stress… but was it the strain of maintaining a lie?

Outside, the corridor and rooms began to fill with people, heat, and noise. I wandered around looking for evidence of a hoax, but what was I looking for? Trips and wires? Smoke and mirrors?

Out of ideas, I started making my way to the pre-arranged spot at the side of the stage. Before I was even halfway, though, I saw a familiar lanky figure moving down the corridor. There was my man. *Busted.*

I pushed my way through the crowded hall, trying to keep the figure in sight. Just when I thought I had him, a black t-shirt demanded to see my pass. While I fumbled for it, the figure glanced at me over his shoulder and ducked around a corner. I broke into a half-sprint, hindered by the crowd. When I got to the corner, the figure was gone. I was sure of a hoax.

The show was mediocre despite the sense of nervous anticipation in the audience. Were it not for the possibility of a ghost sighting, I don't think they would have demanded an encore. What would happen if Fletcher didn't show? Would a riot break out?

Vacate returned from backstage and launched into a track from the new album. There was disappointment in the air, and the band knew it. They were just going through the motions.

Until, everything went quiet.

Scott Fletcher appeared as he must have in the black bag into which his body was ultimately zipped. The vomit that had spilt from his mouth had spread into his hair, which stuck out at an odd angle. I could see through him to the Marshall stack behind, his body translucent and his failed liver and tar-soaked lungs visible through his tattooed skin. He grinned maniacally and, it seemed, straight at me.

Lifting his guitar above his head, Fletcher screamed, "Heeellooo, Melbourne!" before launching into "Sonic Love Story." Acoustics no longer had meaning. Fletcher's music was connecting directly to my soul. The air was electric. The speakers had stopped pounding bass notes through the floor, but sound surged through my chest cavity, my limbs, my brain. It was as if Fletcher was playing just for me, an audience of one. In the following days, hundreds of fans would tell the same story with cult-like glazed eyes.

Wainwright passed out. Li put down his guitar and walked offstage. We had proof that rock was finally, definitely dead.

And the crowd went wild. ✳

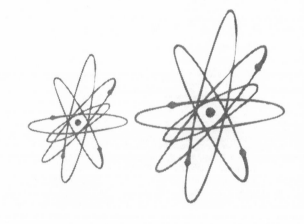

Power Chord

GERRI LEEN

A DARK STAGE IS BACKLIT BY FIRE.

People stream to the pit in front, abandoning the bar and the side rooms, while those on the balcony crowd to the rail. There is a moment of hushed anticipation. Conversation ceases, and little fire-sticks go up as people hold them to the incipient arrival of the band.

Figures are silhouetted against the flames as the band strides onstage as if the darkness is nothing to them. They pick up instruments or sit down at their stations without fumbling, warming up guitars, keyboards, and drums with little picks or taps or raps. The speakers surround the crowd; no static crackles, only raw, elemental sound comes out as the first real note is hit.

The crowd screams in one voice—one discordant, slightly hysteric voice.

A woman on the edge of the crowd is picked up; she screams as she is passed down the sea of people. No one drops her. Hands grope her as she makes her way toward the stage. Her cries change to giggles, and it looks like this time she'll get all the way up to the musicians.

The bouncers at the front come out. They catch her as she's tossed toward the stage. The musicians don't miss a beat. Their eyes glow red as the crowd roars disappointment at the bouncers.

The anger feeds the amps, blows power into the air as the music gets louder.

The crowd yells approval, and more people are lifted and passed.

"They love it here," the master of the place comments to the man sitting next to him. They are in a darkened box near the balcony. No one can see that the boss has this guest, this unassuming man—shabby even. God hated to be recognized when he's slumming.

God sighs and the boss notices the Almighty's foot is tap-tapping in rhythm with the music.

"Guess those harps get old, huh?" he asks.

God sends him a look that says he'll un-make him if he doesn't shut the hell up.

"I'm just saying."

God looks around at people who are laughing and crying, filled with emotion rocketed into them by the band, and his frown says plenty. People are grabbing each other, kissing, groping, pulling one another down into a pile that begins to undulate like snakes.

"They appear to be having a little too good of a time," God says with a frown.

"What? That. Pffff." The boss laughs at God's expression. "They're just acting up."

"What happened to eternal torment? Lake of Fire? Endless suffering?"

"La la la, I can't hear you." He leans in, feels God lean away a bit. "The band's playing. I was feeling lenient."

God gives another hearty sigh, and the air smells fresh, like the air in Heaven, air the boss hasn't smelled for so damn long. He breathes out heartily, pushing away the bittersweet, clean odor with the familiar stench of sulfur and brimstone.

God looks at him with ever-patient eyes for a moment, then his expression grows stern. "But this really isn't the deal we had. Heaven for reward. Hell for punishment."

The boss shrugs. "If you want them to be miserable, move

the club upstairs. Deprive them of this." His eyes gleam as he watches God.

"You know what some of my flock would say to that."

The boss laughs. "I also know that some of your flock have been inquiring about excursion packages down here to catch the act."

God looks peeved.

"We could work something out. I know Michael and Asmodeus have a commission plan they'd like to pitch to us." It was Michael's idea, really, but the boss decides not to tell the Everlasting that. He may need Michael's help someday, and ratting him out as the mastermind for exploiting the departed is not the way to get that.

"Michael's always hustling, I'll give him that. Not like some of my other angels, content to float on clouds and soak in the divine presence."

"You made them. You fix them."

"You mean re-make them. I don't do that. Faulty designs do not mean termination. You're living proof of that. All things have their uses."

And the boss knows he's tons more useful to God than some of those lazy-ass angels. "Still, maybe we should have a work exchange program. Put the fear of God into them, as it were."

God laughs softly. "Can you see Asmodeus in Heaven? Manning the Pearly Gates, perhaps?"

The boss grins. Asmodeus has been known to bite the heads off from those who don't answer him the way he wants. "You'd have a lot less scammers, that's for sure."

"May be something to this plan." God leans back, waving at the boss as if stopping him from saying more. "Let me enjoy this. I so rarely get a chance to slip away."

"You know you're welcome any time."

"I'm not returning the invitation. I banished you for a reason."

"About that. It was really quite a long time ago, and I've considered the error of my ways."

God lifts an eyebrow, but otherwise his attention is riveted on the band.

"All right, perhaps not the error, per se. But the… impetuousness of my acts."

"There is no reentering Heaven."

"Fine." The boss throws his drink back, gestures angrily at the serving imp to bring him more.

"Don't sulk. I hate it when you sulk." God actually looks a bit guilty. "Try not to think of it as exile. Consider it a business partnership. Who else could I leave in charge to run this?"

The boss looks over at him, shaking his head in disbelief. Does the Almighty think he was born yesterday? "Shut up and listen to the music."

"*Tone…*"

"Shut up and listen to the music… please?" He feels like sticking his tongue out but knows it will get him nowhere. God loves to take the high road.

The imp brings drinks for two; God almost reaches for one then waves her away.

"Nice try," the boss tells her, making a mental note to give her a hefty bonus for quick thinking and smacks her on the ass.

"You never stop."

"What? Harassing my employees? Would you expect any less in Hell?"

"I meant trying to corrupt me."

"One could argue that coming down here to groove to the house band *is* a form of corruption."

God smiles. "One could also argue that I'm merely inspecting—the fact that it's when your most popular band is playing is pure coincidence."

"Yeah, that would fly in Peoria."

"Fortunately, it wouldn't be argued in Peoria. It'd be argued before the Council of Saints and Archangels."

A council God runs. Everything really is loaded in His direction.

"Fine," the boss says. "Coincidence. Nothing more."

God is clapping madly as the band finishes up. He stands and yells, "Play 'Steamy River'!" as everyone else in the room. The boss soaks in the ambiance—he really isn't sure he wants to return to Heaven, even if it's in his nature to try to trick or wheedle his way back in.

The band launches into "Steamy River." The driving beat of the song has the crowd on their feet—most of them. The ones still copulating are in danger of getting trampled.

"Great song," God says as he jumps up and down like any other head-banger. "Written by a good Christian boy, you know. I'm sure he has no idea it's being played down here—and at quite this tempo."

"How did you know it was being played here?"

"You think Michael doesn't work both sides of the fence?" God grins. "He tells me what happens when he's down here. You're not as clever as you think you are."

"Maybe not." He pouts. "But you still miss me. Admit it."

God stops jumping, reaches out, and touches his shoulder. "I do miss you, old friend. That doesn't mean I'm going to bend on anything." Then he heads down to the pit, and he's picked up and body-passed, and everyone who touches him cries out in a mixture of bliss and pain.

The boss sits back. Smiles as he watches the Almighty make it up to the stage—the bouncers not even trying to stop his progress. God nods at the demon band before disappearing in a blinding flash of white. Several of the closest members of the crowd scream out, hair on fire from the flash.

Hair on fire. The boss sips his drink and sits back. Nothing new there. Just another day in paradise—one version of it, anyway. ✳

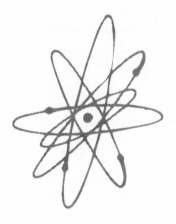

Water Sprite

C.A. COLE

BRANT HAD BROKEN UP WITH HIS LAST WOMAN more
than a year ago, his fifth major breakup since his marriage shat-
tered fifteen years earlier. He'd turned on Dylan's most recent
CD, *Modern Times*, prior to sunset. While setting the wicker
table in the corner of the kitchen, he crooned along to the bluesy
music, singing the line about his love turning up again. Though
he'd laughed at the air-guitar players back when he was the
singer in a local band, he grabbed the salt shaker and held it as if
it were a mike and he was on stage singing to the hordes of teen
girls in big bells and tight shirts.

At any moment, his new woman friend was set to arrive for
dinner. So what did he feel when Brindy, his high school girlfriend, the one he'd searched for in that swarm of girls, his first
love, stumbled out of his coat closet and into the cabin's great
room where he was stirring stew?

"Brindy?" he said, not sure if he was surprised because she was
there, or that he recognized her after thirty years. She'd always
reminded him of an inverted mop. Her hair stuck out in thick
dark plugs of curls. She'd been as skinny as a broom handle,
but not because she didn't eat. If they cruised into a hamburger
joint, John Wesley Harding blaring on the car speakers, she'd eat
all but a bite of his burger. He twirled his long skinny fries, sort

of like her legs, in pools of ketchup. She polished off those, too, starved.

Brindy and Brant. It had a ring. He ached to give her one, but she said she didn't believe in going steady, pushed her ropey hair out of the way, and said she didn't believe in being tied down. She didn't even relent when he played "Lay, Lady, Lay."

Now, under the harsh light of his kitchen, little stitches of sadness creased between her eyes. "Brant?" Her voice was almost a squawk. "No one calls me that anymore." She blinked like a newborn getting used to air on her exposed skin. "I'm just plain 'Beth' now."

Of course. Her real name was Elizabeth, Beth Rindy... Brindy for short.

"Well," he said and stirred his stew a half circle. What he wanted to know was where she had come from, what she was doing in the middle of his secluded cabin. And could he stall the woman friend who was probably driving up the hill that very instant?

Brindy sidled up to the counter that separated the cooking section from his living area. "I was listening to that and shut my eyes for a second." She nodded toward the speakers that dominated his great room. "Are you real?" She extended her fingers as if she wanted to touch him but didn't dare.

"Real as you," he said and leaned the wooden spoon on the stove top. She looked real. Her jeans, straight legged and tight, fit well. He could tell she was thin, although no longer a mop handle, more as if she'd feel good under him. Her black and white top made him think she'd escaped from a prison.

"But..." She searched his face with her mud-puddle eyes. Maybe she didn't recognize him. He supposed he didn't look much like his eighteen-year-old self. Back then, he'd had shoulder-length hair that drove his father bonkers and a reddish moustache that had circled his lips and formed a beard on his chin. The image of his old self made him smile—what with his current hairline creeping back to his earlobes and barely enough of it to run his fingers through. Sometimes he experimentally

flipped his chin, remembering his hair in his eyes and how
he'd toss it back before breaking into "Black Magic Woman."
He'd perfected that hair move long before Cheap Trick elicited
screams from the junior high girls at the edge of the stage.

He was falling into Brindy's umber eyes, so much so that
he almost didn't register the gravel crunching outside, didn't
notice the flash of light before Gretchen cut her motor. He
hadn't installed a doorbell, hadn't expected company to sneak
up, but here he was, emotionally naked, lights blazing, and the
most beautiful woman he'd ever met in front of him as if she'd
dropped out of the sky, as if someone—God, aliens, he had no
idea—had decided he'd waited long enough for happiness.

There was a spongy tap as if the door were constructed of
gingerbread.

"Um," he said, "why don't you go back in there and wait for
me?" He pointed to the bedroom. In anticipation of Gretchen's
visit, he'd thrown three cheap pillows on the gauzy yellow
spread. He wasn't sure the black pillows matched, but he kind
of liked the bumblebee look of it. His wife had done all the
decorating the years they were married. Until recently, when his
daughter, Julia, started churning out the babies, he'd inhabited
the back rooms of other people's houses and hadn't given one
thought to what color he wanted to sleep under.

When there was a second, more solid knock, Brindy patted
the counter and made her mouth into an "O." She twirled as if
she weren't wearing rear-hugging jeans but was dressed in pet-
ticoats, full and swirly. She balanced on the balls of her purple-
sandaled feet like a dancer, which she hadn't been when he knew
her… but who knew what she'd done in the ensuing years?

At the threshold to his bedroom, she threw him a look that
said, How can you be more interested in whomever is on the
other side of that door than you are in me? Me whom you
haven't seen since half your life was over? Me whom you've
always wanted and always loved?

Gretchen was real, a fleshy presence, while Brindy was a
mirage, a dream, his neurons misfiring. Some kind of delayed

flashback. Had to be. How could she stroll out of his closet? Last he'd heard, she was living in California with her husband, son, and two dogs, happily and forever married. Forget about lonely Brant. Forget about Brant's half-formed dreams of a mop dancing, twisting and twirling like something from a Disney movie.

He gave his bedroom door a forlorn look and twisted the knob to admit Gretchen.

"It's freezing out here," Gretchen said and scooted in. "What took you so long? A ghost?" She giggled and slipped out of her bomber jacket.

Gretchen was short, not exactly chubby, but rounded. A pleasant roundness, he had to admit, not all jutting bones and elbows... but he wanted Brindy. Not the lushness of Gretchen's fingers on his forearm.

As the last cut of the album warbled into oblivion, he picked up the remote from the coffee table and hit play. The initial chords of "Thunder on the Mountain" reverberated. Gretchen shook herself, said, "Ahh," and two-stepped around him.

At 48, he hadn't picked up the dancing habit, no matter that his seven-months-pregnant daughter teased him that if he wanted to be popular with women he should learn. "And aren't you always telling me how you were in band? And you can't dance?" Julie would tease him. "But," he'd tell her, "we were playing. We didn't have to dance." Back then, he hadn't had to do much except smile and flip his hair to have his pick of girls. Prerogative of the singer, especially when he was blond with a golden scruff of a voice. But he'd only wanted Brindy.

His daughter had suggested he learn to cook, too. The last few years, he'd either eaten at the diner or microwaved a dinner while wondering why he'd bothered building a kitchen. It didn't appear he was ever going to have company; the women dispersed with his thinning locks. His voice was still good; at least it sounded okay to him in the confines of the shower when he belted out "I Want You to Want Me." Even his flesh and blood didn't visit longer than a half hour. Julia would put her older boy down on the floor while the in-between kid wobbled against her legs. Brant followed the two-year-old around, prying cigarette butts, stray nails, wood scraps, and whiskey bottle caps out of his grip. "Dad," Julia said, "you've got to keep this place in better shape. What if some lady wants to spend the night?"

Just that very morning, he'd bought a new vacuum cleaner that actually sucked and cleaned the floor of all the debris his solitary life generated. With that and fresh sheets on the bed, he'd felt ready for anything. Anything but a ghost from the past roaming into the present.

Gretchen grinded her way across the room.

"Dinner?" he said, running back to the stove to stir. Julia had instructed him not to neglect the stew—most of which was from a can with a few tomatoes and other add-ins—or it would burn and put a damper on the evening.

Gretchen held out a bottle of wine. He put it in the refrigerator.

"It's red," Gretchen said, lunging for the bottle.

"No corkscrew."

What did she expect? He drank beer and whiskey, just like the old days, except now he didn't use the liquor to wash down pills.

She tut-tutted and retrieved a Swiss Army knife from her purse. "I was a Girl Scout," she said. "Always be prepared." She pulled a condom packet out of her back pocket and waved it suggestively.

"Guess you are," he muttered.

"Maybe we should use this first," Gretchen said.

"Now?"

"Sometimes, you know, it isn't as much fun after eating. Indigestion."

"The stew'll burn."

"We can reheat it," Gretchen said, standing on tiptoe to see into the pot. He'd borrowed this dented one from his mother, the one she used to make batches of sauerkraut. The pan gave off a slightly sour smell. Gretchen wrinkled her nose as if his cooking wasn't quite up to par or she could smell cabbage fumes too. She twisted the burner off. "I've been thinking about this all day," she said, breathing into his new blue shirt and stroking his leg.

He goose-stepped away. "Hey, well…"

She crowded him, leaned into him, and licked his lips with the tip of her tongue. Her breasts jutted into his chest. He couldn't help noticing how full they were, how soft they felt pushing against his ribs.

"Let me…" He pushed her away gently. "Be right back."

He adjusted his jeans but instead of going in the bathroom, he tipped open the door to his room. Brindy, cross-legged, perched in the middle of his yellow bed looking like she was picking berries in a summer field, although he could see goose bumps on her arms.

"I thought about getting under the covers," she said, "but didn't know how that would look."

"Like you in my bed." The interior door didn't lock. He wanted to stroke his hands up and down Brindy's arms, sing a few bars of "Lay, Lady, Lay," not lean his back into the door to keep intruders out. "Where did you come from?"

"I was at home, listening to that," she said, lifting her chin in the direction of the living room. The Dylan album thumped along. "That very album, and suddenly, I'm here, listening to the very same song. I don't mean the one that's playing. 'Spirit on the Water.' That one. I didn't miss a beat."

"Oh," he said. That was the tune he'd played over and over, the thought of Brindy at the edges of his consciousness. Brindy. Brindy was his spirit on the water. Brindy. She was always on his mind; he'd sung those words along with Dylan.

"I guess it reminded me of you, and I sang the one line, and poof, here I am." She pressed her lips together. "How do you think I go back?"

He half-sat on the bed, not close enough to touch her, but close enough he could feel eddies around her body. "Do you want to go back? I mean, right away?"

She shimmered, as if she weren't completely in the room, as if she remained in California, a sea breeze blowing through the screen door—it was only late afternoon there. Fall, same as New York, yes, but light, warm.

She cocked her head, listening. "Maybe I am there. Daniel just got home. He took the dogs for a run. I should have gone with him, but I was dancing, daydreaming about you. Danny doesn't do Dylan, doesn't much like rock," she added as if she were comparing. "But you've got company."

"If I had known you were coming, do you think I would have invited her?" He reached for Brindy's hand just as Gretchen pushed the door open.

"What are you doing?" Gretchen asked. She dived on the bed next to him, almost on top of Brindy, who scooted back, curls bouncing. Gretchen grabbed one of the black throw pillows, fitted it behind her neck, and fell back on the bed. "In here's better than out there."

Did Gretchen not see the other woman, barely any space between their skins? Or did she not care? She played with a button on her paisley blouse.

Brindy leaned closer, her knot of curls pressed into his scalp. He drew a breath. Gretchen grinned and unbuttoned the third button on her shirt, wriggling it slightly off her shoulders.

"Does she see me?" Brindy shaped her lips as if she were blowing the words at him instead of speaking.

"Seems not."

"I think it seems hot, too," Gretchen said and undid the next button. She crawled toward him, her hand on his thigh.

"She can't hear me," Brindy said in normal tones as she shifted toward the foot of the bed, away from him. "Do get rid of her."

"Yes," he said, looking over Gretchen's curved back into Brindy's eyes.

Gretchen knocked him over and crawled on top. Sure, he would have appreciated it in the past, sure he liked the fantasy of two women in his bed; but he knew Brindy wouldn't go for that, certainly not the first time they'd touched in over two decades. He grabbed her hand. She laced her fingers through his and said, "If I'm not really here, I guess I can do whatever you want."

"What we want," he said.

"What?" Gretchen asked. "What do we want?"

"Not this," he said, forcing himself to sit. "Not now. Herpes," he said. "I got herpes."

"I've got the condom," she said, ripping the package.

"It's too bad for that. Really." He tried to tug her off the bed.

Brindy leaned forward to give her a shove, but her hands stopped short. "Maybe I shouldn't touch her," she said. "It might wreck the space-time continuum, or whatever did this."

"Don't do that," he said. "Now that I've found you again—"

"Now that you've found me? I didn't think you noticed me back when you sang in that band, back when I was in junior high." Gretchen readjusted her blouse. "'Again?'"

"That was a lifetime ago. Didn't know anyone remembered. Let's get your coat." He helped her across the room and out the door.

"We can eat. I mean, I drove all the way out here. We can have some wine. Talk a little."

"Don't have time."

"Don't have time for what?"

"It's not personal," he said and winced, using his famous dump line from his former life. "I'm sorry. Just… you have to go." He shoved her out into the dark. "I'm sorry. I just can't."

"But—"

"Sorry," he said again and bolted the door. "Sorry."

There was no sound from the bedroom. Maybe Brindy had been a dream, a hallucination, a momentary staunching of blood to the brain. The last album cut, "Ain't Talking," was playing. What if the sixty-two minutes of the album was the arc of time they'd be in sync? What if she disappeared as soon as it was over? He'd replayed it once, but maybe her husband back in California had, too. It was a risk, but he had to stop the disk. Had to start over.

He hit stop, then play, and, with trepidation, with the anticipation of more than twenty-five years, pushed open the door to the bedroom, hoping she'd still be flesh and blood. ✳

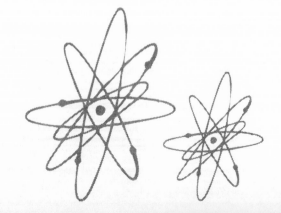

Window Dressing

DEV JARRETT

BRAND SMILED AS HE WATCHED THE GIRL GUZZLE the diet soda he'd given her. "I dunno *why* I'm so thirsty! I guess just being here is making me nervous. Sorry!"

He tried to look indulgent, picking up his own drink. "No problem. I always get cottonmouth in an interview. Nice to see I'm not the only one." He took a sip and she smiled, her face reddening easily. Brand wasn't sure if it was a legitimate blush or just a reaction to the stuff he'd slipped into her drink—nor did he particularly care. He was hardly able to keep his mind on the interview, but he knew he had to at least maintain the charade until the drugs really took hold of her.

"It's just *so* way awesome that you agreed to do this! I mean, Brand Reynolds, lead singer of Inferno, sitting for questions from me! I mean, when I asked my brother—that is, I mean, the publisher—what we needed to do to really get some circulation, and he said to try to get an interview with you, I knew he was just being a smartass. But then when I called and you said you would… oh, man, I thought, no *way*! Oh, he's going to be so frickin' jealous!"

"I'll make sure you have a few Inferno souvenirs when you leave, too. That should really stick it to him." Brand smiled his patented Evil Grin, the same grin that he'd worn for every album cover and photo shoot Inferno had had during the seventies, eighties, and nineties. She giggled, downed the rest of her soda, then picked up her notebook again.

Brand relaxed. The interview questions were always the same. He could probably answer them in his sleep. He looked at the girl, trying to remember what she'd said her name was. Erin something? She was very young, probably still in high school, and quite pretty. Her eyes were growing watery, but with effort she focused on the words written in the steno book.

"Mmm-kay, the whole devil-worshipping theme that Inferno had? Did that ever, like, cause any kind of, y'know… personal problems for any of you?"

"Of course. I mean, it was all just theatrics, just for the shock value—and in retrospect, I think it paid off. But there were times when some of the fans left weird offerings on the doorstep. All in all it was good fun. Some fans sent us strange things in the mail, too. Bodily fluids, mummified chickens, all kinds of stuff. There was one very disturbed young man who sent us a skull."

Her eyes went pleasantly wide. "A human skull?"

Brand nodded. "His parents' house was right behind a cemetery, and he just went out there one night and dug it up. Said he wanted me to be his emissary to Satan, or something."

"Oh, my God! What did you do?"

"We turned it over to the authorities, of course. The whole inverted-cross, 666-thing was all an act. It's just comic book evil. Window dressing. Any skulls and bones we used were just plastic props. The same thing as Ozzy biting heads off bats, or Gene Simmons and those blood capsules. Good fun, like I said."

Brand knew how interviews worked. It was a give and take situation, so he was making an opening for her to ask about the "Raising Hell" tour that Inferno had shared with Kiss and Black Sabbath. She was obviously new to the interviewing game and didn't take the bait. Instead of riding the segue to the sordid tour stories that everyone seemed to love, she bounced to the rumors that Brand had gone back to making recordings.

"Whispers are going around that, after fifteen years of living the good life, you've finally gotten back into the studio. Have you been laying down tracks again? My publisher's saying that Inferno may be coming back on the scene."

Of course whispers were going around. Brand had started them. He wanted to record again. He thought he still had the fans to fill an auditorium.

Both Ozzy and Gene had done the reality TV deal and had made it work for a while, but so many of the people he'd run with back in the high times had simply disappeared into the woodwork. Some were still trying to work, but it was pathetic. Brand found it hilarious to see his hard-rocking brothers of yesterday showing up as the opening band for .38 Special on the state fair circuit. He promised himself he'd never do that. Brand knew he still had the stuff to share a stage with Rob Zombie or Nine Inch Nails.

After all, that's why he'd agreed to this. If he wanted to make his way back to the top, he had some dues to pay.

Her shining eyes were beginning to look heavy-lidded. Back in the eighties, when he and the boys were getting stoned every night, having coin slots for eyes was always considered the point that they were actually baked. It was the time to either change to coke for the night, or go crash with some anonymous chick.

Brand was starting to get nervous. How long since he'd last done this? Eighteen years? Twenty? He thought he'd probably waited long enough. Time to make his move.

"Well," he said, "how about I take you down to the basement? I'll show you the studio."

This was unheard of. According to all the cognizant authorities—*Rolling Stone, Spin,* and *MK Magazine*—the basement studio of Brand Reynolds was the sanctum sanctorum, and no one had ever been taken down there. Journalists had always been more likely to get into Brand's bedroom than his basement. The bedroom was for fun, but the basement was where the real work got done. The idea that no one was allowed down there was a carefully cultivated lie, because Brand had, in fact, taken several people into the basement. And beyond.

The girl wobbled to her feet and giggled. She picked up her steno book, and nearly overbalanced. A pen with a pink top was stuck in the spiral coil across the top of the notebook. She snickered again.

"Uh, what did you put in my soda?"

Brand grinned. "Just some ice, my dear." He took her gently by the arm. "Come on downstairs, and see the studio."

There were always dues to pay. No matter what, no matter where, always dues. Like his mom had told him so many years ago: *There ain't no such thing as a free lunch.* Somehow or other, you always paid for it.

Before Inferno, when he was just an angry kid in Indianapolis, he'd wanted so badly to succeed, but nothing had ever happened. He played, he sang, he wrote songs that all his friends said really rocked, but no one in the business ever noticed. His frustration and anger grew, and his songs grew darker. At the height of his frustration, crying silently one night in his parents' garage, he admitted to himself that he'd give up *anything* for a shot at the big time.

The next week, he was playing with some guys at a nightclub. They were the opener for some suckbag headliner band who'd never amount to anything. A guy in the crowd had reached out and slipped Brand a business card. The next day he'd called the guy, and they'd set up an audition. It went perfectly, and the guy had agreed on the spot that his new, upcoming record label would represent them.

Inferno was born. When he got home from the audition, he found out that his mother was in the hospital. Ovarian cancer.

The album was cut and released, and Mom's condition was fairly stable. The chemo was hard and had worn Mom down, but at least she didn't seem to be getting worse.

Child of Dis, their first album, was well received by both the public and the critics. It went to number one on *Billboard*.

That same day, Mom contracted pneumonia. Cancer wasn't killing her, but the chemo had taken out her entire immune system.

Three weeks later, *Child of Dis* went platinum and Mom died; drowned by the fluid in her lungs. Although Brand was out of his mind drunk or high most of that time, he was sure Mom would have understood. She knew there was no such thing as a free lunch.

Brand had just begun paying his dues.

The phenomenal success of Inferno was unexplainable. They lived in the fast lane in every sense of the word. They played, sang, and partied. And after each tour, Brand had gone home to the house he'd had built in Santa Barbara. After six or seven weeks of silence from his house, he brought the rest of the band over and they went into the basement studio for a few days. Pizza delivery guys, delivery guys from the liquor store, and guys delivering other stuff in the middle of the night were the only ones seen going to and from the house, and then—hey, presto!—a new Inferno album would come out.

The due-paying continued. Brand always paid, because he loved the life, and he loved himself.

Over the years, Inferno's stage shows and public personality became more and more outlandish and extreme until they finally, literally burned themselves out. Two of the band members ended up setting themselves on fire, and Brand and Jackyl, the drummer, had nearly overdosed. A few weeks at rehab, and Brand had retired to his Santa Barbara home, where he'd stayed for several years.

All that time, and he hadn't really done anything until a couple of weeks ago. He'd gone into the basement.

Then he'd gone into the subbasement and made the deal.

He'd had to. He'd been channel surfing, and he saw a familiar face. Jackyl. His real name was Charles (Brand had never known. Go figure), but everyone he worked with these days just called him Chip. He was now a successful record producer, sitting on the geek-side of the table. VH1 had done one of those "Where Are They Now?" shows about him, and had brought up Brand. Jackyl had kind of shuddered and said, "I'd just as soon forget about that time in my life. I still have nightmares. Brand... well, what can I say? Brand was the real thing."

And his eyes had looked positively haunted.

Brand took the girl downstairs to the basement. Framed gold records lined the stairwell wall, unnoticed by either Brand or his interviewer. Her focus seemed to be taken up entirely by keeping her feet under her, and his focus was on the task ahead.

At the bottom of the stairwell was a soundproofed door. Brand pulled it open and flicked a few switches on the wall, illuminating both the control room and the bandstand in the next room, divided by a wide window. The control room was full of computers and reel-to-reel dinosaurs, and tables covered with LEDs, dials, and slides. The room beyond, where the band played, was uniformly gray. The floor was the same color as the egg crate foam that lined the walls and the ceiling. Black cables crisscrossed the floor, held down by strips of duct tape.

Over everything, in both rooms, was a uniformly thick layer of dust. Nothing in the studio had been touched in years. A pervasive scent of stale, still air clung to everything.

"Wow," the girl slurred. "I guess those rumors were just rumors, huh?" Despite the drugged quality of her voice, Brand heard a distinct undercurrent of apprehension.

"Well, the truth of it is that I'm not in the studio *yet*. You see, before recording, you've got to be inspired."

"Inspired," she said owlishly.

"To be truly inspired, I always have to go to the subbasement."

"Subbasement?"

"The subbasement. That's where I always find my muse."

"Your muse."

"Oh, yes, and my muse is very demanding. You see, there's no such thing as a free lunch. Somehow or other, you always end up paying for it."

"… somehow or other," she parroted obviously intimidated now. Her eyes rolled with fear, but she couldn't seem to get her body to follow her directions. Brand led her across the room to another door with one hand wrapped around her shoulders.

"Watch your step over those cables," he said. The steno book fell from her grasp unnoticed, and Brand stepped on it.

He opened the far door and clicked on the light beyond. A much narrower stairwell fed downward, lined with rough, unfinished walls of cinderblock and mortar. He gently prodded her down the stairs ahead of him, to a landing with another soundproofed door.

With his hand on the doorknob, Brand turned to the girl. "You're new to the idea of interviewing, so I'll let you know a little secret. No celebrity ever tells the whole truth in an interview. We can't, if we want to maintain any sense of ourselves. If I made all my secrets public, there'd be no *me* left for me."

She blinked at him, not comprehending.

"I didn't tell you the exact truth upstairs. While a lot of the Inferno stuff is just an act, some of it... well, some of it's true."

Her brows furrowed at this news. She struggled to understand.

"It's not *all* window dressing. You see, there is a price for fame."

Brand opened the door, and the putrescent smell of decay rushed out. She pulled reflexively back, gagging. Her will, smothered by the drugs he'd given her, was weak, and when he pulled her into the room at the bottom of the stairs, her slack body obeyed.

He turned on the lights, and a series of low-wattage bulbs popped dimly to life. At the far end of the room, where the light didn't reach, something heavy shifted. A slithering sound whispered from the corner, followed by a low, groaning hiss.

"Not all window dressing?" She seemed on the verge of finally understanding, but it was too late for her. It had been too late for her to begin with.

"No, it's not all window dressing. Fame comes at a very high price." He gripped her shoulders. "That price must be paid in blood."

"Blood?"

Brand turned to the corner, where those sliding, whispering

sounds had begun to sound more urgent. He raised his voice. "My life from before. I want it back. I've brought your payment."

A cold, reptilian voice spoke in the darkness. "The first payment."

"Yes, the first payment."

The voice hissed again, and Brand could almost hear the smile in its answer.

"Very well. Bargain struck."

Brand shoved the girl forward into the darkness. Her shriek was quickly muffled when something either covered her mouth or slid down her throat.

Brand didn't want to know. He turned away from the rustling, frenzied slithering, and made his way to the door. He clicked off the lights, closed the door, and went to the studio.

When he passed the steno book on the dusty floor, he picked it up and turned to a blank page.

He had a new song in his head, and he started writing it down as he walked back up the wide stairway that was lined with the framed gold records. ✳

Birds

SOU MACMILLAN

ME & CONEY, WE SAW THAT SHIT HAPPEN. It's like three in the morning and we're driving home from Cleveland, Kitty and Noey passed out in the back 'cos they drank 'til they screamed at each other during load-out and Coney's the only one sober enough to drive the van—when Coney says, she says, "What the fuck was *that*?" and stamps on the brakes. It's like a fuckin' meteorite zooming past us, and the van's skidding out in the gravel of the median strip, spinning, and then we're facing the city, watching it.

It's some kind of fireball the size of a tank; you can't miss it. The other cars, they're all pulled over on the side of the road, watching it, too. Then the thing gets some air under it—heads up into the clouds over Cleveland, and you know it's tearing up the miles 'cos it looks small all of a sudden and then disappears. And just as Noey's pulling himself off the floor next to me, say-ing, "What the hell, Coney?" there's this amazing BOOM and the whole goddamned sky lights up like daytime. Then Kitty says from somewhere in the back, "Oh, that sounds bad. That sounds real bad."

Cleveland's not gone, but we all think it is at first, 'cos the lights are all out.

We figure to go to Sandy's, 'cos she's a mom, right? And people
with kids, they've got that preparation thing going on—breakfast, school closings, sneakers that fit, you know. Also, Sandy's
always got food made and we're all getting hungry, but we know
we gotta get as far from Cleveland as we can. None of us can say
why we don't want to stop, we just know. And then Coney says,
after we've been driving for a while, she says, "How come, do
you think, no one's driving out of the city?"

Noey's been dialing numbers on his cell, trying his friends in
Shaker Heights, his sister's apartment on Euclid, the bar we just
left an hour ago. No one picks up. He keeps trying for a while,
and then we hit a patch with no signal and he gives up to dig
around in his bag for his pills.

Noey says, "We stop next. I've gotta get my prescriptions
refilled, okay?" I tell him yeah, we'll find a drugstore, and he'd
better not have a seizure on stage 'cos it freaks out the girls. He
asks, "Do you think it was a bomb?" Then Kitty asks, "Do you
think it was the only bomb?" Coney says, "Maybe it wasn't a
bomb—nothing caught fire, right?" She says, "It really looked
like a meteor, y'know?"

None of us says anything else. No one else thinks it was a
meteor.

Sandy doesn't think it was a meteor. She says she saw some foot-
age on TV and it looked like a bomb. She'd know, too, after the
time she spent in Israel. But there hasn't been any TV for a few
days, it went out with the electric. She says she'd like another
look to vouch for it.

She's kneeling on the living room rug next to Noey while he
twitches. There hasn't been a drug store open for a few days,

either. She thinks we should press on with the tour—safest place is to keep moving. But we should find Noey some of his pills before much longer; this shit's ridiculous. She says, "You can't cross the country with a brain-damaged bass player and no pills. It's been less than a week and he's a fuckin' mess." Her kids push their toys around them on the rug like people go into convulsions in the living room all the time. I dunno; maybe they do at Sandy's house. She wonders out loud if she's got any valiums left and if they're good anymore.

That night Noey tries Cleveland again. He hasn't got an answer yet. Kitty says no one picks up in Chicago. She says, "I think everyone's gone there, too."

Me and Coney, we sit with maps and figure out the dates. If we leave out the big cities, there's seven dates left to play in twenty-two days. Huntington's the next stop. Coney figures we can break into a Walgreens and be there day after tomorrow, on time.

But then Noey won't take the pills.

After all the bullshit involved in breaking in the back window of the pharmacy and then scrounging through what someone who broke in the front had left, and finding what's probably the right pills, he won't take them. He says he doesn't want to take anything he's not 100 percent sure of, it took too long to figure out the right mix of chemicals. Him and Kitty get into it, her shouting at him, "What? Falling down pissing yourself is better?" and him insisting that he can't go into a coma when all the hospitals are like ghost towns, yeah, it's better. It's a really shitty drive to Huntington.

Huntington has lights. Turns out everyone has lights now, we just happen to be in Huntington when they come back on. Whatever. It means we can plug in. We don't ask questions—the bar's full. We load in, we soundcheck, Noey has a four minute fit on the nasty wood floor, we all proceed to drink.

There's a steady stream of people who turn up to drink and talk. It's all theories and circumstances—sunspots, cell reception, a lot of phones are out, all the big cities ring to no answer. The grid got knocked out for a while and the electric's just come back up. But everyone's nervous—there's no news, no TV, no radio, either. One guy says his friend drove out to Pittsburgh after he couldn't get his girlfriend on the phone, and he hasn't come back yet. No one who's driven out has come back yet. There's no word, just guesses. People are getting drunk to fill up time until they get answers and have something to keep busy with. No one's been going to work 'cos the power's been out, and now it's Friday night. They want to know what we've seen. There just isn't that much to tell. We get on stage around ten.

And everything's fine until it suddenly isn't. We're playing stuff off the CD—songs that hit the radio a few months ago. People are familiar with it, they're enjoying themselves. Some of the kids in the front are singing along, even. We're having a good time, four or five songs in.

Then the bass cuts out. I look over at Noey and he's standing there with this faraway, glassy stare like he gets right before he falls down. And then... well, then he's just not there anymore. But that really makes it sound too simple—he kind of... kind of *explodes*.

I blink and there's a fuckin' ton of little birds all over the place. His bass hits the floor with a slam and a rising hum of feedback, in the middle are all these little brown birds, sparrows, flying like they're in a centrifuge where Noey was just standing, flying around and around, and then they break all at once, and make out for over the crowd. I stop playing to stare. Kitty and Coney stop to stare, too. The whole bar comes to a grinding halt. The birds—there must be a few hundred—they bank off with this insane precision, and go out the front door.

Kitty says, "Oh... Well, that's new." Coney drops her sticks and walks real slow through to the door. The crowd parts for her without a word. She looks outside and then turns back in. She says, "Well. Well, he's gone, I think."

Uncle Dave, the soundguy at the Asbury Park gig, doesn't believe word one we have to say about Noey. He thinks we're joking, making light of the fact that our bass player split on us. He tells us, "I remember working with these bands at Fort Apache—someone would get pissed off and make like they were boycotting the session. They always turned up in the end, though. Don't worry, he'll turn up. Always do." It's also clear by the way he keeps looking at me practicing that he hopes Noey shows up.

I've been attached to Noey's bass like we were together in the womb since Huntington, trying to write lines to play that Coney can cue off of. We're both nervous about the set tonight. She says, "He was really stunning, you know?" And I don't know if she's talking about his playing or the thing with the birds. We're sitting in a booth to the side of the bar, me with the bass, her tapping on the table, and it feels like it might just come together. Doors don't open for another hour, so there's that.

And then there's the gasp out of Kitty at the bar. She's knocked her drink into her lap, rushing to point at Noey.

"Yer bass player's here. Told ya," Uncle Dave growls from the soundboard.

"You assholes left me in Huntington—what the fuck?"

He's filthy and wearing someone else's clothes. You can tell, 'cos his sleeves are too short and he's got the backs of the sneakers folded down under his heels to make his feet fit. Coney and me, we're out of the booth in a second. Kitty stammers, "You. You—" and can't get anymore out. Coney says, "We thought you… what happened to you, man?" He asks her to buy him a beer. His wallet's gone missing with his clothes.

It takes three beers for us to understand that he has no idea what birds we're talking about, that he came to without any clothes on, behind the bar yesterday and had to steal clothes out of a dryer in someone's cellar. He hitched all the way here to meet us. He's really hurt that we left him behind. Coney tells

him that we looked for him, and we really did. He thinks we're
fuckin' with him about the birds, that we ditched him 'cos he
seized on stage. Kitty shakes her head and leaves. By the time she
comes back with clothes out of Noey's bag, he might believe us.
Kitty says, "Hey, do you want some of Sandy's valium?" He says
no, he just had three drinks. Is she trying to kill him?

We get almost all the way through the set when it happens
again. There's the reverberating bang of the bass on the floor and
the cyclone of sparrows that nearly beats the door guy senseless
before he opens the door and they shoot through like a geyser.
That's the end of the set.

Josh, the guy who set up the show, comes to pay us while I'm
packing up Noey's gear. He's pale as snow. He says to Coney,
"I was up in Princeton after the Flash." That's what people are
calling it now: the Flash. He says the whole town's empty—except for the crows. Day after the flash, he was out there with
his roommate, walking around to see what happened. Nothing
but a sea of blackbirds. Trees were full of them, lawns covered,
every roof black with birds, a sea of inky feathers. And while he's
gaping at the birds, he realizes that the roommate is gone. One
minute she's there, next it's just him and the crows and her car
keys where she was standing. He called for her and then when
she didn't answer, he got in the car and drove back as fast as he
could. A day after the power came back on she showed up at
their apartment. Still has no idea how she got there. She won't
leave the apartment.

We spend a good two hours looking for Noey and then lock
ourselves in the van for the night. Maybe he'll find his way back
to the last place he saw us.

It happens again in Weston, before we get on stage, even, it happens. Phones aren't picking up in Springfield, so we decide not
to go there. It happens in Canton. It happens in Sturgis, too, but

this time when he explodes, I pick up the bass like this shit happens all the time, which I guess that it does now, and we finish the set. That night at load-out the van is covered—*covered*—in bird shit. "This is completely uncool," Coney says when she sees it. Kitty says, "At least it's not fish. I mean, picture it," she says. "Noey goes bang and all of us scatter trying, to scoop him into a glass of water. We'd have to set up an aquarium before soundcheck." Coney thinks it might be better than this.

What's really bizarre is how it gets so normal so quick. It's our fuckin' finale now. Or our mid-show climax. Word's gotten out—crowds are turning up just to see the magic exploding bassist. He's been getting mad admiration. The girls hang all over him from the minute he shows up.

News is starting to filter in, more stuff like Princeton. One of the bar tenders tells us Ann Arbor's doves as far as the eye can see. The drummer from the opening band says that they left Austin after watching the Congress Street bats have at it with boat-tailed grackles. There's a story going around about a payphone in Boston that was answered by the call of a million blue jays. I sit at the bar and listen to the stories while watching Noey try to go about his business as people interrupt him at it.

He looks rough. It's not just that he's barefoot again; he's looking threadbare all over. The girls don't help it. They descend on him at the stage during set-up. They all want to touch him, they reach for his face, pet at his hair.

In the bathroom he and I stand at the sinks. He doesn't want to go out there yet, he says it's too much. He just wants to play and enjoy it. He says after the show tonight he wants some of Sandy's valium; it's got to be the seizures that do it, it sure feels like it is. He'll try the pills. He just wants to play. And the flying, he remembers it now, it's making him tired. The coming to and not knowing where his shoes are is pissing him off. "The girls, they don't get it," he says while washing his face. "It's like being pulled apart. But they think it's something else, something freeing. It takes everything I've got not to lose parts of myself." He wipes his face on the sleeve of his stolen sweatshirt. "Do you know? This one girl begged me to teach her how."

The place is packed tonight. It's a long space, but skinny, with a straight view of the back door from the stage. The door guy's been told that it has to stay open—it *has* to. He says he knows, he'll keep it open.

We're all the way through the set before it happens. For a minute there when it dawns on me we made it through to the last song, I think that maybe we'll get off easy, that it won't happen at all, that we'll have just a quiet, regular show. But then there's the moment—the bass cut, the clatter of the instrument hitting the stage, the throb of feedback, the batter of wings. Coney smacks the big cymbal and thank you, goodnight. We start to unplug as Noey flies away.

It's girl squeal that gets my attention. There's still a knot of girls in the middle of the floor, and they're all crowded around this one girl who's holding something. I put down the cable I'm winding and walk over to see, and when I get up close the girls all shush up quick. I ask real nice, "Hey, whatcha got there?" and she turns to face me.

A sparrow. She's holding it with both hands as it struggles to get free. "Oh my God, let it go!" shouts Coney from right behind me. "Let it go!" she yells and lunges for the girl, but the girl's faster than her. The door's still open and she runs right out. Coney starts chasing her, but someone knocks her down. The girls who're left pile on top and pound on her until she stops moving. I see Kitty take off out the door, so I go to Coney, pull her limp and muttering up off the floor. I hear myself screaming, "What have you done! What did you do that for?" All the while I pray that the girl loses her grip on the sparrow.

Moorhead is a fuckin' nightmare. We get there half an hour before we're supposed to go on and the agent is bullshit we missed the seven o'clock load-in call. Coney tries to explain: the drive through St. Paul and the assault of magpies, how it was like driving through a black and white blizzard. She takes him outside to see the van and the spiderwebbed windshield. He has no sympathy, not even for the day-old bruises on her face. He has a packed house and we're late. He yells at Coney that we're unprofessional, and where's our bassplayer? "He'll show up," Kitty tells him in the small flat voice that's all she's been able to muster since yesterday. She says, "He'll show up," without any confidence. Coney starts to cry and goes around to the back of the van. I tell the agent we're fast, we don't need a soundcheck. We'll go on on time, just start the opening band, we'll be ready by the time they're done. He says, "Just use their gear. Don't bother to unload," and storms back in.

The place is full beyond capacity and sweating, the crowd is all staring at me holding the bass. After the first song someone realizes that Noey isn't with us. There's a mutter through the crowd of, "That's not him," and, "Who's that?" By the third song they're turning from curious to angry, not paying any mind to the music at all. We start the fourth song and a bottle hits me square in the chest. I'm standing there stunned when Kitty pulls the bass off me and starts pushing me backwards toward the green room. "Come on," she's saying. "We have to go. Come on!"

People are climbing onto the stage, chasing after us. Coney leads us through the stage door and puts her back up against it, yelling, "Hurry!" while Kitty and I try to find something to wedge in it. Kitty gets a chair under the doorknob and I push the couch against that. We climb out the window and run for the van.

We can see the van across the blacktop, there at the edge, parked by the vacant lot, and we run at top speed. Coney's crying again, I can hear her sob as we run. Someone's yelling back behind us, rounding the venue. We're almost there. Coney pulls out her keys and trips at the same time, and the keys fly out of her hand, clattering across the pavement. She and Kitty both dive for them and fall on each other. I'm pulling the two of them off the ground and the crowd is gaining on us, and I've got Kitty's arm, and Coney's getting up from all fours, and they're close, and—

From the grass of the vacant lot, hundreds of sparrows come up all at once, flying between us and the mob, pecking at angry faces, beating at them with their wings, screaming their tiny high curses in a language of brown birds. It's enough. It's enough time to get in the van and floor it for the highway.

We haven't seen him since Bismark. He was there, circling over the auto glass shop, a thing of feathers and a collective call, the sound of a needy wheel turning. He swooped twice and lighted for a second on the van. When he rose, he dispersed in all directions. There are no more shows left, and we haven't seen him since Bismark. ✳

The Music of the Spheres

Ken Scholes

ABIE FINALLY GAVE UP ON THE RADIO when five passes yielded nothing but shit-kicking music and indignant talk show hosts who tried too hard to be a cool they would never attain. Silence was preferable, so he gripped the wheel and watched the headlights swallow highway.

When he saw the hitchhiker ahead, he considered it well-timed kismet. At least, Abie thought, it would be someone to talk to. He edged the Ford to the shoulder and hit reverse. The dark clothed figure stepped into the scrub, out of the way, as he braked. The door opened and Abie adjusted the guitar on the back seat to make room for a rucksack and what looked like a cello case. "Climb in," he said. "Toss your stuff in the back." Without a word, the hitcher pushed the gear into the back seat and pulled the passenger door closed.

"Where you headed?" Abie eased the car forward and back onto the road.

"Tahoe," the girl said.

Abie went for a second look. Maybe it was her height, maybe the way she carried herself, but with the hood pulled up and the bulky overcoat, he'd been convinced it was a guy. Maybe that was the goal, he thought. Out alone on a Nevada highway, truly the middle of nowhere. Probably not a good place to be a girl.

"So where you from?"

She stared out of the window away from him. "Could we listen to the radio?" The shit-kickers still ruled the airwaves. He sighed and drove in silence. Thirty minutes later, he picked up another hitchhiker. This time he wasn't exactly sure why. He intended to drive past the dark clothed figure but found himself pulling over. He even climbed out of the car and moved his guitar to the trunk.

This one climbed in with a rucksack and a violin case.

"Where you headed?" he asked this one over his shoulder.

"Tahoe," she said. Both girls hid their faces in shadowing hoods and looked away.

He shook his head, trying to shake off the strangeness. It felt like an uncanny deja vu, and yet he felt calm. Almost like that slight floating feeling after his first cigarette in two weeks.

Thirty minutes later, he stopped again. This time, he moved everything to the trunk and even helped the newest addition load her harp case. He had no idea how it all fit. It seemed like something out of a bad commercial with clowns and cars, in reverse.

"Let me guess," he said. "Tahoe?" The slightest nod of the hood and he climbed back into the car.

Abie Kincaid felt too good to wonder much. Three tall girls, each with musical instruments, each dressed alike, twenty miles apart on a deserted highway in the middle of the night. No big deal.

Instead of wondering, he daydreamed about the shows he would play. Someday. He had a pack of songs he'd written, along with the covers he'd learned. He'd fed himself a solid diet of folk and alternative rock. Dylan and McLean, the Goo Goo Dolls and Matchbox 20. It was, he thought, only a matter of time. So what if Jessica thought he was terrible? She'd be the first in the line, he knew, when Abie Kincaid shoved the shit-kickers over to the right far enough for him to have his own corner of the airwaves. His daydreaming ate up an hour.

"We need to stop." When the three hitchhikers spoke unison, their voices were liquid, blending into a tone that ran over his entire body like a warm, soft tongue. They gestured to a small roadside bar. He pulled up and parked.

"How long, ladies?"

The first one he'd picked up turned towards him. "We've been untruthful. We are not going to Tahoe." He suddenly thought that perhaps this was their stop. His stomach sank as the inexplicable feeling of well-being drained away like so much bath water. "Where *are* you going, then?"

"Midway."

He scratched his head, remembering senior history three years ago with Mr. Frunk. "The island?"

The second one shook her head. "No. Northern Idaho. On the border."

Relief flooded him and he smiled. "Oh. I can take you there."

"Yes," the harp player said. "We thought so." The slight buzz became a full-on drunk. "We might need a map," he said.

"And currency," the first said.

"And a new car," the second said.

"Bring your guitar," said the harp player. So he did. They all walked into the bar and when they pushed back their hoods they were each uniquely and stunningly beautiful. One had copper-colored hair, one was brunette, the last blond; each wore their hair short. Their eyes wouldn't allow him to find their color —they were deep and wide and undulating. Every man in the bar stopped what he was doing and watched, slack-jawed. Every woman did the same, only with hard glances that said *step-off*—or something like it. One hitcher moved to the wall of slot machines. Another headed towards the pool table. The harp player took Abie's arm firmly and steered him towards the stage. A country western band was wrapping up an old tune about cheating hearts.

The owner came over in a hurry.

"My friend is a performer," the girl said.

"Sorry, miss. We already have a band for the night," the balding bar owner said.

Abie watched the magic work. A slight smile pulled at the corners of the man's mouth. His eyes glistened. He was catching whatever drunkenness she had tossed Abie. "They can play later," she said.

"I reckon so," he said with a grin. He walked over to the amp cord and yanked it out of the wood-paneled wall. The lead singer came over, red faced. The room buzzed danger.

"What the hell you doing, hoss?"

"Change in plans."

The girl laid her hand on the singer's arm. His face remained red, but the anger left it. He blushed. Then Abie was on stage, tuning his guitar and doing a mic test. The girl opened his guitar case at the foot of the stage and fixed her gaze on him.

Abie lost everything in the room except for that pair of eyes. He lost the music. He lost the lyrics. He lost his soul. But he sang. Christ almighty, for the first time in his life, he truly sang.

When he finished, the guitar case overflowed with bills. The line of people, red eyed from crying, hoarse from screaming his name, slipped out of the bar into the dawn. "We have to go," the harp player said, dumping the cash into a whiskey carton the owner had provided. The other two joined them, each with plastic sacks of cash. Near as Abie could tell, everyone, including the owner, must be going away with empty pockets. The slot machines were dark now, too, and silent.

They pulled onto the highway as a nondescript sedan with tinted windows pulled in, then exited a short time later, just outside of Reno. They helped themselves to a used Chevy at Slim's Quality Pre-owned Cars and Wedding Chapel. They left Abie's car and two thousand dollars cash in the space where the Chevy had been, then turned north. The girls talked more now, but still not much. Their hoods were down. "Where are *you* headed?" the redhead asked.

Abie's high had peaked with the show. His face hurt from the grin. "Midway."

The blond harp player laughed. "Before you picked us up."

Abie glanced at her in the mirror. "Seattle."

The brunette chimed in: "Home of Nirvana."

They all sighed, even Abie. The miles spun away beneath them. They stopped for food, for gas, and for restrooms. They ate in the car, on the road, occasionally looking backward.

"Why are we going to Midway?" he asked as they passed through Sand Point. "We're not. We're going just past it," the blond said.

"But why?"

They answered in unison again. "We have a performance there."

Abie laughed as their combined voices washed over him, and he enjoyed the growing lump in his jeans for another forty miles. Twice in Sand Point and once in Bonner's Ferry, he saw more nondescript sedans waiting, for no apparent reason, at intersections. At one point, during a more secluded stretch of road, he thought he'd seen a black helicopter in his side mirror, low over the trees, and silent. His traveling companions seemed quieter. They'd seen it, too, he thought.

They turned off for Midway, a small, out-of-the-way border crossing. It was choked with black sedans. The helicopter was there. Men and women in dark suits milled about.

"Do I turn around?" Abie felt panic eating away at his calm.

"No," all three said.

"We don't have time," the redhead said. She sat beside him in the passenger seat and looked at the sky, studying it carefully. "We only have an hour."

Abie pulled up to the stop sign in front of a guard station. A border patrol officer stood behind a man and a woman wearing dark suits.

"Where are you from?" asked the man the group.

"Where are you headed?" asked the woman. Abie saw the snipers on the roof now, saw the men against trees just inside the forest. All this side of the border. The Canada side appeared to be business as usual.

He started to say *Nevada*, but the blond touched his shoulder from the backseat. The redhead leaned over him. "I'm just a poor wayfaring stranger," she said, "a-traveling through this world of woe."

"But there's no sickness, toil, or danger," the blond said, "in that bright world to which I go."

The man and the woman backed up. "Please step out of the vehicle," he said, reaching under his jacket.

Three car doors opened. Three voices joined together: "I'm going there to meet my mother/she said she'd meet me when I come." It became song. "I'm only going over Jordan./I'm only going over home." Abie watched as the three women converged on the two suits. As they took slow, deliberate strides, he watched rifles raised and pistols drawn. He held his breath. They continued singing. One by one, the guns dropped. Then the hands that held them. And then the bodies attached to the hands until the asphalt, roof, and forest were a kindergarten classroom strewn with sleeping children.

They climbed back into the car. Abie felt the draw of the song and felt his euphoria battling the drowsiness that stole over him. He also felt the words. The desire to join in had gripped him from the start, but he'd held back.

"Drive," they said. And he did.

They left the highway not far into Canada and drove down a dirt road until it ended in the forest. A creek murmured on their left, and a trail wandered off on their right. The hitchhikers grabbed their packs and their instruments.

"This is it?" Abie asked. "Your performance is *here*?"

They nodded. His soul became a leaking balloon, elation rushing out from it. "You're more than welcome to watch." The redhead smiled at him.

"Bring your guitar," the harp player said.

"Fifteen minutes to curtain." The brunette broke the fern barrier and moved down the trail.

They went at a good clip; Abie followed after. Somewhere behind him, he thought he heard a car door slam. They walked for ten minutes then stopped in a clearing.

The instruments came out with practiced speed. He sat on the edge of the clearing. "Three minutes," the blond said.

Silence. Stillness. The sound of beating hearts. The sound of wind rustling leaves. Of grass bending beneath the weight of bugs. Of footsteps on the trail behind. And then music exploded. It burst from the instruments in a perfect unified chord. It burst from the throats in a honeyed tone that permeated the air. Abie watched, and the suited men watched, too, from where they stood at the end of the trail. They were helpless to act.

In the beginning was the song. They sang it, each voice strong and blended with the others. A song about long ago and far away, vast distances in space and time. A song about Four who became Three because of terrible war far from home. A song about a song; one sung to bind the darkness in the cosmos and halt the Hater's spread.

Abie had never heard anything like it. And yet he knew it. A song about long traveling in night to find the next binding place. The words pushed at his lips and pulled at his tongue. His fingers fumbled with his guitar case. Still he held back.

A song about a new Fourth found in the desert.

"Join us," the blond harp player whispered to him, and he gave in to it.

Drawing his guitar like a great flaming sword, he strummed and added his note to their chord, added his voice to their choir, joining their war. He stood with them now in the clearing and watched the suits watch them. Their faces were washed with love and hope and wonder. The Three spoke into his mind now. *This binding will hold ten thousand years,* they said, *if we but sing true.*

The ecstasy burst within Abie like a hundred collapsing suns, the heat pouring in on itself. He felt his sneakered feet leave the ground and saw that they were lifted up. White beams shot from their instruments, and from their mouths and eyes. As the Four raised, their hair flowed upward as if caught in a gravity-defying waterfall of light. The performance reached a crescendo and Abie knew, just as the girls did, that it had been a success. He knew other scheduled performances waited ahead of them. Other worlds were locked in the raging war. But first, to rest in the place that he was made for and made from. He smiled, and they smiled, too.

Then light took the Four and carried them home. ✷

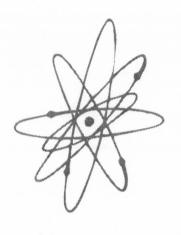

Interstellar Overdrive

STEVE LIBBEY

March 1968

THE TENEMENT THAT MY COUSIN GENE had chosen as a hide-out had the makings of a human-scale rat's maze. I spent ten minutes wandering through dingy hallways, graffitoed lobbies, and mysterious stairwells, but I finally found our keyboardist in the basement of the flat with his head buried in the innards of the Mellotron. Stacks of magnetic tape loops were piled at his feet. Expensive stacks, too: those loops of tape contained the sounds of instruments recorded for playback by the keyboard, and they were only available from the manufacturer.

So I pointed this out: "Hey, Einstein. Shouldn't you take better care of your toys?"

Theo wiggled his hands at me without removing his head. "Making progress, man. You're gonna dig this."

I picked up one of the loops between thumb and forefinger. A label on the non-playing side read: *Cello, single. Mellotronics, Birmingham.*

"Huh. Birmingham's not far from London, is it?"

"Baby, nothing's far from London. You can fit the entire country inside Texas and still have room for a lynching or two."

I winced. "Watch it. Our hosts are going to think we're as bad as the rednecks."

Theo settled back on the chair. His white-boy afro jutted out at odd angles and wobbled as he moved. "They want to believe that. Let 'em! It's our schtick: crazy Texans."

"I was born in Kansas."

"We keep trying to forget that." Theo winked at me. "Get a load of this."

He flipped the power switch of the Mellotron. Cooling fans roared to life. He adjusted the volume knob of his amp and pressed a key. A saxophone wailed one note, warbly in a groovy way.

"So?"

"That's not it. Hold on." He pressed another key: same saxophone, lower. He swore and counted three keys to the left. The sound of a woman crying out in ecstasy filled the room.

"Holy shit, man."

Theo grinned back at me. "Now *that* will be trippy. Imagine it coming out the PA at the warehouse, hundreds of watts of '*Ohhh*!'" He pressed the key a few more times to demonstrate the different groans he had recorded.

"Am I mistaken in detecting an English accent in that young lady's exclamation?"

"Not at all, young sir. Her name was—er, is—Penny. She was super cooperative. I reckon she'll be at the gig."

"To hear Ollie talk about it, the entire population of London will be there." The surly Londoner had bragged about the event ever since we'd arrived, eager to show how much hipper London was than Texas: Joe Boyd's fabled UFO Club was being reborn.

"And you were the one who thought we should save the plane fare. We've only been here three days and it's blowing my mind."

I had to concede. "Yeah, it's way gone. Makes it hard to go back to Dallas."

"Who's going back?" Theo waggled his eyebrows.

"Me." I held up my hand with the wedding band. "Remember? Six months to go?"

Theo waved his palms. "It's cool, it's cool. Your old lady's groovy, Ty. You'll have the first Rebel Rouser spawn."

"Don't remind me." In truth, I was thrilled and terrified by the prospect of fatherhood, and already the band had taken a backseat to my impending responsibilities. Since junior high, there had been no question that Julia and I would be together. When the rabbit died, we got hitched at the courthouse in hopes of derailing any complaints from our families. Thus far, all we had experienced from them was detached support. I had a feeling that I would have to keep playing guitar in the Rebel Rousers just to make sure the little one had doting adults in attendance. As much as we played up our wild-man reputation, down deep we were just good-hearted Texas boys.

Footsteps resounded on the creaky basement stairs. A mop-topped beatnik, complete with combat boots and rose-colored glasses, ducked his head as he entered the low-ceilinged room. Under his arm was tucked a cardboard box. His scraggly blond mustache curled over his lip as if it threatened to dampen his ability to speak.

"'Allo, cats!" The accent wasn't English, but it was European and unidentifiable to my ears. "As promised, here are your tapes." He set the box down on the corner of the Mellotron and undid the flaps. A nest of tape loops bulged out.

"Cool. Hey, Anatole, meet Ty."

I shook Anatole's hand with Texan firmness; his grip was limp and damp like a fish.

"Bonjour," he said. "You are American, no?" He whisked his fingers at the rolled up sleeves of my white tee shirt: my usual attire, which looked parochial in this year of kaleidoscopic fashion.

"Yes I am."

"How ginchy. What do you play?"

"Guitar, mostly."

"And I build sound, mostly." Anatole's fingers fluttered in the air. "Experimentalism. Sound sculpting. Electronic manipulation. Metaphors freed of their verbal fetters. Are you down with Stockhausen?"

Theo interrupted before I could speak. "Oh, yeah, man. Totally on that wavelength. Ty is a fiend for some stompboxes."

Anatole raised an eyebrow. "*Oui*? What do you use, a little fuzz? Wah pedal? Echoplex?"

"Um…" I had a feeling I was going to disappoint him. "Just a Fuzzrite, actually. The airline busted my CryBaby wah."

"Show it to me."

My gear had been shoved into the corner of the basement space where our host band rehearsed. Their guitarist had a glorious Marshall stack that dwarfed my own rig at home, accompanied by the latest and greatest Roger Mayer pedals and a real Echoplex. Anatole's shoulders sank a bit when he saw my modest gear. He picked up the wounded wah pedal like a sick cat.

I shrugged. "Well, you know, they say tone's in the fingers, right?"

"Quaint." He curled his mustache. "No, no, the tone is in the ether. Musicians are the priest-kings who cozen it down out of the grasp of the gods, so that mortal man may sip of the nectar." He produced a screwdriver and began to loosen the screws of the CryBaby's bottom plate. I gave Theo a helpless look.

"Anatole invents electronic effects for all the best musicians. Like, the Pink Floyd, Hendrix, Arthur Brown… even Beatles."

Circuitry exposed, Anatole held the pedal up to the light like a newborn and inspected it. "Dirty. Cheap wiring. *Oui*, yes, Beatles. You have heard of them."

"We've heard of them all," Theo insisted. "We're not from some podunk burg."

"I like the Yardbirds," I offered lamely.

"Piff. Americanophiliac wankery. No offense." Anatole pointed at me. "You should take back the blues from them, you Yanks. What have you planned for the Happening?"

He meant the psychedelic festival, the UFO Club, the reason for our trip. "Ah, just our set. Theo has the Mellotron making porn noises."

Anatole seized my shoulder and leaned in so close his nose nearly touched mine. "The fire is yours to wield, if you dare! Loud guitars, feedback—these are so *last year*. Ask me what I can do for you."

"Ha. Um. What can you do for me?"

He stuffed a card into my shirt-pocket. "Come to my work-shop tomorrow at noon. I will be ready for you then." Anatole turned his back on us and charged up the stairs. "Tomorrow, my friends!"

I shook my head back and forth. "What the hell was that?"

"Genius, man. That guy is certified. We're lucky he's taking an interest in us."

"I'll be lucky if I get that wah back."

"Just be cool, okay?" Theo's expression softened. "You know this is our big break. Texas is too small for us, man. We belong with these people. They're forward thinkers, on the edge, and now the labels are snatching up anything that even smells like them. Just the fact that Anatole De Vos is working on your gear is enough to make A&R scouts call. Don't act all shy again. I want to tour Europe."

I thought of Julia's expanding belly. "When?"

"Whenever! Now! Get excited, brother!" He pulled me into an embrace. I patted his back awkwardly. Theo grinned at me. "I'm glad you're here."

"Sure. Me, too. It will be interesting."

I left Theo to his new box of tape loops and went to wake up Gene.

Permanently dusty and cobwebbed windows in the hallway dif-fused the afternoon sunlight. The door to the flat hung open, issuing a vaporous reek of clove cigarettes and pot. Young, flashy lounged on the couch, at once elegant and disheveled, listening to a turntable that spit out music that seemed to be nothing but random guitar noodling. They looked me over with an air of disdainful curiosity.

"Looking for Gene," I said.

A waiflike girl in blue pointed with her cigarette. Apparently, I was to follow the smoke. In the tiny bedroom, Gene had propped himself up with pillows on a mattress. A slender girl with wild hair slept nude beside him. My eyes strayed from her ass to the book in his hand: *Dharma Bums.*

"You aren't kidding about this wanderer thing, are you?" I asked.

"Tyson!" Only my family used my full name. "What it *is,* cuz!" Before I could stop him, he stood up; fortunately for propriety, he wore his wrinkled army pants, an audacious choice of pajamas for a deserter.

"It is what it is," I said, glancing at the sleeping girl. He grinned like a tiger. "Does anyone here even know what mornings are?"

"For squares and grandmothers. But you can't beat a spot of Earl Grey to wake you up. Care to join me?"

"She won't mind?"

"Not likely. Besides," he said, tugging a red and green striped shirt over his head, "when's the last time we really visited? Family reunion?"

"Yeah. Middle school."

I half expected Gene to lace up his army boots, but instead he had found a proper pair of cowboy boots. The on the couch hadn't changed their position. Gene ignored them as we left the flat.

"I wonder who they were?" he said with a grin.

On the sidewalks, the differences between Dallas and London struck me again: the dense, claustrophobic sky, never free of clouds; the ancient streets; ironwork strewn casually about, hardly considered the old world status symbol that it was back home; the crowded buildings fighting for space; patches of green cultivated against the gray concrete incursions; and most of all, sidewalks that were actually in use by pedestrians. As much as I wanted to appreciate the authenticity of my surroundings, I couldn't help feeling as though I had stumbled onto a movie set.

Gene and I settled in at a coffee shop populated half by

young, aimless and half by old, aimless geezers. Gene struck me as awfully relaxed for a man on the run from the U.S. Army and I said so.

"It's easy to lose yourself here. Better to be AWOL than dying of malaria in the jungle."

"Your folks know where you are?"

He blew a raspberry. "Are you kidding? Pop would disown me and turn me in—in that order. He'd rather I take a bullet than shame the family." His expansive shrug said everything he felt about his family. "London's my scene now."

"Well, I won't narc on you."

"I know." He grew quiet for a spell, and I sensed that Gene had said his piece and that was the end of that. I had sweetened my tea with cubes of sugar until it tasted like sugar water. We watched a dapper young man ride up on a scooter, park, and strut into the coffee shop.

"Those are big here," Gene said. "Me, I prefer a solid hog between my legs, but I don't want to mess with the paperwork. The tube is good enough for me."

"Like the veins of a big steer," I said. "I can't get over how dense it is here."

"You mean *alive*." Gene's eyes lit up. "You can feel it, can't you? The world just feels closer, like we're sitting on top of the pulse of everything, like... hell, like Dallas is just an imitation. Or an outpost. This is where it starts."

"Well," I said, feeling a bit self-conscious with my drawl, "I don't know about that. These folks didn't invent rock 'n' roll, did they? Or blues?"

"They made it their own. They *conquered* it."

"Christ, you and Theo both." I slurped back the rest of the tea. "Okay, fine, I get your drift. You and Theo should find a pad here and work up a proper British accent."

"Stop screwing with me. I'm serious."

"Me, too. You're both bouncing off the walls like kids in a candy store. I bet the band would follow him if Theo stuck around."

Gene narrowed his eyes at me. "But not you."

"Not me. Don't make a big production of that. Let events run their course."

"I'd rather raise a kid here than in the bloody desert."

Bloody, I noticed. That didn't take long. "You're on the lam, man."

"If I wasn't AWOL, that's what I'd do."

I sighed. Drama everywhere. My cousin and Theo wanted to condense their lives into a single flashing point. Yet what would next year be like? Ten years from now? My thinking had already changed. It was changed forever when the results came back positive.

My gaze settled on a pair of chicks nestled in the corner booth. Both possessed the wan complexion I had seen in English girls, as if the sun were an invading force that they had successfully repelled from the shores of their island nation. In the process, they had also armored up their hair with unnatural colors: pale, bright orange. One wore a smartly cut jacket with a colorful vinyl patchwork of avocado and pink; the other, a psychedelic version of a schoolgirl uniform. Their high, rouged cheekbones and pouting lips would have made any man desire them in his arms, just for a night. Only the faintest desire stirred in me, though, a mere reminder that I was still a young man, a musician, a lord amongst the peasants in this rock and roll kingdom. Guilt and resignation chopped off the head of my libido as quickly as it reared up. I felt old, all at once. I should have been having more fun.

Gene had followed my glance. "They'll be at the gig. Should we talk them up?"

"No. I mean, you can."

He shrugged, a fisherman in well-stocked waters, complacent in the bounty offered up to him.

The exterior of the apartment complex hosting the party was as underwhelming as the flat where we were staying. Inside, however, was another story.

Whether the decorations were put up solely for the party, or the party was being thrown to justify the decorations, the interconnected suites were a Dante-esque panorama of decadence and display. Ollie lumbered up the stairs ahead of us, nearly blocking our view, his wide shoulders stretching the fabric of his tee shirt to the limit. He had just quit a job at a steel mill, he told us, to make more time for his social life. Whatever else he did for money remained a mystery because he expressed little interest in sharing the details of his own life. When we were suitably intimidated, Ollie became our gruffly determined tour guide. I had taken a shine to him while we rode a classic double-decker bus to a restaurant and he nudged me to direct my gaze out the window and towards the sky. "Big Ben," he grunted, almost begrudgingly, but I realized he knew a tourist would want to see it. Ollie made sense to me, the way Texas good old boys did, and I felt a bit guilty that I preferred his company to that of my cousin.

"Let's hit the living room first," Ollie said, steering us down a narrow hallway to an unmarked door plastered with a collage of nude model cutouts *sans* heads. I noticed he made a point of placing his hand on a pair of breasts as he pushed the door open.

The living room of the main flat was crowded, lit with a rainbow of colored lights and blaring music from hefty sound system, yet Ollie had chosen well for our entrance. Heads turned, folks pointed, conversations paused. We psychedelic Texas cowboys made the scene with our Stetsons, snakeskin cowboy boots, tight jeans, and tighter tee shirts. More than one London girl made eyes at us during our crossing of the room to the makeshift bar. Ollie grinned ear to ear, pinched girls' bottoms, talked loudly, and seemed to enjoy the notoriety of hosting the wild Yanks.

Within moments, questionable drinks and more questionable pills appeared in our hands. London appreciated a spectacle,

particularly one with style, and in a perverse way, their artifi-
cial hipness engendered a genuine hospitality that touched my
transplanted mid-western heart. I soon found myself in a circle
of guitarists, swapping gig stories and naming blues songs with
solos we had copped. A bloke (I couldn't think of him as anything but) named Dave and I hit it off and promised to meet up
for a jam. "One Tele cat to another," he said drunkenly.

"Damn right!" I responded to the toast, my drawl gone far
south. The pill-and-booze combo had done its work with the
speed of a plains twister.

Eventually I mingled further, led by Dave and the other guitarists from one room to another, where fellow musicians held
court with star struck girls. More than one chick took my lack
of flirting as an open challenge; a busty number wedged herself
into the loo with me. I fended her off with as much tact as I
could muster.

Theo had no such scruples, nor a jealous wife back home, and
he disappeared into a dark warren of rooms whose furnishings,
concealed by bead curtains, may have consisted of nothing more
than a bed. I was willing to bet that the two girls under his arms
had yet to complete high school, though heavy English fare had
plumped them up to squeezable proportions.

Head spinning, I found a remote modular couch and curled
up with an abandoned bottle of proper Jack Daniels. I closed
my eyes and let the sounds of music and conversation pound at
the misty wall thrown up by the booze and the pills. I couldn't
formulate complete thoughts without letting them slip away into
free association—surely an effect of the mystery pills—so I let
my mind drift past vistas of imaginary landscape and unlikely
housing. A vast shape loomed over me in my little trip, calling
my name over and over.

When I opened my eyes, they took a good minute to fully
focus. "Dink?"

Dink grinned a lop-sided, eager beaver greeting to me. He
had joined the Rousers two months before this gig, when the
drummer who had founded the band was bussed off to boot

camp. Fresh out of high school, and thus the youngest member, he greeted every experience with wide eyed enthusiasm. Right now, he appeared to be laughing at his own joke but ready to share.

"What?"

He flopped down next to me. His breath stank of potent English ale. "You will never guess what just happened to me!"

"You met Ginger Baker."

"No! I mean, I did, yeah, he was here earlier. But seriously, I just got the most amazing blow job ever!"

"That's nice."

He giggled. "No, wait. It gets better! Remember what my dad does?"

Such trivial facts were particularly hard to summon up at this moment, but I gave Dink a chance. "Ah, damn it, he sells... shoes, right?"

"Furniture. But, no... what does he do in his spare time?"

This rang a bell. "He's a Klansman, isn't he?"

"Right." Dink looked as though he were about to burst. "And this chick—she was black!"

I had to chuckle. "Your old man would pop a vein."

"Or worse."

The kid had made no bones about his estrangement from his folks. Suddenly I wanted to be his big brother. I pulled him close for a bear hug. "Want to really get his goat? Put the moves on her. Grab one of those rooms and get it on."

"Seriously? Seriously? You think I can?"

"Hey, if she sucked you off, she's probably horny for more. Give her a poke for your asshole dad."

"Wow." Dink sat back, amazed.

"Welcome to the wild and woolly world of rock and roll, buddy." I tousled his hair. "Now get."

Dink leapt to his feet and saluted me before disappearing into the dark shapes of partiers. I settled back into the cushions for another few pulls on the fifth of Jack and congratulated myself for having struck a small blow for the civil rights movement.

Weariness took over as my drinking buddy. I was too doped up to get much out of a conversation with strangers, let alone bandmates, and seeing Dink in his mood of perpetual awe gave me the weird sense that I was only renting this euphoria. It would dissipate and leave me blinking in the gray light of a London afternoon, wondering why I wasn't at home with the woman I had married. Every time Julia sent me off to traipse across the country with the band, I had the perverse desire to refuse and barricade myself in the bedroom with her; and at the same time, to declare our marriage over and go to live in perpetual adolescence. Theo, three years my senior, did so. Dink had a good decade of road tripping in him before he wound down. I was only twenty-five; how could I have aged so quickly?

Was it a victory or a defeat?

I dozed off in this polarized frame of mind until someone shook my shoulder: once, gently, and a second time with determination. It was Dave, and his cheerful English smile was gone.

"Trouble, chap," he said.

"What? What?"

"Your lad's got a gang on him."

My eyes stung. Dave offered a hand to get me on my feet. "Okay, I'm up. What's the story?"

"That drummer of yours and six greasers. They dragged him out of a bedroom."

Dink. Christ, I sent the kid to his own demise. "Let's go!" I took three uncertain steps and collided with the doorframe. The room spun.

"Bloody hell." Dave caught me. "You won't do him any good in your condition. Where's that gorilla you popped in with?"

"Ollie. He'll know what to do." We stumbled into the main party room. Partygoers had gathered in the doorway to watch the altercation. I got a glimpse of a half dozen guys thugged out in black leather, a topless black chick pleading with them, and a defiant Dink. Ordinarily I wasn't afraid of a fight, but the pills had queered my sense of balance.

Dave seized the arms of the nearest two and demanded to

know Ollie's current whereabouts. They shrugged, too blasé to
be interested, but a girl extended a long, quavering arm towards
the suite of bedrooms. "In there," she said.

Dave and I banged on the doors of the bedrooms, those that
had them, and burst the doors open. Couples in the midst of
coitus shot us accusatory glares. We didn't bother to apologize.

A cry rose up from the fight. Panicky, I kicked a door open
without knocking. Ollie's wide back, no longer encumbered
by a shirt, was turned to me. His trousers were loosened and a
mop-topped blond head bobbed between his legs. He propped
himself against the wall with one hand and gripped a beer bottle
with the other, grunting with satisfaction.

"Ollie! Man, we need your help."

His head jerked around and for a moment his face contorted
with rage. I held up my hands. Behind me, Dave blurted out:
"One of the Yanks is in a row with the Totter Street boys!"

The girl kneeling before Ollie peered out from his thick
legs—and even in the dim light, I could see it was in fact an effete young man, pale cheeks red with excitement, cravat disheveled in classic dandified style.

"Whoa, that's a dude," I blurted.

Ollie blinked in confusion. A shadow crossed over his face,
hiding desperation and fury.

"Bloody fucking hell!" he roared. One meaty hand shoved the
boy against the wall, hard. "God damn fairies. A bloke can't even
drink in peace." Ollie hitched up his pants. "Where's my fucking
shirt?"

I pulled Ollie out of the room. He shook his head to clear it.
"Where's the scrap?" A gasp from the onlookers was his answer,
and he bulled through them. "Make way!"

The situation had deteriorated. Dink was on the ground with
his arms over his head to protect from kicks from motorcycle
boots. Without stopping, Ollie plowed into the fight. The two in
his trajectory tumbled onto a couch—a soft landing, but Ollie
followed up with swift and powerful punches to their midsec-
tions. Only he rose from the tangle.

Dave smirked at me. "A master at work. That big ape once boxed semi-pro."

"I can see that."

Ollie squared off against the remaining four thugs while the girl helped Dink to his feet. A ferocious grin split Ollie's fat face. I could see that the fight was the perfect nightcap for him, especially after his little gaffe with the queer kid. In his defense, I could imagine how drugs and alcohol would make it hard to tell the actual gender of some of these fey, androgynous British kids. Were it one of my close friends, I would never let him live it down, but Ollie had a rage inside him that would not welcome my teasing unless it was backed up with fists. That was too rough a game for me.

Instead, I watched him beat the hell out of the suddenly un-enthusiastic. Dink, bless his heart, removed his shirt and placed it around the girl's shoulders, a gentlemanly gesture that belied the ugliness propagated in the South by men like his father. Despite the shouts, the spurts of blood, and the crunch of bones, I had a dazedly cheerful feeling about this trip.

Anatole De Vos' laboratory could have passed for any one of the dozens of decrepit auto repair garages that crowded the East End. Such squalor in Dallas would have had a coating of dust; here, it was unidentifiable grime that must have first coughed forth from the steeples of Dickensian factories. In my eyes, it was as delightful as a manicured garden.

The address on the card wasn't represented on the street. I peered in cloudy windows of three buildings until I settled on a door that seemed the mostly likely culprit—it was blaring Cream's "Tales of Brave Ulysses."

My knocking rattled the door in its frame. Brave Ulysses sol-diered on, undiminished, but now it inherited new sounds that I didn't recognize: additional feedback howls, swoops, chattering tremolos, gulps of overlapping echo. The song ended but the feedback continued. It sounded like there were three rock bands practicing, *sans* rhythm sections.

The door wasn't locked, so I went inside. Anatole's shop had indeed been a garage, once; pulleys still hung from the ceiling. He had papered over most of the windows and lit the place with candles, colored bulbs, and flickering broken televisions set to mid-channel.

In the middle of the room, on a grate that covered the mechanic's pit, Anatole crouched in a circle of guitar amps arranged like Stonehenge. Each amp had a guitar positioned in front of it, and each had a pedal board chock full of mysterious metal boxes, ranging from the size of a paperback book to a toolbox.

Cables and cords interwove so thickly that they created a carpet in the space between the amps where Anatole sat and twiddled knobs on a vast, archaic mixing board.

Anatole pointed at a sunburst Gibson Les Paul propped against a Marshall stack. "Pick that up, my friend."

I did. The Paul had seen better days: someone (I could guess who) had routed it out for a middle pickup, but the cavity was empty but for a surfeit of wires, some alarmingly disconnected.

"Move!" Anatole shouted over the noise.

"Huh?"

"Body motion! Make the guitar sing to you."

I knew what he wanted. The proximity of a guitar to a cranked amp could control the volume and swell of the feedback. I was no stranger to the sound of an overdriven amplifier, but Anatole had taken it to a wild, non-musical extreme. I turned around to interpose my body between the amp and the guitar, and its feedback fluctuated weirdly through the various effect boxes. With a few steps and turns, I generated a variety of odd sounds, aided by the electronics and whatever Anatole was doing on his board. He flung his hand in the air as though he were an orchestral conductor.

We noised out for a good ten minutes this way until the room went dark and silent. Anatole cursed in French and I chuckled.

He lit a Zippo and headed for the fusebox across the room. The lights came back on, as did the amps with a wallop, but he flipped a switch on the mixer to cut off signal to the guitars. The amps hummed along in cheerful, tube-driven innocence.

Anatole fetched a beer for me from a small refrigerator. "You have a knack for exploration," he said with the kind of disarming grin he might give a girl post-coitus.

My cheeks warmed. "Ah, yeah. Well, it's good fun, you know."

"It's more than mere fun." He opened a bottle for himself. "Come with me."

Tapestries demarcated his workroom from the larger testing area. A worktable stretched across the entire back wall. Tools and wires hung on a pegboard; circuit boards, transistors, and metal boxes evoked an industrial landscape in miniature. Anatole rescued a blue box from underneath a nest of wires.

"Here is the magic," he said. The box had been spray painted blue. It was large enough for a sandwich, maybe. Two knobs and a footswitch adorned it.

"What's it do?"

He set his bottle down. "You know how Beatles produced that wonderful effect, by varying the speed of two tapes with a hand on the flanges? So that the voice seems to swirl?" He mimed the movement. "This produces such an effect simply through electronic manipulation."

"Yeah?" I turned the box over in my hands. Something rattled.

"*Oui, oui.*" Anatole was sorting through the piles again. "But that effect, it is not what you need for the happening. Rather, I will entrust you with a very special project, my friend." He spun around, his face abruptly dark and tight. "I can trust you?"

"Sure thing, man," I said as cool as possible, though I found myself increasingly weirded out. "What ya got? A wah, maybe?"

"Hmph." His body seemed to close in on itself like an elderly man's might, and it struck me that Anatole had more years under his belt than he let on. From another pile, my Crybaby wah appeared. "This one, it is yours. But follow me."

We passed through a narrow doorway leading to an even narrower set of stairs that led upstairs. The second floor loft had none of the clutter of the first floor. A cheap Eko guitar had been plugged into a wide black box and a small Selmer combo amp; an uneven circle of deteriorating store mannequins surrounded the rig in clusters: three dummies, and then two, and then four. The illumination came from sunlight streaming through the dusty windows. Anatole began to fiddle with the only light bulb, dangling from its wiring.

I hefted the Eko and admired the ugly mother-of-toilet-seat top. I stepped on the pedal's single footswitch and strummed an open G.

The chord wobbled in the air of the dark room, and even though the Selmer had little power, I could feel the waves of sound splash across my body. It was like a symphony of the Leslie rotating speaker cabinets and tape delay units and fuzzboxes all at once, and I got excited. How many British chaps had one of *these* in their arsenals? I'd be happy just to listen to one played at full blast.

"Non!" Anatole nearly tackled me in an effort to yank the cable out of the guitar. *"Imbecile! Idiot!* What are you doing?"

"Hey, now," I said, suddenly irate. "Watch it."

But he had turned his back to me and unplugged the black box. "This is not a playground." He had tugged his cuffs over his palms and he cradled the box in his hands as though it were a hot potato. A faint reek of burning circuitry wafted from the unit.

Now I felt guilty. "Damn, man, I'm sorry. I just assumed—"

"No, no, you were correct: this is intended for you. But you must not activate it carelessly. Wait until you are onstage."

"It's fragile?"

He thought for a moment, glancing about the room and seeing something he didn't like. *"Oui.* Somewhat. Let us try some other pedals for you to show off." Before I could speak, and before I could remove the Eko, he hustled me out back down the stairs. The mannequins returned to their silent vigil.

The Rebel Rousers gave the set a cursory run-through, skipping over the portions of the songs left open to free-form jamming—which left only twenty minutes of actual music. Based on what we had observed in the London scene, experimentation was the rule, not the exception. This excited us to no end. Back home, we were shoving our ideas down the throats of audiences half populated by frat boys and bikers, and only our ear-piercing volume prevented them from hurling spent beer bottles in disgust.

I tried out Anatole's bounty of effects pedals on every song: the flange-simulator (which he called "The Ladder of the Heavens" and I thought of as "the whooshy sounding box"), the compact delay, a selection of weirdly-voiced fuzzes and octave fuzzes—but not the mysterious and volatile black box. No one seemed to mind that my hissing line noise had quadrupled. Theo gushed at me after each song: "Far out, man!" "Dig! That's the now sound!" and so on. I had to admit that Anatole's inventions made my playing otherworldly, which thrilled me. I was eager to get in front of an audience.

We took a beer and piss break. Gene wandered down, now wearing a denim suit embroidered with flowers and American flags. "Groovy tunes," he said.

I grinned. "Psychedelia, Texas style."

"Them boxes ain't Texan," he said, pointing at Anatole's effects with his bottle. "You're probably the first American to make those sounds."

Theo, Dink, and Horace came back down and resumed their stations. We all looked at each other, indecisive.

"Run the set again?" Theo asked.

"Naw," Dink said. "Let's try that there Ritchie Valens cover with Ty's new toys."

Theo wagged his head. "Yeah, groovy. Can we hear that one?" He indicated the mystery box, which I hadn't even plugged in.

"No can do," I said. "It's delicate. I promised Anatole I

wouldn't use it until the show tonight."

"What if it's broken? Shouldn't you test it out?"

"Well…" He had a point. "For a bit, maybe, just to make sure everything's copasetic. I *am* curious how it'll sound through this rig." The guys watched eagerly as I plugged it into the signal chain, at the very end, right before the amp.

We had added "Come On, Let's Go" to our set as a fifties standard re-imagined with acid rock guitar and howling organ, so that the simple, tonic chord progression took on a primal power. Instead of playing the chords cleanly, I left the fuzzbox on for a wicked, dirty snarl. Gene nodded along with the beat, lost in the noise and the volume, as Horace belted out the words with his raspy drawl. Amongst the dandified British bands, we would stand out as rowdy as our reputation implied.

When the refrain came along, I stomped on the switch of the mystery box. My guitar's volume doubled, the wave effect began. The room seemed underwater. I saw Theo's eyes go wide. To hear the full range of frequencies, I played the chord progression with fat barre chords, holding down both top and bottom strings. They shimmered like a curtain of fire.

I switched it off when the verse came in. Even through the rest of Anatole's effects, the guitar sounded insignificant in comparison to the mystery pedal, but I resisted the urge to kick it back in.

The song ended, leaving us panting and sweaty in the dank basement. I felt as fatigued after playing one song as I had after the entire set.

Theo just shook his head; I had never seen him at a loss for words.

Hearing the mystery box in the context of a full rock band had indeed been overwhelming, as though we had crossed some threshold that divided amateur acts from major label acts. The air weighed down on us, heavy with potential.

Dink broke the silence. "Killer diller," he said, standing and stretching.

"I gotta get one of those," Theo said huskily.

"Maybe we can share. How'd it sound, Gene?"

But Gene had left sometime during the song. Maybe the mystery box wasn't as impressive to non-musicians. As I began to pack my rig, I fought against an unwelcome sense of disappointment. Gene was family, but so were the Rousers, in their own way, and it was our own rock and roll world that we now inhabited.

The Midnight O'Clock knew a driver for a local delivery company who was careless enough with their trucks—"lorries"—to enable this bloke to sneak one out of the lot after hours, and this is what we loaded our mutual gear into. I quite liked the Midnight O'Clock boys—younger than us, long haired and pale, naïve, hedonistic, and possessed of mysterious funds for embroidered Edwardian jackets, looming amplifiers and American guitars. Trevor O'Clock, as he dubbed himself, assured us as we piled guitars on top of amplifiers that he had a shipment of prime acid on the way from a "very special gentleman."

"The last time I dropped acid, I punched out Horace," I told him. "Whiskey's my drug of choice."

Trevor O'Clock touched my arm in his fey way. "Trust me. You Yanks have never had the like. Timothy Leary would give up his citizenship if he knew about this batch."

"I'm not sure." I was beginning to feel like a mother hen, but this gig was at the famous UFO Club, what was left of it, and I didn't want to open the doors of perception and let the entire band stumble through whilst attempting to play our set. Pot and alcohol had treated us fine thus far.

"Suit yourself. You might change your mind when you meet him. Your cousin wanted to be included in the festivities, didn't he?"

I shrugged. "Haven't seen him all day. Maybe he's already there with your man."

"That's odd."

While some of the lads clambered into the back of the delivery truck, I opted to split the cab fare with Ollie. The battered taxi appeared to be as old as the geezer behind the wheel.

Ollie wore his usual workman's clothes: plain white tee, brown jacket, trousers, and a plaid wool cap. He chewed on his lip as the cab lurched away from the curb.

"Thanks for the help last night," I said.

"Cheers, mate. Nothing to it." He didn't smile.

"Ah, well, usually I can keep my boys under control, but, you know, on the road it's like a vacation, and once the drugs and girls get in the mix—"

He opened his mouth to speak and closed it, leaving only a silence.

"Yeah, so, wow." I cast about for something to say. "Guess you Brits have a thing or two to teach us about getting our groove on."

Ollie turned his bulk in the back seat to face me. "What's your meaning?"

"Huh?" I blinked. "Nothing! I mean, it was a hell of a shindig, you know?"

"Go on, say it."

My heart had started to race. Men like Ollie used violence as a means of communication sometimes. I was no wimp, but the man was a Neanderthal in a hat.

I offered him an innocent grin. "Just what I said. Lots of drugs, lots of booze, lots of wild shit. Just the sort of party we like."

"Huh." Ollie scrutinized me like prey. "A lot of booze."

"And pills, don't forget the pills."

"You could hardly stand," he said without levity.

"I was three sheets…" A blurry image came to me at once: an effete boy on his knees before Ollie. I knew why he was so touchy. "Anything could have happened. Pure, unadulterated freak out."

"A bloke can make a mistake."

"I know I sure did. I could barely recognize who I was talking to, half the time."

He narrowed his eyes.

"So," I continued, "there ain't no need to dwell upon strange shit that could have happened to any of us while under the influence."

"Right." Ollie settled back into the seat and folded his arms, satisfied. I had passed some sort of test.

The cab raced through streets ancient and new, amongst looming facades lit with dim, incandescent street lamps. At night, London seemed even more ancient and knowing. Generations of Londoners had lived and died behind those rain-streaked walls, cloistered like rats in their nests

We bypassed the forest of beautiful old buildings and colorful main drags to enter an industrial part of town. As big as London was, I recognized a few of the warehouses and garages. We were driving through Anatole's neighborhood.

"I think Anatole works just down that lane." I pointed out the window.

Ollie grunted. "Yeah, I been there with the Midnight lads."

"He's got some far out gadgets."

That elicited only a shrug from the big man. I settled back into the seat.

Joe Boyd's UFO Club had risen to prominence as the central locus for the London psychedelic scene. Somehow Boyd had crafted the space to be "a happening" in the truest sense of the term, and it was hot from the get-go, not only for scenesters looking for the next party, but also as a neutral ground for the artists and musicians. The crowd was so hip, so groovy, that even John Lennon and Paul McCartney felt comfortable attending shows without bodyguards. It was probably the only place you could rub elbows with a Beatle and not have a horde of screaming girls in the way; instead, you were treated to a barrage of guitar feedback from the Pink Floyd, Soft Machine, or even dodging fire from the flaming hat of Arthur Brown.

Yet the success of the club was its doom: the Irish dance

hall it had been utilizing, the Blarney, was not prepared for the increased police pressure on the club (no doubt antagonized by their "spot the fuzz" contests). When Boyd's partner, Hoppy Hopkins, landed in jail on drug charges, the UFO moved to the Roundhouse—an expensive, dilapidated circular hall. Rent was too high to carry on with the usual range of bands, as the Pink Floyd and others found fame and were priced out of reach for smaller venues. The previous October, the Roundhouse shut down.

Now, five months later, was the "rebirth of the UFO Club"— and so the entire population of , freaks, and deviants would be in attendance. The Pink Floyd had signed on to headline the show; we and the Midnight O'Clock were support. From the rumors that had reached us, the new UFO Club could feature a crippled mime act and still pack the house.

Bright lights silhouetted a crowd that spilled out onto the sidewalk surrounding the four-story brick building that appeared to have once been a warehouse with offices. Whomever the original occupants had been, their sign now read, in glowing pinks and oranges, set off by a mounted blacklight, "UFO." Painted flowering vines rose up the brickwork and bloomed unlikely, exaggerated petals. A massive painted eye looked out from the tops of each side of the building, as if keeping watch for the fuzz. Every window glowed with a different color.

"Damn me," I said.

"I worked on some of the renovation. He done it up proper," Ollie said.

"You mean Boyd?"

He directed the cab to the back loading dock. "Naw, mate. De Vos."

"Anatole?"

We pulled up next to the Midnight O'Clock's borrowed lorry. The boys were already pulling out their gear, grinning from ear to ear at the sight of the psychedelicized building. I paid the cabbie and caught Theo's sleeve. "Pretty groovy," I said.

"Way, way out," Theo said. He looked as though he were go-

ing to burst out of his own skin with excitement. I took hold of
my guitar cases and followed him inside. Ollie obligingly hauled
the Marshall stacks as though they were bags of groceries.

Anatole had taken pains to decorate even the service entrance
with someone's sloppy abstract paintings that still reeked of oil.
A young woman in tight bellbottoms guided us to a staging area
behind the curtains of the stage. I parted them to peek out at the
space. The main room had been the warehouse space. Blacklights
illuminated the painted steel poles spaced at even intervals. The
stage itself was a cluster of circular platforms from two to five
feet in height. Behind them was a shelf for the backline of amplifiers. PA stacks to the sides and monitors nestled between the
platforms. It was an impressive performance space. Theo nearly
pissed himself.

Trevor O'Clock rushed up to me. "Hey, man. Remember that
cat I told you about? The time is now."

We made our way towards the front of the building. Anatole
had knocked out selected walls to give the impression of a series
of caverns. Already the dimly lit rooms were brimming with
London kids in various states of intoxication. A pair of twins in
white pulled their matching poodles out of our way.

A hand waved us into a storage room lined with wooden
crates. My pupils expanded to make out details in the candlelit
darkness. Our mysterious contact leaned against the crates and
lit a cigarette. The hooded eyes and gaunt features of Syd Barrett
basked in the hand-held lighting ritual. His body disappeared
in a plain black shirt and jeans, far less ostentatious than the
partygoers.

Trevor grinned like a schoolboy and introduced us. Syd's
handshake was weak, uncommitted, but he gave me a friendly
smile. "From the States, are you?"

"Texas."

"Groovy. How are you finding London?"

"Totally far out," I said, grinning, and Syd laughed.

"You haven't even started your trip." Syd withdrew an antique
billfold from his pocket. Inside was a sheet of stamps with the

image of an eagle. He peeled one off for each of us. "Drop right before your set," he said. Then, sporting a jester's grin, he helped himself to one.

Trevor giggled and accepted the remainder of the sheet from Syd. I tucked my stamp into my pocket. Loose-limbed and blinking, Syd held his candle up to study the room. "This must be the only room Anatole hasn't turned into a cartoon," he mumbled and ran a hand over the crates. The stencils caught my attention: wheat grain. Was the previous company a grain distributor? It seemed to be an impractical business to run in the depths of London's East Side.

We returned to the staging area. The Pink Floyd's gear was being unpacked by Anatole's stage crew, who all wore sky-blue armbands. Syd brought out his double-bound black Telecaster from the case and I dug out mine, a beat up '58 from my uncle, and we swapped. Syd's had been purchased recently with fresh funds from their recent successes, though he had already put it through the wringer. I strummed it a bit and dug the fight the neck gave me, as if issuing a challenge to play like a madman. Syd turned my guitar over and over in his hands, staring at every ding and crack in the finish. At last he ran his fingers up and down the neck. "She's wonderful," he said.

"My uncle named her 'Irene' after his ex-wife. How'd you know she was female?"

"You can just tell with a guitar, if they're a bloke or a fine dolly, y'know? If she moans in your hands, well, that's some Yankee magic there." He returned the guitar to me with care. "I look forward to hearing her tonight."

I noticed a collection of unmarked metal boxes with knobs and switches with his amps. "Anatole's got you hooked too, eh?"

"Oh, yeah, mate. Dig this one." Syd produced a large black box from another freight case. It was identical to the mystery box Anatole had given me. "Brand new, a secret weapon. He won't even tell me what it does."

"Not so secret, I'm afraid. I've got one, too. Anatole's using us for some advertising, I suspect."

"So how's it sound, then?"

I tilted my head and tried to remember. "Hard to say. Wobbly like a tremolo, but there's much more going on with the guitar signal. And there's some echoing... you just have to hear it."

Syd nodded with interest then his face went blank, and I knew the acid had already kicked in. I squeezed his bony shoulder. "I'll catch you after your set," I told him. "Stay cool, pardner."

"Righty right," he said, face twitching minutely.

No acid for me, I decided at that moment. I was already spooked by the enormity of the shindig—why make it worse?

The blue banded soundmen and stage hands appeared en masse, ready to set up our gear. Since we Rebel Rousers were sharing amps with the Midnight O'Clock, all we had to do was shove our gear further away from the Pink Floyd's, then watch guitars uncased, tuned, plugged in, adjusted, and so on. The romance of rock and roll had not yet taken hold; rather, our preparations were more akin to shaving and brushing your teeth before the big date.

My pal from the party, Dave, appeared with a garish cocktail, a cravat, and a grin. Apparently he was tight with the Pink Floyd, judging from the way Syd rejoined reality long enough for handshakes and a little chat. Dave noticed me and gave a salute, and when the Pink Floyd had to attend to their instruments, he sauntered over.

"Lovely gathering," he said. "Have you eyeballed the birds here yet?"

"Birds?" Or Byrds? Or Yardbirds? Or—"Oh, chicks. Not yet. I'm spoken for, you know." I flashed my wedding band.

Dave gave me a quizzical look. "Ah, pardon me. I didn't expect a chap your age to be settled in already."

"I ain't too fashionable in that regard. But, you know, what can you do?"

"Except the right thing, quite so." He glanced at a cluster of . women "Lennon's hitched, too; doesn't stop him in the least."

"Stops me," I said, and paused. In the middle of the cluster, peering over his round glasses and laughing, was John Lennon himself. Those surrounding him didn't seem star struck, and in fact Lennon was listening more than talking, and drinking liberally from a pint. I tried to spot his wedding band but failed. Still, I felt a thrill of excitement to think that a Beatle would see our set. That, at least, would impress the folks back home.

Before I turned away, I saw Lennon tongue one of the LSD stamps and give everyone a fiendish leer.

I listened to the Midnight O'Clock set from backstage. The UFO Club was packed with beautiful, hip, drugged out Londoners, a capacity crowd beyond our wildest dreams. As much as I dug their music, I couldn't linger in the crowd as our friends tore through their set with glorious bombast. Before a gig, my place was backstage, holding my guitar, thinking about as little as possible. Theo had the Mellotron open again, poking at the capstans with a pencil. Horace and Dink smoked a joint and zoned out to the music.

Anatole appeared in front of me. "Tyson! Why haven't you plugged in the effects?"

"Ah… hadn't occurred to me. We've got time."

He knelt down where the pedals sat in a heap and began to chain them together with short cords. "You must line check them all! These are unique inventions, not mass produced garbage. They are delicate, breakable… they have to be tested!"

I didn't try to analyze his logic. "I did that earlier today. Everything works."

His head jerked up. "What are you saying?"

"Tried 'em all, even that weird one. It's cool, man. Relax. You make boss stuff."

I could see he was trying to rein in a sudden rage. "You mustn't… I told you… *Merde!* It's too late. I shall test them myself." He snatched my guitar out of my hands and plugged it in.

"Go on, find yourself a drink. I will take but a moment."

Anatole had turned his back on me as he knelt among the devices. I had an urge to kick that back with my cowboy-booted foot, but I resisted and instead took his advice. There was a cooler of beer tucked into a corner stocked with Watneys Red Barrel. I used my lighter to pop the bottle cap and wondered why the hell Anatole had freaked out about something so minor as my effects rig.

The beer had a sharp tang that made my muscles tense and eyes water. Skunked, I thought, but usually skunked beer tasted soapy—and usually it came from a keg. I took another sip, winced, and set the bottle on the floor.

When the Midnight O'Clock ceased their clamor, the room went nuts with howling and applause. I wandered back to our gear. "If that's not a sympathetic audience, I don't know what is," I told Theo, who had been watching through a break in the curtains.

"They're going bonkers," he enthused. "A controlled, psyche-delic riot. It's the acid."

"You got some, too?"

Theo's eyes were unfocused. "Man, *everyone* is tripping. I don't know how Anatole can afford to throw a free concert and include free acid, but I am glad as hell to be here."

"I'm not. Tripping, that is." Yet the lights shone a little too insistently, casting off colors in the corners of my eyes. "I think."

"Osmosis, baby." Theo grinned as a pair of stagehands hauled his Mellotron out to the stage.

Anatole had found a stand for my guitar. I regretted my cantankerousness towards him. The stompboxes had been strung together following some logic only he understood. At the tail end of the chain was the mystery box.

I strummed my guitar, unplugged, to get acclimated to the movements of playing. A few pentatonic runs and a few barre chords warmed up my fingers.

"Tyson, my friend," a voice spoke behind me. Anatole put a hand on my back and leaned in. "Use the effect at the end of your set, for at least three sustained minutes. Perhaps during a jam, *oui?*"

"We were going to end with a quick little rocker," I told him. "I take a short solo in the middle eight—"

"No, no. End your set with a freeform jam. It is… what the crowd wants. A total freak out, yes, do you see? Take them out of this world."

I scratched my head; my hair had begun to tingle. "We got a little of that, I guess…"

Anatole had waved Theo over and repeated what he told me. Theo nodded with enthusiasm. "Far out, no problem, man. Just pull the plug on us when our slot's over."

"Hey now," I said. "We had a setlist worked out."

"Screw the setlist!" Theo's eyes bugged out at me as Anatole looked on, satisfied. "Screw hierarchies. This happening is about freedom. That's freedom of expression, freedom of thought, feeling—"

"Transcendence," Anatole interjected.

"Transcendence, art, love, sex, heat, it's all here. Man, it's *all right there!*" Theo jabbed a finger at my fretboard. "Make them come with freedom. A musical orgasm!"

I longed to be home watching TV with Julie. "Okay, okay. Transmission, got it."

"Transcendence," they said in unison. "Just let it flow," Theo added. "Don't be so uptight. Let your hair down, man." He plucked the Stetson off my head. "And no redneck shit, 'kay? Solid?"

Forty minutes, I told myself. Then I was going to hit someone.

The stage hands set us up quickly. A few microphones had been set up for the vocals, and one to hang over the drum kit, but otherwise the bass, guitar, and Mellotron had to rely on the overpowered amplifiers brought by the Midnight O'Clock. I didn't mind, since that meant my amp would be loud enough to elicit some juicy feedback.

Beyond the stage, islands of colored light illuminated the

cigarette and pot smoke hovering over the tightly-packed crowd in the otherwise dark room.

Although the sounds of the Midnight O'Clock had dissipated, their energy seemed to remain in the bodies of the audience, who jerked, swayed, shouted, and gesticulated at each other in the hunched-over, self-absorbed posturing of a drug-user blessed with an urgent, chemical epiphany. The acid hung over the kids like a psychic cloud, discernible through the primal shift in their body language; the difference between a grazing herd of cattle and a herd on the verge of stampede. We were safe on the stage, an inviolate space that didn't require bouncers to protect, yet I felt uneasy at the intensity of the hungry stares. Were Londoners so thirsty for music? I doubted it. The scene had gone from groovy to spooky, and I knew we had the power to take it all the way to an unrestrained freakout if we chose. It was a dream gig, in other words, but dreams could turn to nightmares.

"It's time," Anatole announced. "Remember what I told you. Give them madness! Give them fire!"

Horace and I exchanged looks, and he giggled in his usual stoner way. Theo stepped onto his platform as if he were a preacher in a cathedral.

Before the rest of us could assume our positions, Theo kicked on the Mellotron with the tape loop of the moaning woman. A sea of hands arose as the amplifiers blasted her ecstasy out into the crowd. Theo laid some strings underneath, thick dissonant chords that resolved into gratifying major chords. The kids pushed forward to scream at him, echoing his tape-loop lover. Young women tore off their shirts, caressed themselves, and howled in sympathetic orgasm. It all happened so fast that I had the sense of being an onlooker at a traffic accident.

"Fuck, yeah," Dink shouted from the drum throne. He tore into a drum fill and then a deep, groovy beat—which was not one of our songs. Apparently we were starting the set with improvisation. Horace leapt in with a walking bassline that adhered to a classic blues structure, which was fortuitous because I was too addled to follow something complex. I had to take a moment to watch for his root, a sign that I had to focus. He was in A, an easy key, so I stomped on the Fuzzrite to get a bold snarl out of a bent string.

The crowd roared with approval. Everyone in sight of the stage was dancing—or rather, grinding against each other to the beat. The topless girls were groped or initiated groping themselves. One brunette locked her eyes onto me and moaned every four bars, like clockwork. I wished our platforms didn't separate us from each other so I could confide in Horace: Is this really happening?

Dink propelled us forward, breaking up the beat and inverting it. In the spirit of freakout, I activated a green, three-knobbed pedal of Anatole's. My fuzzy guitar sound swooshed as if flying back and forth over our heads. The effect became absurd when I played all the strings, so I switched to long, drawn out notes.

We vamped on the riff for ten minutes until Theo waved us down. He ended the song with the same female sex sounds.

"Groovy," he said into the microphone, and nothing more. Grins paraded across his face, thanks to the acid, as if he were experiencing emotions at ten times the normal rate.

Theo called out one of our rock songs. We bashed it out, and then another, and another, to my relief. All that freeform jamming in front of the strange crowd set me on edge. The audience surged forward and pulsed as one to the driving beats.

During a break, Theo replaced his rack of Mellotron sound tapes with another rack. He pressed a key and a bizarre yodel emitted from the amplifiers.

"Give 'em something fast." Dink tapped his foot on the platform for a moment, chose a tempo, then kicked into a rollicking, Hendrix-style beat. I followed suit with thick, funky, ninth chords. Theo's Mellotron whooped and rang with strange, altered sounds from Anatole's archives.

Dink pushed the beat, becoming more and more frantic, just as I started a guitar solo. To keep up, I began turning on the effects, one after another, until I had an echoing, swooping, hic-

cuping, octave-shifting cacophony coming out of my amplifier
entirely unlike anything I had ever heard. If it hadn't been for
Horace's solid bass lines, the song would have degenerated into a
wall of noise.

Anatole flailed his arms at the side of the stage. He pointed at
my feet, where the pedals lay. His meaning was clear: the mystery box. I waited until a turnaround came before pressing my
foot down on the switch.

The room—the whole building—*tilted*, as if a giant hand
had lifted it by a corner. Gravity seemed to slide back and forth
across the floor like liquid. I saw the audience members grasp-
ing for purchase, holding onto the columns or each other. Even
though my knees wobbled, I didn't fall over; I had never surfed
before but I imagined this was similar. My heart raced with
fear and excitement, mingling together in a heady mix. When I
twanged the low E, everything shook.

Out of the corner of my eye, I spied Anatole holding aloft
a box with an antenna. Instead of grooving to the music, he
frowned with concentration and directed the antenna to all four
corners of the room. Then he shouted at one of his stage hands,
who bustled off.

Were they recording the gig? I hoped so. Heck, it could be a
live album, though I rather doubted the mind-blowing results of
his inventions could be captured on vinyl.

I went on experimenting with different notes through the
mystery box. Deep notes produced a seismic shift; high notes,
especially high inversion chords, a lightness in gravity as though
we were in space. A giggle escaped my lips; it was just too insane
and ego-gratifying. I could only imagine what Hendrix or Clap-
ton could accomplish with one of these!

Suddenly the lights went out and the music stopped, except
for Dink's drumming. He petered out and looked up from the
kit with a heartbroken, hangdog expression. "Is that it?"

"I think so." The room remained dark for a few pregnant moments until the roar of backup generators presaged the return
of power. A stage hand swooped in on my pedals and began to

unplug them. Without a word, he yanked the plug from my guitar, gathered the pedals up in his arms, and trundled off into the shadows. Feeling lost, I wandered back behind the curtain, where the boys from the Pink Floyd huddled smoking cigarettes with my new friend. Ollie loomed over them, larger than any of them by half again, uttering his grunting laugh.

Syd came forward and stroked my shoulder. "Flash," he said in an appropriately distant voice.

"Wasn't me. It was the electronics."

"Oh, man," he said into the room. A stage hand strapped a guitar onto him.

"Have fun. They're warmed up for sure. Me, I need some air."

Syd laughed as if I'd intended a joke. He let a stage hand guide him onstage. I pushed past Theo and Dink, whose out-stretched arms threatened to engulf me in an acid-soaked gloat-ing session. Instead of sharing in their exultation—it *was* a truly remarkable set we had played—I wanted silence, peace, solitude. For just a few minutes.

The stink of smoke had pervaded the service corridor. I rushed down it, desperate for fresh air. A stage hand stood by the door, fumbling with a chain and a padlock. I reached for the knob of one of the double doors.

"You can't leave," he said.

"Just stepping out for a spell."

"No, you misunderstand. No one leaves. Mr. De Vos' orders."

I gave him a tight smile lacking warmth. "Open the door, pal."

"Truly sorry, but I mustn't."

"Ah." Taking a deep breath, I reared back, planted my boot in his chest, and shoved. The Brit's eyes went wide as he fell on his ass.

"Never say 'no' to a Texan," I said. While not born and raised in Texas, I was a resident now, and that state had a lot more macho cachet than Kansas. With a manly puff of my chest, I opened the door.

Instead of the night sky and industrial lane I had driven in on,

I saw colors.

"Colors" was a weak term to describe what was outside the UFO Club. Raw color, detached from lightwaves, the very essence of a color itself—it made no sense to me except that I had an instinctual reaction to the massive abstract structures of color coruscating about each other. The prismatic spectrum we knew was merely a metaphorical construct that gave the loosest sense of what "red" or "violet" might be. Surrounding the UFO Club like an ocean was Color itself, in all its inhuman, chaotic majesty.

A sound accompanied the swirling maelstrom, a granular white noise so clear as to seem visual, defining the ridges and valleys of the color storm. Not loud, but pervasive and eerie.

I stared and forgot to breathe.

Someone seized my shirt and dragged me back. The stage hand slammed the doors shut and padlocked them decisively. He fixed me with an accusatory glare.

"Seen enough?"

"What—what the *hell* was that?"

He shook his head slowly and said nothing.

"A light show?" I imagined some kind of fancy spotlights pointed at the building. "Oil projection?"

"Go back inside," he said gently.

I couldn't order my thoughts—I had been dosed with acid, I was sure, from the sip of strange-tasting beer I had taken. Once the Pink Floyd finished their set, I could retreat to the van, go back to the Midnighters' flat, and sleep properly.

The skronk of a guitar and bass echoed in the distance as I returned to the backstage—the Pink Floyd had started their set with feedback and noise, and odds were that it would not proceed much further into tonality.

I cast about for water, but none was to be found—only questionable beer bottles. Trevor O'Clock waved me down to tell me something, but I stopped him with a single word: "Bathroom?" I must have looked as if I was having a bad trip, because he led me by the arm to a filthy lavatory and waited outside the door. I put my head under the water faucet and turned the knob. A few drips came out. No water pressure.

"Son of a bitch!" I yelled.

"You all right, mate?" Trevor peeked in the door.

"Just thirsty as a goddamn cowboy. I need a regular glass of water. You limeys have that shit here, don't you?"

Bless his heart, he didn't rise to the provocation. "I'll find you something. Have a rest." His head slipped back out of the doorway. I sat on the toilet seat and held my head in my hands. The thing was, other than the trippy hallucinations I saw when I opened the loading dock doors, I felt fine. A bit wired from the gig, but the usual symptoms of a bad trip were absent. Hell, I could have even survived without the water, but for the moment, it epitomized normality for me, and I just wanted the Brits to provide something other than madness and surreality.

Trevor returned with a glass of water. I drank it eagerly. "The Floyd are in rare form," he enthused. "I've never seen them like this. Bloody amazing."

"Don't wait up on me, man. Go dig it." Trevor hesitated, so I gave him a smile. "I'm fine, really. Thanks."

"Right, mate. Come on out when you feel fit." And then he was gone. Solitude held a great appeal to me. My only true connection to this place was Gene, who was apparently as AWOL from the night's gig as he was from the Army. Theo, Dink, and Horace were captivated by the sophisticated London freak scene. Far from home, exhausted in a strange bathroom, I yearned to be home in the arms of my wife, in the silence of our bedroom. I wanted to feel her stretching belly and imagine what the future might be.

Honestly, what was the band to me? A chance to play some tasty licks on the guitar, drink until I was woozy, and romp around the countryside with the boys. Child's play, really, the adventures of young men striving to avoid adulthood.

At that moment, I decided to quit the band. My heart lightened at once.

I stood, empty glass in hand, to return to the backstage and take it all in one last time, when the building shook. Hard. I caught myself on the stall door, dropping the glass in the process. Out in the hall, the audience howled with... approval? Fear? Madness? The walls shifted before my eyes, snakes of pure color rising out of the peeling paint, as though the lightshow outside had invaded the building itself.

The corridor outside was a flurry of activity. Anatole's stage hands dashed back and forth with handheld devices. They wheeled a large, elaborate metal contraption that spit sparks and beams of pure color. Anatole himself ran alongside it, shouting orders. When they came my way, I grabbed his arm. "What the hell's going on?"

He shook my arm off in a manner both exultant and aggravated. "Revolution, *mon ami*! Just watch history unfold!"

My jaw hung slack as they pushed the thingamajig out to the stage. The Pink Floyd had reached a crescendo of sound, a wall of pulsing noise that could hardly be called music but for the instruments from which it originated. I rounded the corner to see Anatole goading Syd on, until color beams synced with the music and washed over the writhing audience like an ocean tide.

With a grand gesture, Anatole threw a switch on the device.

The music stopped, the lights cut out, and the building screamed.

A shockwave ran through every surface of the place, sending vibrations up everyone's bones. I nearly tipped over. Syd did, flat on his face, and Anatole clutched his switch to retain his footing.

Silence settled over the hall, quickly eaten by a thousand murmurs of confusion. Anatole shouted in French at a stage hand who was already struggling with an oversized fuse box. The lights flashed back on and a squeal announced the rebirth of the PA. Anatole was quick to snatch Syd's microphone.

"My friends, my good friends, do not fear. Together we have crossed the threshold from the stultifying lives of our past to a glorious new future."

Anatole gave the crowd with a smile of paternal kindness. "*Oui, oui*, you are disoriented right now. It will pass. In but a few moments, we'll cast open our doors and embrace... destiny!"

Someone sidled up next to me. "What the hell's he on about?" John Lennon adjusted his wire-rim glasses, which had been bent from an impact. "Some kind of prank?"

"Beats me. Maybe he set off explosives."

"Not while I'm here." There was nothing jovial now about the Beatle. "Fucking artists. I should have stayed at home."

"You should split. I would, if I could. I might still."

Lennon raised an eyebrow. "You know where the back door is?"

"Sure." I led him to the loading dock door. The stage hand had finished chaining and locking it.

But Lennon had found a steel bar and wedged it inside the chain. I took one end, he took the other, and we twisted the chain taut enough until one of the links broke loose. The chain rattled to the floor.

Lennon grinned that myopic grin at me. "Not bad, hey?"

"After you." I held open the door for him, but he got only two steps before recoiling and cursing.

Beyond the door was no longer London's East End.

A floral aroma wafted past us into the smoky confines of the UFO Club. As we stared, dumbfounded at the shimmering landscape before us, Anatole resumed his rant, which echoed along the brick walls to our ears:

"A new world awaits you, a Garden of Eden crafted by the hippest, grooviest God you can imagine."

The otherworldly, impossible colors I had seen surrounding the building had retreated to form the arch of the sky, moving in vast, shifting sheets that gave off a faint, bell-like tinkling at the edge of hearing. The woolly clouds that floated beneath them caught the light as a halo about their edges.

"This world has no police to club you; no Man to keep you down; no money to taint you; no racism to blind you; no guns to kill you. *Non*, my friends, this world has only that which we bring to it: love, art, *Peace*."

Stands of improbable, fleshy trees dotted the countryside,

resplendent under the vigorous sky. Bulbous fruit depended from their branches, and the leaves were oversized as if painted by an Impressionist's brush. Small, winged shapes flitted about the branches above and the thick flora below. A stream bisected the hills in the distance.

"Bloody hell," Lennon breathed. "You'd better call me a cab."

"I kinda doubt they know this address." We both stared at the panorama before us. Lennon just shook his head in amazement. "I see it, too," I assured him.

A great shout went up. Anatole's stagehands had opened the doors to the new world, and the London kids were discovering it too, though under the influence of far more drugs than Lennon or I. As we watched, freaks, hippies, scenesters, and artists scattered across the lawn, arms open to the kaleidoscopic sky over their heads. I caught a glimpse of Syd, his Telecaster still hanging over his shoulder, walking with his head craned back and mouth agape. His bandmates trailed behind him, hunched over, not transported like their leader. Taking up the rear, Theo and Dink giggled and pointed.

I turned Lennon to face me. "You all right if I leave you for a second?"

"Is anyone all right?" He pushed his glasses up his nose as if he hoped they would show him London again. "That mad bastard's screwed us all."

"Well…" I didn't have a response. What did celebrity mean in a place like this? I only had a feeling in the pit of my stomach that I would soon need allies, and Lennon appeared to share my sense of outrage. "I'll find you again."

"Right then." He paused. "What's your name, mate?" I told him. "Thanks, Tyson," he said earnestly. I clapped him on the shoulder and waded into the crowd of gawkers.

My bandmates had straggled away from the Pink Floyd. I found the two of them standing over a curious shrub that seemed to lean away from their insistent hands. Theo saw me coming and greeted me with a look of astonishment. "Man, get a load of this *plant*." Dink repeated the word over and over.

I rubbed my eyes. Neither of them were in any state of mind to process what was going on. "Stay put," I told them, and went looking for Anatole De Vos.

Anatole was pretty easy to find, thanks to his megaphone and need to pontificate to his hallucinating audience.

"Open your mind and let the sky in," he suggested from the middle of the pack. "Your dreams, they run free here. Everything is free here!"

I pushed through a guard of stagehands and shoved his megaphone aside. His eyes took a moment to focus on me but I started right in on him: "Can the bullshit, man! I'm not stoned, tripping, drunk, or high—but I am *seriously* pissed off." Hands seized me, but Anatole waved them away. He leaned in close to me.

"Tyson, my friend, please relax. Our brothers and sisters are in a delicate state right now, digging their new home. I will explain everything soon."

"'New home'? You'd better explain that right now."

His voice dropped further. "Since you are one of the architects of this achievement, I'll give you the scene in a nutshell." He cleared his throat. "The black boxes I gave you and Syd were not mere effects pedals. When activated in sequence, at a certain volume level and in a specially treated structure, they open a rift in the fabric of space itself." His voice rose with excitement. "I discovered this entirely by accident. You can imagine my terror, to find myself here alone. When I—" A stagehand interrupted him to whisper in his ear. Anatole became serious. "You and I shall speak later." He dashed away, followed by his crew. I gawked at him in disbelief, but a plan had begun to brew inside me.

The great irony of this predicament was that I, by sheer dint of cussedness, found myself the leader of a small band of musical celebrities and colleagues. John Lennon—John freakin' Lennon—listened attentively as I related my brief encounter with Anatole to him and a small group of *compadres*: Horace, Trevor O'Clock, Dave (I learned his last name was Gilmour and he was considered hot shit in London), a few Mods and Rockers who had cast aside their petty squabbles in the face of weirdness, and a pack of girl soccer players (they called it "football," which gave me strange mental images) who were as tough as nails. These like minds were easy to spot in the crowd of tripping, euphoric freaks, because they looked more pissed off than their fellows.

Dave raised a finger after I related my story. "You do realize that sounds like a load of bollocks. I mean, Anatole's explanation. You and I both know sound is just... sound."

"Not when you're on acid, mate," Lennon said. "There have been days in the studio where I thought Paul and I were about to fall right off the planet."

"Your perceptions were altered."

"But what if it's more?" Lennon waved a hand at the sky. "I mean, this is like Descartes to the bleedin' Nth degree, isn't it? We can only perceive the world, not experience it fully."

"Was that really Descartes?" one of the soccer girls piped up.

"Whoever fuck it was said it, what I'm saying is that this— place—may have been here all along, waiting for people to perceive it. And that *is* something sound can change. Not to mention drugs."

"Rubbish," Dave said.

Lennon bristled but I cut them both off. "Until we know exactly how Anatole zapped us here, any theory is open to discussion. More to the point is how we're going to get back. Because"—I met each person's eye—"we *do* want to go back home, right?"

"Hell, yeah," Horace said.

"Me mum will be worried sick," the soccer girl said.

"My bloody *wife* will be worried sick... and my bleedin' son." Lennon's voice rose. "Not to mention the band and the rest of the civilized world. I mean—" He softened his tone. "I mean, no one's got the right to take us from our loved ones, no matter who we are, you know?"

There were nods of assent. "Good," I said. "Now the question is: What do we need to know to change this situation?"

"What De Vos did to hijack us," Dave offered.

"And whether he can reverse the process," Horace said.

The soccer girl spoke up. "And whose arms do we need to break to make him do it for us?"

I thought I saw the solution approaching us. "Just a minute," I said. I stood and waved both arms, and when Ollie saw me he came over. He was all smiles; he shook my hand and tipped his hat to the assembled group.

"Brilliant, innit?"

"Brilliant, sure. Have a seat, Ollie. We're working on a plan."

Ollie lowered his bulk to the ground. The soccer girls shifted uncomfortably at his proximity.

"Right," he said jauntily. "What kind of plan?"

"Escape plan," Lennon said. "We're buggering off."

Ollie gave the countryside a scan. "Where to, you figure? 'Cause I don't see anything Anatole ain't got for us right here."

I had expected Ollie to be angrier than he was. The drugs were throwing off everyone's reactions. "He means back home. Anatole's been working on this scheme for ages, which means he learned how to come and go as he pleased from this place."

"Like Sir Richard Burton," he said.

I didn't catch the reference. "What if we send a delegation to negotiate with Anatole?"

"Talk him out of kidnapping?" Lennon asked.

"Sure. Why not?"

Lennon grinned viciously. "Because what he needs is a boot in the head. Let's take your big friend here and beat some sense into the stupid git."

Ollie stood. "Right then," he said.

I shrugged and stood up as well. "That *would* make an impression. Why not?" I ground my fist into my palm theatrically.

Before I could move, meaty hands enveloped my throat and held me aloft. The weight of my body dragged on my neck; the pain was excruciating.

"'Ere's what I think of your 'plan,' you fucking wanker." Ollie gave me two agonizing shakes and threw me to the ground. My shoulder took the brunt of the landing with a bone-wrenching crunch, and my vision turned black for a moment.

Ollie loomed over me. He fetched me a brutal kick to the midsection that took my breath away before bodies interposed themselves between him and me.

All I heard was his snarl: "Stay the fuck away from Anatole, if you know what's good for you."

I buried my head in the grass and let the pain have its way with me for a minute, until the weirdly metallic scent of the alien ground cover brought me back to reality. I rolled over. Lennon, the soccer girls, and one of the Rockers all peered at me, blocking out the iridescent sky.

"You all right, mate?" Lennon asked.

I sat up. "Not really. What the hell was that about?"

"I think our friend has chosen sides," Dave said. "I didn't see that coming."

They helped me to my feet. I rubbed my sore neck and tried to clear my head. The various London concertgoers had spread across the land, exploring like they were children in a garden. Neither Ollie nor Anatole were in the immediate vicinity.

"What were we saying about beating De Vos up?" Dave sounded even more sarcastic.

"Shut up," Lennon said.

I ignored their bickering, suddenly understanding what compelled the American revolutionaries to go to such extremes as cutting ties with Mother England. Unable to control the situation, they fell to fighting over the position of top dog in our little clique. It made me terribly weary.

The stage hands were handing out sleeping bags by the UFO Club's front door. I trudged over, accepted one, and went to find a bush to sleep against. By the time I had settled in, the mouthy soccer girl knelt down next to me, concern writ on her face.

"Doin' fine," I grumbled.

"Tyson—I'm terribly frightened. Everyone seems to be pretending this is just a dream, but it's not, is it? We've really been taken away from London."

"From Earth, I'd say."

She sagged, and I recognized the tell-tale signs of female despair. For all their bravado, I could see the girls were only eighteen, probably still in high school. This girl had dark brown hair that had been teased into a flip—an affectation that seemed especially pointless now.

With an effort, I propped myself up and put an arm around her. She wept, quietly, and I held her and thought of who might be comforting Julia in a day or two. She told me her name was Catherine. When her hands strayed southward, I gently placed them back in her lap and laid back down.

"You can rest here if you want," I told her. After a moment's hesitation, she nestled against me.

Our first night in Peace, as Anatole had dubbed it, didn't so much fall as it did dim. The color bands that wavered across the sky blurred and darkened to a velveteen texture. A trio of tiny moons rose, refracting pink light. The effect was beautiful but unsettling, a fresh reminder that we did not belong here.

Catherine clung to my hand as we walked the land surrounding the UFO Club. The acid appeared to be wearing off, and not a few concertgoers wept or panicked. The stage hands seemed to have become a police force of sorts; they calmed down those freaking out and comforted those who broke down. When Catherine and I approached one pair of stage hands, we got such a hairy eyeball that we backed off.

Once we got out of earshot, I said, "Ollie must have squealed. They know there's trouble brewing."

"Surely they expected it. What will they do?"

I shook my head. "Don't know. I haven't seen any guns yet. It would be tough to conceal a homicide here."

Catherine shivered. "Please don't speak of such things."

"Sorry." But morbid scenarios passed through my mind as we returned to where the group had met. Only Horace had remained, munching on an apple distributed by Anatole's stage hands. He held it up as we approached.

"They have apples here?" Catherine looked hungry.

"Fallen from the Tree of Knowledge, I reckon. All we need now is a naked chick and a dude missing a rib." Horace chuckled. "I'm kidding, of course. The goon squad had some packed away."

"Food stores," I said. "But how long will they hold out?"

"Until the first harvest, hopefully." He pointed towards the UFO Club. A pair of tractors had been wheeled out of the garage.

"You're shitting me."

"Hey, you're from Kansas, right?"

I winced. "Kansas *City*. Not a farm."

"Well, I suppose they'll find someone to drive it." Horace finished the apple, considered it for a second, and tossed it far. "There, I just planted an orchard."

Catherine and I settled in next to Horace. He shared a ham sandwich and a pear with us. I swallowed a few bites. "Anatole may be a genius when it comes to electronics, but he doesn't have a clue when it comes to people. These kids aren't ready for a pastoral life, regardless of how much they idealize it. If they didn't have a bangers and mash shop on the corner, they'd starve."

Horace nodded. "My uncle worked on a dairy farm. He used to complain about twelve hour days, shit up to his knees, bruises from uppity cows... sounded like hell."

"They have civilization for a reason."

"Like a proper loo," Catherine said, standing. "Do I have to go back to the club?"

"We left water pipes back in London. You'd do better to find a private bush."

She cursed and left us. Horace raised a questioning eyebrow at me, but I shook my head. "I'm just being a gentleman. There're enough wolves among this flock of sheep already."

Horace considered this. "Ty, seriously. Do you have any idea how we're going to get home?"

"Short of strong-arming De Vos into flipping the switch to reverse, if that actually works, no. This is way beyond me."

"But you're not going to give in?"

"And starve to death with these bastards? Hell no. But that doesn't mean I have a plan." I sighed. "Yet."

Horace squeezed my shoulder. "I'm with you, no matter what happens."

"Thanks, man." I hesitated. "Horace, I should level with you. Before this nonsense kicked in, I was going to quit the Rebel Rousers."

He grinned. "You think we didn't know? Theo was spoiling for us to move to London and hire that Dave cat to take your place."

"Oh." I flushed. It seemed inconsequential now. "Well... er, good."

"It's cool, man. No one expected you to play rock star after the kid was born. I mean, come on."

"Right." I had to chuckle a bit. "Thanks."

Catherine returned with her soccer contingent and sat in their midst, away from me. That was fine, I decided. The girls reported their findings: several fields demarcated for planting; stagehands recruiting kids to help unload seed and fertilizer; fights being broken up; Anatole revealing stockpiles of food, clothing and tents; lots of fornication; lots more folks coming down from their acid trip; and Ollie stuck to De Vos' side like glue.

So Anatole had his pastoral utopia after all, complete with ruling class, peasants, and euphemistic name.

Once the girls had finished with their report, we sat in silence. The air had not cooled much since daytime—most of us used the sleeping bags as cushions. Trevor O'Clock and his bandmates found us in the dark and settled in; their reports matched the girls', with one additional piece of information: the word amongst the population was that Peace was, indeed, a paradise—in part due to the massive stores of acid, bales and bales of it, in the UFO Club basement.

"So everyone will just trip their brains out and let Anatole have his way?"

Trevor spread his hands. "Seems like it. The absence of pigs is pretty appealing, I have to admit."

"A little boring, if you ask me," Stan O'Clock said.

"No cops, lots of drugs, plenty of birds up for a shag—I could get used to it." Trevor became apologetic. "I mean, I'd still rather be home."

The soccer girls spread their sleeping bags in a cluster and curled up. I listened to Horace and the O'Clocks repeat themselves for a while, until I became convinced I had to take some sort of action. My bruised neck ached with the thought of it but I got up and walked towards the club.

The UFO Club had become the de facto castle of De Vos, it seemed, though plenty of folks lounged inside, revisiting their acid trips or lounging on the furniture. No one seemed worried. Judging from the laughter, they regarded this displacement as a wild turn of events to liven up an already lively night. Hipsters populated the main room as if waiting for the next act to come on stage. Probably De Vos expected the night's bands to be the in-house entertainment in perpetuity. Generators provided electricity to the room, though the question of how much fuel he had stored had no apparent answer.

Back when the UFO Club was in London, Trevor O'Clock had mentioned to me that there was a back stairway to the offices where the promoter would dispense our gig money. I had a feeling that was Anatole's enclave. Lo and behold, a weary stagehand stood guard at the foot of the stairs. He woke up enough to scowl at me.

I crooked a thumb back towards the door. "Hey, man. They're playing demolition derby with the tractors. You cats might want to do something about that."

The stagehand ran off, cursing, and I mounted the steps. The upstairs offices had been renovated with far more care than a one-off nightclub ordinarily receives, with fresh paint, new light fixtures, clean carpet. At the top of the stairs, a conference room held Anatole, Ollie, and a handful of stagehands, all bent over a map of the region we had landed in. Anatole spoke quietly and insistently as he stabbed the map with a fingertip. All but one person nodded along in agreement. The dissenter began to make his case, but a dirty look from Ollie shut him down. Could the big man have been in on this scheme all along?

The frustrated stagehand turned his head to glare at the wall, enough that I could see his face: it was my cousin Gene.

I blurted out his name without thinking. All heads turned towards me. Ollie jumped out of his seat, fists clenched, but Anatole stilled him with a hand on his arm. His fingers stroked the man's bulging forearm, which struck me as odd, though I was more worried about another beating.

"Tyson, oh, wow, man. You're not supposed to be up here." Gene left the room to approach me.

"So Peace already has rules? What a bummer."

Gene's expression cautioned me to shut up, but it was Anatole who spoke up. "It's fine, my friends. I know about Tyson's scheme. He is expressing legitimate concerns, which I promise we will address in time."

"The only address I care about is my own: in Dallas." I pushed Gene aside and leveled a finger at the inventor. "You realize this is tantamount to kidnapping, right? Or hijacking. Or... something illegal. Plenty of us don't appreciate having our rights trampled."

"I'll trample you, mate," Ollie warned.

"Fucking try it, big man," I said. My ears burned with anger. "I'll break your goddamn limey face and feed it to you." Gene tried to restrain me, but I had run out of patience and ideas. "I have a child on the way! I can't lollygag around here with your acid casualties!"

"Please, Ty, can it."

I slammed Gene into the wall. "Fuck off, traitor! You knew Julia was expecting. You *knew!* How could you?"

Gene turned an imploring face to Anatole. "Hey, man, Ty has a point. Can't we—"

"*Non!*" Anatole thundered. "Peace is mankind's finest achievement, the chance for a perfect society. We cannot let petty concerns interfere with the greatest experiment in history."

With a howl, I lunged at him across the table. Ollie reached out for me, but Gene already had a grip on my belt and hauled me back. Together we practically tumbled down the stairs. My head reeled from the fall and the bruises spoke out in hot pain at the bottom of the stairs. I stumbled as Gene pulled me towards the backstage.

"What are you doing?" Gene yelled into my face. "That lug outweighs you by a hundred pounds. They taught me to kill with my bare hands, but I *still* wouldn't try to fight him." He sighed. "Man, you're as stubborn as every Bigelow."

"Look who's talking. What did he say to convince you to turn on your own family?"

Gene flushed. "I thought you'd be cool with it."

"I don't run from my commitments."

"Oh, so I do? The Army was bogus.. Kill or be killed. That's not how man was meant to live. You might not want to hear it, but Anatole's right about one thing. The only way to find peace in this world is to get *out* of this world." His gaze wandered off. "I watched my best friend die, cut in half by a VC landmine. He couldn't talk, but he didn't have to. He wanted to say, 'Why? Why kill me, world?' You know what the *why* of it was, man? Bullshit American imperialism. Just politics! Never meant a thing to me or Scott. That's my *why*, going AWOL. There's real peace, here, cuz."

I blew a raspberry. "You won't last a month frolicking in the fields. I know you."

"Ty, I've changed. I've seen things. Peace is what I want— Peace has what I want. Besides, if I get antsy, I can just—" He stopped abruptly.

"Aha." I smirked at him. "I knew it. The door isn't closed, is it? You boss men can get back to Earth."

Gene rubbed his face. "You're not—"

"... supposed to know that we're not really trapped? I'm sure. De Vos had it worked out, didn't he? Freedom, peace, a new beginning. And an escape hatch if things go south. Figures."

"It's just good sense," Gene implored me. "We can jump back for medical supplies, fertilizer, food, whatever the colony needs to get through the first few years. After that, no one will want to go back. Problem solved."

"Is that your logic or Anatole's?"

That shut him up. Gene led us to a cooler where some beers still held out. He took one (I still shied away from potential LSD exposure) and drank it down.

I pressed my advantage. "Not too different from the Army, is it? Trapped in an exotic location, told what to do, survive as best you can. Only instead of gooks, you have lonely chicks who'll fuck you for solace."

"That's unfair."

"To who? You? The women in your hippie harem? Me, perhaps?" I shook my head. "I can't believe we're still arguing about this."

"We're Bigelows," Gene said, and I knew he was beaten. I let him stew for a few minutes as he downed another can of strong British beer. "So what do we do?" Gene asked at last.

"Well..." I paused. Where did my responsibility lie? To Horace, Lennon, Dave, Catherine, the rest of the dissenters? Towards the innocent kids who would wake up from their dream to discover they had been kidnapped? If someone wanted to stay here, it was no different than buying a farm out in the Kansas plains—with the exception of the lightshow sky, of course.

"Maybe we could negotiate with Anatole. Get him to agree to let folks head home if they aren't up for the experiment."

Gene shook his head. "That idea was already shot down. He's dead set on keeping Peace together."

"Without guns? Are they going to whine people into submission?"

A mischievous grin lit his face. "Well, he may be a gun-hating hippie, but I did bring a little souvenir from the Army." He hitched up his shirt to reveal the grip of a pistol. "I figured it would come in handy for hunting."

"Hunting Belgians. Well, that solves that problem. Gun to head, 'send us home!', zap."

"It's not so simple. The smaller transportation rig by his office is pretty elaborate—it's not like making a phone call. Anatole would have to cooperate, and you have no way of knowing where he sends you. Could be limbo."

"Oh." Buoyed by Gene's example, I took a beer for myself. "Have you seen it work?"

"Sure. He sent someone back for the apples."

"Could you operate the controls?"

Gene looked alarmed. "Me? I mean, I saw the sequence of switches, but he scans something, adjusts something else—I'd be terrified to lose someone."

"But you can do it."

"Maybe." He frowned. "Can't we come up with a different idea?"

"Anything else involves shooting the people we need to get home."

Gene and I returned to the little encampment. Everyone was awake again, huddled around a campfire. Lennon and the Rockers sat together; he had one of their jackets, evoking the famous old photos of the young Beatles. The Midnight O'Clock had gathered together as well. I half expected to see Dave or the Pink Floyd, a gathering of friends before weirdness struck. But Theo and Dink were missing in action.

Everyone tensed when they saw Gene's uniform.

"Folks, meet my cousin Gene. Don't freak out, he's going to help us."

"Why should we trust him?" Lennon barked.

Gene drew himself up. "Because Anatole has a way back to Earth and I know where it is." Gene explained quickly what he had told me. The group became excited at once.

"Well, let's go!" Lennon said. "I fancy a sleep in my own bed tonight."

"I wish it were that simple. Anatole is the only one who knows how to set the machine. He keeps that knowledge to himself so he can control us—all of us." Gene looked around meaningfully. "I reckon on staying in Peace, but it ain't right that you folks are here against your will. I'll do what I can."

"Well," Lennon said, "what *can* you do?"

"I can sneak some folks past the guards so that we can take a crack at that transporter. Thing is, I can't guarantee that it will send us back to London."

"Where else would it go?" Trevor asked.

Gene shook his head. It was all he needed to say.

Something struck me. "Anatole doesn't make the trips himself, does he? He sends you guys."

"Right!" Gene became excited. "Hey, sure, I get it. The transporter on the other side must be pre-set to reach Peace, like on auto-pilot. Yeah, yeah…" He screwed up his face in consideration. "One person could go for help if they get through."

"And send back a whole lorry full of bobbies," Lennon said.

All eyes converged on me.

Trevor broke the sudden, pregnant silence. "I'll do it. I'll volunteer." He smiled at me. "If something goes wrong, you'll need Ty here. Best it was someone who has nothing to lose."

"But you're—"

"I'm the right bloke for the job. Now, let's hop to it, hey, lads?"

Lennon's Rockers rose in unison. "Right. We'll keep De Vos' boys occupied."

Catherine and her girls joined them. "We're up for a scrap, too."

"Then Ty's with me. We'll get Trevor inside, and… and hope for the best."

Gene didn't sound especially enthusiastic, but the tide had carried us to action, at last. We stamped out the fire, organized ourselves, and made off for the UFO Club. I fell in beside Trevor.

"Are you sure you want to go through with this?" I whispered.

"Aye aye, captain. My father's a barrister, knows the entire police department by name. I'll have a strike force kicking down De Vos' door before he can shag a hippie."

"All right." I realized what was nagging at me. "I haven't seen Theo or Dink since we got here."

"They struck out with a lot intent on exploring the hills and that stream." Trevor pointed in a direction; we had no cardinal reference points. "That's the last I heard."

I pulled Horace aside to share this news. He nodded sagely—I had forgotten how sensible he could be when he wasn't stoned. "Should I search for them?"

"No," I said. "We'll need every man we can get in a minute. I suppose they'll turn up when we've put the kibosh on Peace."

"Rebel Rouser to the end," he said with a grin. I returned it. "Yee haw. Stick with Lennon. Don't let that famous face get mussed up, right?"

"He looks more like a thug right now. I'm not sure this hippie shit ever agreed with him." Horace was right. Lennon seemed to relish the opportunity to be the big dog.

We had reached the front entrance of the UFO Club. Lennon swaggered out in front of the pack like Marlon Brando in *On the Waterfront*. "'Ey, you wankers! Me and the boys fancy a taste of your beer. Open up."

Anatole's stage hands gathered together to repel the Rockers and their famous new leader. Meanwhile, Gene, Trevor, and I crept around to the side entrance, where not long ago we had been unloading gear. The corridor stood empty and dim in the Peace nighttime. We let our pupils adjust to the darkness while the sounds of violence echoed from the front of the building.

We crept along the dark corridor. By the time we reached the stage, a group of stage hands, led by Ollie and De Vos, were spilling out of the office staircase and dashing towards the outside. We threw ourselves flat behind the Midnight O'Clock's Marshall stacks.

"Looks like they have a use after all," I said when the coast was clear.

Gene stopped us at the bottom of the stairs with two upraised fingers—a signal he had learned in the military. As we waited, he mounted the stairs casually, making no effort to conceal himself. For a moment he was out of sight, then he called down the stairs: "All clear. Come on!"

The room set aside for the secret transporter was concealed by a tapestry and a thick, oak door. No more than ten by ten and windowless, the room gave the impression of a tomb. Trevor blew air out his cheeks.

In the center of the room, rods ascending from a metal plate formed a wall-less booth. Wires struck out to a console in the corner, large enough to house four or five of the black mystery boxes we had been tricked into using. The console itself was covered with switches, knobs, dials, and meters.

Trevor shook himself once and stepped onto the metal plate. "Like this, yeah?"

"Yeah. Keep your hands and feet inside." Gene crouched at the console. I stood behind him and watched his hands waver over the controls.

"Anatole left a setting on here," Gene said. "Think it's London?"

"You'd better be certain of this, man."

He bit his lip. "I told you it was risky. We can abort the mission." For all his nervousness, Gene's training had taken hold. "Give the go ahead."

I looked Trevor right in the eye. "Now or never," I said, trying to keep my voice steady. "Still sure?"

"Just close my eyes and think of England." Trevor looked younger than ever. "Ready steady go."

I wiped sweat from my brow. Gene had been in combat—he knew what it was like to risk someone's life with a decision. Not me. My heart was threatening to burst out of my chest.

"Don't keep a lad waiting," Trevor said.

"Go," I gulped. Gene hit the switch.

Electrical arcs crackled at the tips of the rods. Trevor shrank from them, covering his head. Blackness filled the space, delimiting the transporter in a perfect, abstract rectangle, and absorbing the light around us. The last I saw of Trevor was his mouth, open for a silent scream.

The room shook once then was still.

"Okay," Gene said, standing. "Let's split."

"But can't we—"

"No. We won't know if he made it until he comes back. It was De Vos' design."

I felt utterly helpless. The final image of Trevor had been seared into my mind, and I was sure we had doomed him.

Gene, a few steps ahead, pushed me back from the staircase. "They're back already! We're busted, man." The wooden staircase protested under multiple sets of feet.

"Is there another exit?"

"A window with a fire escape." He pointed down the hallway. "Move now!"

"But you—"

Gene drew his pistol and cocked it. "I said move 'em out, cowboy."

I ran for the window. Behind me, Gene shouted something and opened fire. The stage hands howled in fear, and that's all I heard, because I was out the window and down the rusty iron fire escape as quickly as possible. The jagged iron rungs stung my hands as gravity tugged my weight down to the ground with a stunning wallop. I investigated my aching hands and waited to hear more shots.

None came.

I hesitated. Gene was up there, fighting for my sake. It wasn't right, yet I couldn't easily rejoin him without wading through a dozen or more angry guards. I called his name. But the face that poked out of the window was broad and angry: Ollie. He worked his arm out and pointed an object at me. A bang sounded, and dirt exploded a yard from my foot.

That clinched it. Trevor was our only hope. I turned tail and ran for the hills, literally.

My back itched, anticipating a bullet from Gene's gun. My legs pumped harder than they had in any football game. I was running for my life now, because the lone gun in Peace was aimed directly at me.

Peace's hills appeared to be bucolic and rolling from a distance; up close, they were scraggy accumulations of outcroppings, crevasses, boulders, and caves, all wreathed in a thick quilt of coarse moss. Leafy bushes, different from those near the club, clung to what soil they could and raised dark leaves to the variable sky. The stench of rotting vegetation had settled over the hills, though it lacked the comforting musk of Earth flora.

The murmurs of the stream bounced from rock face to rock face, but I hesitated to give in to my impulse to reach water. Ollie was in pursuit, I knew—his thick form had raced across the plain a few hundred yards behind mine—and the stream was bound to expose me to gunfire. Yet Theo, Dink, and their friends had most likely followed the water on their leisurely hike. I was so scared my knees were quaking, but if I led Ollie and that gun to my friends, someone would get shot—and if it didn't kill them right away, I had no confidence that Anatole had provided an emergency room for gunshot wounds.

Thus I veered away from the stream and into a series of channels cut into the rock. The sheer walls rose twenty feet above me, with too few obvious handholds apparent in the night darkness to justify a climb. I ran and cursed the Texas schtick of our band that forced us to parade around in cowboy boots. Great for kicking, lousy for a sprint. My shins ached in a way I had never before experienced.

I was lost and hoped it meant that Ollie couldn't find me, either. Stopping for a breath, I listened for the sound of Ollie's footsteps over my own gasps. The night was quiet—the birds sang no night songs, no insects hummed, no wind whispered through the trees. Either that was *de rigeur* for a Peace night or something was amiss. Perhaps Ollie and I were scaring the typical nocturnal inhabitants.

My chest burned from exertion. If I hadn't been so frightened, I would have collapsed on the spot. When I straightened up, the sound of scree dislodging and tumbling to the ground froze me. A silhouette appeared at the top of the ridge, arms wide to keep balanced. In the gloom, it was difficult to determine whether it was Ollie or a wandering —or Theo. I waited and watched.

The figure turned from side to side, scanning for something, and by the time the pistol's shape became visible I knew it was Ollie. I held my breath.

He crouched, using both hands to steady himself on the edge. For a pregnant moment, I tried to read the body language of his dark shape. Then he cursed and swung the gun my way. I bolted.

Two shots ricocheted off the stone—or was it three? As terrified as I was, I tried to count bullets fired. Gene had used three, I was fairly certain. My father was a veteran; he once bragged to me that the .45 caliber automatic he had used in World War Two was still seeing use in Vietnam. If that was what Gene had been issued, it held seven bullets in the clip and one in the chamber, assuming Gene carried the gun fully loaded. Given his training, I thought it was a safe bet. Soldiers had no fear of their weapons.

Call it two bullets from Ollie, then, in the spirit of caution. That left three bullets in the clip. I ran pressed against the wall under his feet, to obscure his aim. Yet Ollie could keep his head in a fight, and so he didn't shoot again, just kept pace.

From above came a grunt, and I looked up to see him leaping the chasm. He cleared it, scrambled to his feet, and jogged ahead. My stomach sank; he must have found a way down.

I reached a cross channel: to the right, a rising slope and Ollie, to the left, a path farther down into darkness. The choice was obvious so I didn't hesitate to plunge into the shadows. At once I nearly knocked myself out on an overhang. The water that had carved out this curving passage had spread wide through soft stone, leaving behind an arched ceiling bisected by a strip of rainbow sky. I hunched over to avoid a concussion and kept moving into the darkness.

The crunching of my boots on the gravel obscured the sound of Ollie's movements. For a breathless moment I halted and listened and heard only the wind tripping across the crack above—until a cough and the sound of larger boots than mine on the same gravel. Ollie had guessed well which turn I took.

I stumbled as I resumed flight. Ollie called out to me: "You can't get away!"

Throwing caution to the wind, I sprinted full tilt in the dark passage. The shelf cut by ancient water flows hovered at shoulder height, so I prayed the ceiling was high enough to accommodate me. Minutes seemed to stretch into hours in my headlong dash into the bowels of Peace.

Ollie's voice came echoing past me. "Stop bloody running, you wanker! I won't kill you."

"Bullshit!" I shouted back.

"Right, well, I'll do it quick."

"Fuck you!" The rock shelf caught my side, a searing impact. I bounced off and kept going—right into a boulder. It was like being hit by a bus; stars exploded in my eyes. I hit the ground and blanked out.

Only for an instant, but disorientation set in. I dragged myself to my knees and crawled under the shelf. I feared I had gotten turned around, but Ollie's exclamation came from behind me.

"Oi! Cowboy lost his hat, wot?"

Hot, salty blood dripped into my eyes. My hat was gone. Cool air blew into my face, a hint of a larger chamber ahead. I dragged myself towards it.

"Ha! I see you!" A shot rang out, the bark so close and loud that my body believed it had been struck. The pain I expected did not come. My outthrust hands felt the ground dropping in a steep slope ahead of me. With a mighty tug I tumbled into the abyss. Small rocks bruised my skin as I crashed down to the bottom, perhaps ten feet below the passage. An acrid odor of dried feces hovered above the floor of the cave.

"Bloody hell," Ollie, at the mouth of the cave, spoke in hushed tones. "I got him."

I held still and listened to him. He panted heavily and made no effort to leave. Minutes passed that felt like hours.

"You still there?" he asked as if afraid to hear the answer.

"Yeah," I said for no good reason at all.

"God damn it," he swore, though he sounded relieved. "You shouldn't shoot me, man."

I heard him maneuvering at the mouth of the passage. "I promised Anatole."

"Come on. You aren't really a murderer."

"Don't push me, mate."

I laughed. "Or what? You'll shoot me? You're already trying to do that."

"I'll come down there and do it for you!"

Our voices resonated in the space, sullying the silence that had been here for ages. The echoes overlapped, mixed in with the scraping of our bodies and boots. We violated the space, yet some of the quiet sounds didn't seem analogous with our movements.

A primal fear roiled in my gut.

Light flared, small yet dazzling: Ollie had a Zippo lighter out and used it to light a stick. Rocks cast wild shapes against the walls of the cave.

"There you are!" he exclaimed.

I ducked away from the light and found myself staring into the gaping maw of a creature with retracting whorls of fangs as long as my fingers. The thing reared up like a hideous, horny caterpillar the size of a crocodile. Fetid breath hissed out from its fangs.

I flailed my hands to ward it off. It snapped at me, close enough to brush my hand with its teeth. The gravel gave out underneath me and I fell backwards, sickened by my sudden helplessness.

The gun sang out once, twice. In the flickering half-light, I saw the thing flinch and then jerk away. I got my hands and feet under me and clambered up the slope in record time. Ollie got hold of my arm and pulled me over the lip. Together we ran back the way we came.

We reached the crossroads and stopped, panting, watching the darkness for coiling, moving creatures. Nothing came. We finally relaxed and stared at each other.

I pointed to the gun. "Anything left in the clip?"

"No. It's spent."

"Guess you'll have to kill me with your bare hands."

Ollie frowned. "I *could* do it, you know."

"I know." My knees still quaked. "Why haven't you?"

"Dunno." Abruptly, he squatted on the ground. "Seems wrong, don't it? All this fighting."

"That sounds funny coming from you."

"No, it don't. I only fight when blokes egg me on. I mean, it ain't wrong to knock about a fool who's taking the piss, is it?"

"Probably not."

He rubbed his head. "I got a good thing here in Peace."

"Seems that way." I decided to take a chance. "Seems like a place you can be yourself."

"Right!" A momentary grin appeared, to be replaced with a suspicious scowl. "What're you saying?"

"Nothing. That's the point. No one cares what you do here, right? That's the appeal. To you."

Ollie inclined his head in a slow nod.

"If you could go back to London, would you?" I waited for a response. "He's been sending folks back. You know that, right?"

"Yeah."

"But you wanted to stay in Peace. For Anatole." Ollie's head jerked up when I spoke the inventor's name. "You don't have to defend yourself here. Or anywhere, for that matter."

"You have it so *easy*," he snarled. "Got your little wife and kid, got your fat American wallet. Where I came up, they was on you like dogs if you let on you're queer."

Queer. The word hung in the air. For a blue collar tough

like Ollie, homosexuality was the worst possible curse. Even in
Dallas, he wouldn't have fared well. It didn't surprise me that
Anatole was gay, or that Ollie was—but I wouldn't have guessed
that the inventor was capable of such heartless manipulation.

Unless he wasn't using Ollie at all.

"Back in London, you couldn't have shown your feelings." I
made it a statement and he agreed. "You'd be shamed in public,
rejected by your family and friends. All you would have left was
the queers, and you weren't ready to go all gay. Right?"

"I ain't a limp-wristed little pouf. I'm all man."

"No one can argue with that."

"I just don't fancy the company of women. Why should I
have to skulk about?"

"But society forces you to go against your nature."

Ollie sighed. "It does. It bloody well does."

I jabbed a finger at him. "Well, Anatole is forcing me to go
against my nature. I want to see my child born. I want to take
care of my wife. It's not a burden—it's my free will, my choice,
but your man refuses to let me be free."

Then I swung my hand around toward the encampment.
"Back there are kids who *want* to drop out like you—and plenty
of other folks who have a life back home. For chrissakes, John
Lennon is trapped here. Can you imagine the uproar when a
Beatle goes missing?"

Ollie's shoulders sagged. "I can't do anything about that."

"Bullshit. Anatole will listen to you if he cares about you.
Does he?"

"Yeah. I think so."

"Then tell him. He can't just order paradise into existence—he
has to work for it. First order of business ought to be making
sure that everyone in his utopia wants to be there in the first
place. Otherwise you're running a prison."

From his crouch, he looked everywhere but directly at me for
a full minute. Expressions shifted across his face like the water
of a river. I almost pitied him for the agonizing process he was
going through. It would have been much simpler to just kill me

and return to his lover's utopia, pretending that nothing was amiss—until the next voice rose up in dissent.

I had argued a good case, but logic doesn't always mesh with reality. My muscles tensed, waiting for a lunge.

At last Ollie said, "He won't give in easily, you know."

And I relaxed, a tangible feeling of hope easing my pains. "So who wears the pants in that relationship?"

Ollie barked his working man's laugh. "He's about to find out."

Theo and Dink had not reappeared when we got back to the UFO Club. I accompanied Ollie to the office, where at first the stage hands gloated over my apparent capture then goggled at Ollie when he released Gene from the broom closet serving as a makeshift cell. Gene had two shiners, surely the least of what Ollie could do to a man. Anatole was shocked when Ollie told him the story and what he had decided; to give the man credit, he took special note of the news of the fang-y creature.

Yet my logic, conveyed by Ollie, won the day. Anatole had assumed that anyone attending a UFO Club show was ready to abandon a corrupt society and found a new one. Now that his idealism showed some holes, he was willing to patch them up. The next morning, he promised, he would announce to everyone that a one-way trip back to London was available to them.

We retreated to our various sleeping arrangements. Anatole and Ollie left the room hand in hand, something that would have disturbed me on the streets of Dallas, but in Peace it seemed just about right.

Peace lost half of its population the next day. Lennon, the Pink Floyd (with a reluctant Syd in tow), the remaining Midnight O'Clocks, Dave, the Rocker boys, Catherine's soccer girls, and a slew of other bleary-eyed, hung-over partiers queued up to be zapped back to the empty lot where the UFO Club had stood. Horace and I held back, asking after Theo and Dink from everyone in line and others still frolicking on the lawn. No one had seen their party since they departed. I recalled the creature in the cave and fretted some more.

Ollie and Gene came to find me. Evidently they had buried the hatchet. "I've organized a search for them," Ollie assured me. "If those toothy blighters wander about at night, we'll need protection. Peace ain't entirely peaceful, is it?"

Gene patted his gun tucked in his belt. "And now this actually serves a good purpose."

"You're going to stay, too, aren't you?" I asked.

"The only folks who really want me back is the Army. I'd say I'm needed here right now." He chucked my shoulder. "But who knows? I might pop up any time, after I've screwed every chick here."

"Paradise indeed."

I shook their hands. Ollie's smile was so relaxed and happy that I couldn't help but return it.

Horace and I waited for our turn in the transporter. Anatole was all business as he adjusted the dials to account for fluctuations in the ether (so he explained), which made me worry for Trevor all over again. I stood on the metal plate, shaking with the memory of Trevor's silent scream, but Anatole favored me with a final, knowing smile. Whether it was gratitude or relief, I am still not sure.

So I guess I'm done writing this down. It seems utterly absurd on paper—or rather, it belongs here, where imagination holds sway instead of reality. Yet it really happened.

Trevor O'Clock, known to the rest of the world and his parents as Trevor Sartorius, remains missing, presumed dead. Lennon and I kept up a correspondence for a time. The Pink Floyd wrote a song about Peace, booted Syd, hired Dave, and became stars. Gene emerged from "hiding" five years later, to report that Peace had managed to prosper, Theo and Dink had formed a new band with the world's greatest guitar effects, and children had been born—some of which may have been his. Anatole and

Ollie remained inseparable, an odd pair but happy in their color-ful alien home.

Speaking of hiding, I need to locate a safe place for this journal that questing seven-year-old boys won't uncover. ✳

Criminal Air

CHARLES BLANK

"YOU DON'T HAVE TO WORRY about Blackmor after today,"
Scailes said. He sniffed as his assistant helped him with his robe.
They stood three hundred feet above the auditorium stage on a
grated platform, awaiting the moment to be lowered to audience
level. "This is a great day for our great city, and for the world."

"Yes, sir." The assistant brushed black soot off the shoulder of
the judicial robe. "This damn soot is everywhere, all the time.
Soot and grime, soot and grime." Stepping off the platform, the
assistant had a coughing fit.

"Think of all the deaths he caused," Scailes called after him.
"Sure, it's not immediate death—Blackmor didn't shoot down a
crowd of people with a Kalashnikov, but think of ten years from
now, when little baby Timmy is ten and has to have eighteen
tumors cut from the front of his spine!"

Scailes struggled to catch his breath, so he sat down at the
long table on the platform, which was now being cranked down
to a level just above the crowd. Four judges sat to his right and
four to his left, each dressed in a judicial robe. They were allowed to do only three things during this last day of trial: listen,
submit a silent vote on paper, and breathe.

Scailes was leader of the council, just like his father. And his
flanking colleagues were once his father's colleagues. Their habit

was their duty: to remain silent in public, only voicing their advisements to the leader in an adjacent and secure private room.

A crowd of this size had not gathered at a trial for nearly thirty years, not since Scailes's father sat as head of the council. He grinned, comparing this day's events with his father's work so many years before.

Scailes had adored his father, had watched him work the years-long Second Coming Theory trials. Back then, the crowd soaked up his father's wisdom as he argued that the Second Coming Mystery was not the result of an extraterrestrial invasion, or a meteor, or an atomic war, but rather a result of the lord's retribution for a the sins of humanity. Theories still floated around regarding how the first civilization of humanity was destroyed, but Scailes believed his father had won the hearts and minds of the people, as well as the favor of the lord, that day at the trial.

Oxygen masks were available for each of the nine judges. The masks were connected to a large offstage air pump by a thick, translucent, corrugated plastic hose—all of which was manufactured by the Midglee Corporation. A mask was available for the crowd, too: in a coin operated machine, in the foyer, next to the ladies restroom. The air tasted of wet old tires when it was working, though it was currently out of order.

Scailes smiled at the crowd. Though the trial was serious, he could not help himself. He loved being the center of the crowd's attention. He loved being heard by so many people, and his conscience was sparklingly clean.

"Breathe freely, everyone," Scailes called out as he leaned into the gritty, cheaply manufactured microphone. His voice echoed throughout the room, bouncing around like tin. He felt regal. "Let us calm down, let us have a moment of silence, and then let us begin."

The moment of silence began as the crowd hushed itself.

The silence was not pure.

A young girl began to wheeze heavily, loudly enough to be heard throughout the three-thousand-seat auditorium. She didn't stop wheezing, and her teary-eyed mother finally carried her out.

"Will the man on trial please be brought forward?" Scailes coughed something up from his throat and wiped his mouth with a gray handkerchief. He took a long, strained breath from the dusty breathing apparatus.

Two hefty guards in black executioner hoods escorted a frail young man forward from behind the crowd. The young man's wrists were chained, one to each guard. The guards placed him in front of the table, facing the council, facing Scailes.

"You are named Blackmor. Blackmor of Waterville, employee of the Midglee Air Machine Factory." Scailes leaned into the microphone. "You have received a fair trial. Have you any statements before the verdict is issued?"

The young Blackmor spit on the floor.

"How dare you disrespect this council! Are you aware of the seriousness of the charges?"

"I may have broken your law, but I refuse to say I'm guilty. There's no way for me to handle your trialing claptrap. There's nothing I can do in the presence of your lies that will result in both my dignity and my survival. Your trial here is nothing but a farcical performance."

"More disrespect!" said Scailes. He opened a large book of law, which caused a cloud of soot to plume out. He pointed downward at a book-marked page. "Does not the law forbid the adjustment of air into mathematically described compressions and rarefactions?"

Blackmor gave an expression of deep thought about the question and scratched of his chin. After a few moments of this outwardly expressed contemplation, his eyes seemed to twinkle.

"The law forbids music," Blackmor answered, "if that's what you're pushing at."

"And did not I, and probably most of the fine citizenry of this crowd, witness you commit this crime seven days ago in town square?" Scailes asked.

"Yes," said Blackmor, "you were there. But what I have done shouldn't be considered a crime."

The crowd grew restless, and their whispering grew. The whispers were stamped out by Scailes's raised voice over the public address system. "Not only did you perform music at town square, but you had the outrageous nerve to use a phonograph to play the music of Bach, Barcelata, Stravinsky, Bo Ya, Holborne, Blind Willie Johnson, Mozart, and the rock 'n' roller Chuck Berry himself. All of whom the lord cast out of the heavens in the Greatest War for polluting the skies into their current black and poisonous state!"

The crowd's whispering grew louder in response, and angrier.

"As an employee of Midglee—and especially as a man who works in the Air Quality Improvement Department—you should be aware of the implications of pollution."

"I admit that I forced all those tones through the air. But only to prove that sounds do not produce poisonous gases. And Midglee is just a day job, by the way."

"At the moment of the event in question, did you have instruments with you to measure any release of poison?" Scailes demanded.

"Nothing specifically calibrated as such," Blackmor answered, "except my nose, and eyes, and mouth, and a few other senses. The only instrument you need is a half a brain, really. And I have two of those."

"Scientific evidence tells us that poison can be invisible and odorless. It is like the force of starlight that pushes us to the ground. Without government-approved instruments, how can you be sure that you didn't vastly increase the amount of poisons in the sky?"

"The music was beautiful, particularly Mozart's," Blackmor offered to Scailes. Then he turned to the crowd. "Wasn't it?"

The crowd said nothing, waiting for Scailes to answer, and he did: "Yes. The sound could be termed as 'beautiful.' Oh, yes. But evil is often seductively pretty, more often so than not. Beauty is not the argument here today."

"It shouldn't be a crime to perform music!" Blackmor shouted. The crowd booed and hissed. Many stood up and shook their fists.

"My people," said Scailes with a regal tone, "please be calm. Be seated. And you, Mr. Blackmor, shall have no more outbursts. You are far too arrogant for the air around you. How dare you be so full of yourself? The lord is the only one on Earth with the right to make music in *his* way... with the waves of the deep brown ocean, or wind through the tree statues, or by squirrelbots chattering in the streets. How dare you believe that you can push air around better than the lord?"

"I never said I can make better music than the lord," Blackmor stated. "I don't know that I ever spoke about him. But since you asked, I'll respond in that context: I am only arranging the air he has given me. The lord has given us the desire to hear beautiful sounds; also, the lord has given us the ability to make divinely beautiful music. Doesn't the lord want me to seek the fulfillment of my desires and use my talents?"

"If the lord wanted you to make music," Scailes said with a smirk, "he would toss hollow coconuts at your head."

The crowd chuckled along, pleased with the joke. The council joined in the smirking, careful to suppress their laughter.

"Look to the sky," said Scailes, "and you will see the poisons in the air. There sits the blackness that makes men ill. There looms the soot that makes air difficult to breathe. Read your Holier Bible. It is our belief that music creates this poison. It is the truth of the lord."

The crowd cheered. They went wild, making noise to show their approval. Blackmor had his head down but his lips were moving. And underneath the sound of the roaring crowd, he whispered to himself.

"Our government created the myth that music blackens the sky, when it's the air machines that are the reason why."

Blackmor chuckled to himself, having felt a rhythm in this accidental rhyme. He lifted his head and his eyes up to meet the faces of the first row of the jeering crowd, and his words became a poem:

"The men in power
Who quote their bible in haste
Fail to see
It's nothing more than a paste
Made from older bibles,
And a cookbook, besides
And two old movie guides
From something called 1995.
Religion tight as a noose,
The science is quite loose
and the myth is fueled by a bribe."

The crowd was nearly silent. Several people in the crowd coughed. Blackmor looked out into the crowd—he was no longer reciting an improvised poem, he was singing. With each word he had increased in tone and melody:

"Your religion will die someday somehow
But rock and roll is bigger than Jesus now."

With a deep frown, Scailes gave a nod to the guards holding Blackmor. One of them punched him in the stomach. Blackmor doubled over in pain, and struggled to catch his breath.

"Your feeble ideas are nothing but the pollution of the truth," said Scailes. "Read the Holier Bible, young man." Scailes closed his eyes in rapture as the crowd supported his cries. He opened another large book fervently, causing cloud of soot to plume out. He pointed downward. He opened his eyes slowly and read: "On the eighth day of the Second Coming, long after all the clouds had cooled, the lord stamped Chuck Berry and his band of great sinners onto the Golden Record, and sent them on the aether-sailing Voyager into the vacuum of space, where no sound can live. They were cast into the abyss for scorching the skies with music, and polluting the seas with toxic symphonies and rock and roll concerts. And the lord suffocated the followers of Mozart, who went to their horrible deaths blaming the poisons not on their own music, but on the burning of dinosaur oils.ˮ

The crowd bowed their heads and shook them when they heard this familiar story.

Scailes motioned for the council to hand over their votes. They scribbled words and handed them over.

"You are found guilty of all counts: possession of a musical instrument, musical performance, possession of a phonograph, operation of a phonograph, resisting arrest, defamation of an employer, public urination, and finally, for eight counts of playing the Golden Record. What contempt for humanity! Your sentence, however, can be reduced if you tell us how you came into possession of a copy of the Golden Record."

"I will never tell."

"Do you understand the seriousness of your crime?"

"Yes. And it's not a copy."

"Please, Mr. Blackmor, spare yourself. I should have you thrown in the tar pits for what you've said and done here today. Tell me how you came into possession of the Golden Record, and I might be inclined to reduce your sentence."

Blackmor turned and spit again.

"Well, then, that secret will be yours to keep," said Scailes, his voice echoing like amplified tin. "You, Blackmor of Waterville, will suffer the fate of those fools who denied the lord and tried to avoid blame with their foolish theories. It is this making of sounds, this *music*, that hurts us all. It is blasphemy that poisons the skies and our hearts. The lord our God is the only musician allowed to arrange our atmosphere. As head of the council, I demand that you be denied the very resource you have violated. You shall be denied air!"

The crowd cheered and roared with anticipation for the finale of the show they had come to see. The two hooded guards grabbed Blackmor to hold him still. With their large hands, they had no trouble keeping him immobile. And they had no trouble pinching his nose or covering his mouth.

Blackmor could not breathe.

His face turned bluish, giving him an unearthly appearance.

The two guards were expecting Blackmor to struggle; the crowd had hoped for a fight. These guards had executed many criminals before with their bare hands. If the criminal struggled, one of the guards would break the captive's neck with a quick twist and snap.

But Blackmor did not struggle as the guards pinched his nose and covered his mouth. Blackmor stood still. Half a minute passed, and his feet began to tap.

And they were tapping a tune. ✳

Catherine Cole

C.A. Cole has had recent stories in *Crimson Highway, Perigee, flashquake,* and *Bewildering Stories,* and lives in Fort Collins, CO.

Rhonda Eudaly

Rhonda Eudaly's work is featured in *The Four Redheads of the Apocalypse; Written Word Magazine* Issue #4; *Apex Digest* Issue #5; *Flush Fiction; International House of Bubbas; More Stories That Won't Make Your Parents Hurl; Encounters; Cyber Oasis; Small Bites; Apex Digest Online; Aegri Somnia;* "Confessions of a Coffee Fanatic" in *Chicken Soup for the Coffee Lover's Soul;* "Getting Off the Buts" in *The Writer's Ezine,* "The Fast and the Furryous" *Perfectly Plum* (BenBella Books), and the March/April 2006 issue of *Today's Christian.*
ONLINE: WWW.RHONDAEUDALY.COM.

Lyn C. A. Gardner

With master's degrees in English and library science, C. A. Gardner has been the editor at a private maritime museum and currently serves as cataloger for a public library. Thus far, stories, poems, art, and articles have appeared in venues like *Abyss & Apex, The Doom of Camelot, The Leading Edge, Legends of the Pendragon, Mythic Delirium, Strange Horizons,* and *Twisted Cat Tales.* Two stories and a poem earned honorable mention in *The Year's Best Fantasy and Horror* (12th, 13th, and 15th editions). In 2004, Gardner attended the Clarion West Writers Workshop.
ONLINE: WWW.GARDNERCASTLE.COM.

Frank Gibbard

H. F. Gibbard is a lawyer by day and a writer of speculative fiction by night. A couple dozen of his science fiction, fantasy and horror tales have appeared in various anthologies, online 'zines and print venues. His application to the Horror Writer's Association is pending. He also writes a legal history column for the Colorado Lawyer magazine.

Harold Gross

Harold Gross has been writing solo and as Gordon Gross with partner Eve Gordon for many years. Previous stories have appeared in the magazines *F&SF*, *Analog*, *Aeon Speculative Fiction*, and in the anthologies *Star Trek: Strange New Worlds III*, *Absolutely Brilliant in Chrome*, and even a cookbook, *A Cup of Comfort*, with accompanying recipe. Harold was also awarded top honors in the 2nd Annual Phobos Fiction Contest for "RUWattU8" in *Hitting the Skids in Pixel Town* and received an Honorable Mention for "Wreckage" from *The Year's Best Fantasy & Horror* (16th Ed).

Sarah Hilary

Sarah's stories have been published by *Velvet Mafia*, *MYTHO-LOG*, *Heavy Glow*, *Apollo's Lyre*, *Twisted Tongue*, *Four Volts*, *Neon* and the *Boston Literary Magazine*. Her short story, On the line, was published in the Daunt Books 2006 anthology. She won the Litopia "Winter Kills" Contest in 2007. Sarah lives in the Cotswolds with her husband and young daughter.

ONLINE: WWW.WRITEWORDS.ORG.UK/SARAHHILARY/

Cheryl Holland/C.L Holland

Cheryl says: "I work in administration and have a degree in English with Creative Writing. I have been an avid reader and writer since childhood, and have a collection of books on mythology and folklore."

William Devereaux Jarrett III

Dev Jarrett, in addition to being a writer, is a soldier. In the US Army for the last 14 years, he's lived all over the world, but calls Georgia and Virginia home. Currently he's stationed at Fort Shafter, Hawaii with his wife Jennie and three of their children (two older daughters live on the mainland). Dev's been published in several online and print venues over the past year, and his first book, *Family Tradition*, is now available from Sam's Dot Publishing.

Lee Johnson

Lee says: "Hi, I'm Lee Johnson, easily described as a drunk layabout, or a 'student'. I'm currently finishing a creative writing degree at Manchester Metropolitan University, which for the last 3 years has forced me to get up at the crack of noon and write about whatever I like, usually while getting plastered. I'm making the best of it though… I also write for a few low-key magazines around the UK. To keep my supply of ideas flowing steadily, I often take educational trips to Amsterdam, one of which spawned this story. The majority of it, though, is true. So I'd like to thank Hudson, Craig, Fester and of course, Adrian, for being there, and thank you all very much for reading. You look lovely today, by the way."

Gerri Leen

Gerri Leen's work has appeared in *Fusion Fragment, Mythology, GlassFire, Shred of Evidence,* and the *First Line,* and has had stories accepted by the *Sails & Sorcery* anthology, *GrendelSong, Renard's Menagerie,* and the *Fantastical Visions V* anthology.

Steve Libbey

Steve Libbey is a Portland-based author and musician. Building websites by day, he writes fiction and stabs at a guitar when the sun has set. His first novel, *The Bloodbaths,* was published by Subatomic Books in 2007. Meanwhile, he co-writes the *Secret World Chronicle* novel series with Mercedes Lackey. He is hard at work on the sequel to *The Bloodbaths,* as well as a post-apocalypse book featuring a Siberian cowgirl.

ONLINE: WWW.STEVELIBBEY.COM

Sou McMillan

A veteran of the early and mid-nineties Columbus, Ohio indie music scene, Sou MacMillan was the voice behind Caroline/Double Deuce band Pet Ufo, which coined the term Tantrum Rock in the heyday of post-grunge and riot grrl politic. Now she writes and knits like a madwoman. Look for her books, *Shallow*

Empire, available from Lethe Press, and *Chrysanthemum*, due for release on Subatomic this year.

AUBRY NEWSON
Aubrey Davis is never without at least one notebook, and her pen collection is not to be laughed at. She is a student at New York University, but is currently living and working in Florida with her fiancee, Evie.

GILLIAN PALMER
Gillian Palmer is a senior at Mount Holyoke College and Cincinnati-area native who is currently looking into creative writing graduate programs. She draws inspiration for many genres from all corners of life, and works best with a classic rock-based soundtrack.

MATTHUE ROTH
Matthue Roth is a novelist and performance poet. His first novel, *Never Mind the Goldbergs*, was published by Scholastic/ PUSH in 2005; his next, *Jupiter*, will come out next year. His most recent book is *Candy in Action*, an introspective look at supermodels who know kung-fu.

ONLINE: WWW.MATTHUE.COM.

KEN SCHOLES
After a long break away from writing, Ken returned to it after logging time as a sailor, soldier, preacher, musician, label gun repairman, retail manager and nonprofit director. He sold his first story to *Talebones Magazine* in 2000 and won the Writers of the Future contest in 2004. His quirky, offbeat fiction continues to show up in various magazines and anthologies like *Polyphony 6*, *Weird Tales* and *Clarkesworld Magazine*. In 2006, his short story "Of Metal Men and Scarlet Thread and Dancing with the Sunrise" appeared in the August issue of *Realms of Fantasy*. Later that year, inspired by Allen Douglas's uncanny painting of Isaak and taunted by his friends and family to finally write a novel,

Ken extended that story and *Lamentation* was born (forthcoming January 2009 from Tor Books.) *Lamentation* is the first in a five book series called *The Psalms of Isaak*. Ken lives near Portland, Oregon, with his amazing wonder-wife Jen West Scholes.

ONLINE: WWW.KENSCHOLES.COM.

J. MICHAEL SHELL
J. Michael Shell's fiction has appeared in *Tropic: The Sunday Magazine* of the *Miami Herald* and two university literary publications. *New Witch Magazine* just accepted a fantasy story and he will also be featured in this years' edition of the *Southern Fried Weirdness* anthology. At the University of South Carolina (BA in English) he studied under James Dickey and William Price Fox.

HORACE JAMES
Horace is a writer of short-stories and unfinished novels. His short story, "The Lizard Pit," has been accepted for the first issue of a new horror zine, *Necrotic Tissue*. In his non-fictional life he's been (among other things) a musician, a parking lot striper, a hi-fi installer, and is currently a computer programmer. He lives in Miami with his wife and son.

CHARLES BLANK
Charles Blank graduated from the University of Iowa in 1998. Since then, he has lived in Minnesota, Texas, and finally Portland, Oregon. Through all this time and space he has enjoyed working for several video production companies.

CHLOE WALKER
Chloe Walker lives in Melbourne, Australia where she battles fickle weather and writes short fiction. Her stories have been published in Aussie magazines and anthologies including *Voiceworks* and *Verandah*.

Printed in the United Kingdom
by Lightning Source UK Ltd.
132701UK00001B/100-108/P